Don't Let Him In

Howard Linskey is the author of a series of crime novels set in the north-east, featuring detective Ian Bradshaw and journalists Tom Carney and Helen Norton. Originally from Ferryhill in County Durham, Howard now lives in Hertfordshire with his wife and daughter.

By the same author

The Drop
The Damage
The Dead
Hunting the Hangman
Ungentlemanly Warfare
No Name Lane
Behind Dead Eyes
The Search
The Chosen Ones
Alice Teale is Missing

Don't Let Him In

HOWARD LINSKEY

PENGUIN BOOKS

PENGUIN BOOKS

UK | USA | Canada | Ireland | Australia
India | New Zealand | South Africa

Penguin Books is part of the Penguin Random House group of companies
whose addresses can be found at global.penguinrandomhouse.com

Penguin
Random House
UK

First published 2021
001

Copyright © Howard Linskey

The moral right of the author has been asserted

Set in 12.5/14.75 pt Garamond MT Std
Typeset by Jouve (UK), Milton Keynes
Printed and bound in Great Britain by Clays Ltd, Elcograf S.p.A.

The authorized representative in the EEA is Penguin Random House Ireland,
Morrison Chambers, 32 Nassau Street, Dublin D02 YH68

A CIP catalogue record for this book is available from the British Library

ISBN: 978-1-405-94509-7

www.greenpenguin.co.uk

MIX
Paper from
responsible sources
FSC® C018179

Penguin Random House is committed to a
sustainable future for our business, our readers
and our planet. This book is made from Forest
Stewardship Council® certified paper.

For Alison and Erin with love

He has always been there.
No one has ever seen him.
Now he is watching you.
You're next.

I

I'm watching you.

I've been doing it for a while now.

You're not big on security, are you? There's no lock on your back-garden gate. Just a latch. I tried it once during the daytime when there was no one around and it made a grating noise when two pieces of old metal scraped together, so I came back and oiled that for you. Now I can let myself in whenever I want without making a sound.

Your house is like most of the others in this town. Quite small and old, but the garden is perfect; it's long and not overlooked by any neighbours, providing you and me with all the privacy we need, and there's a tall fence at the back, with no other houses or flats behind it, just a hill. There are mature trees and bushes for me to stand behind. Perfect spots to observe you, unseen.

I could do without the wind chimes, though. Are you into all that feng shui nonsense or do you just like the sound they make? That metallic tinkling every time a breeze passes through them grates on me, and I have to make a real effort to blot it out but it's worth it for the view. I take a step back and look up to watch as the bathroom light goes on and I get a charge of excitement from this stolen moment of intimacy between us. You shed your clothes matter-of-factly, not realizing you have an audience and I catch a glimpse of the outline of your body as you step into the shower. I can't make out every detail through those frosted-glass windows but they are way less private than you imagine, particularly when it's dark out here and the light is on in your bathroom. You should really put a blind up.

I watch intently as you rub shampoo into your hair, then let the water rinse it away and I get an uninterrupted view of your body as you face the window. I can make out those darker patches on your chest and, too late, I realize that a higher vantage point would have allowed me to see everything. I will watch from the hill next time.

You take your time. Is this deliberate? Do you know I am here? That's not possible but I catch myself smiling at the notion. I know you're careless with the back door. You only lock it when you are on your way up to bed. It's probably unlocked now and I wonder what you would do if I came in? How would you feel if you stepped naked from the shower to find me standing there?

Would you scream?

Would your heart stop?

Would you want me?

I know it's been a while since you've been with a man. Maybe I'm exactly what you need.

But there's somewhere I have to be right now and it really cannot wait.

I'll be back soon, though.

I feel as if I truly know you now and I've made up my mind.

You're special.

You're the one.

You're next.

2

Costa Rica

The poor little sea turtles get confused. Newly hatched, they burst out of the sand, spot the man-made lights, then move inland towards them when they should be going out towards the sea, where they belong. This is fatal. They use up all their strength, while heading towards the mirage of the lights, thinking it's the ocean. When the sea turtles finally run out of steam, they find themselves close to a main road illuminated by street lamps, neon restaurant signs and gaudy bar fronts. Exhausted, they die in their hundreds, not even lasting a day.

If it wasn't for volunteers like Rebecca, none of them would make it. The sea turtles are cute little guys but they don't have a clue. On their own, they perish. And there were so many of them, pushing with their tiny legs as they traversed the beach, struggling for every inch of progress across the sand yet taking themselves further away from their true destination with every kick. That's when the volunteers stepped in. You had to pick them up, ever so gently, turn round and carry them back towards the sea.

It was a simple and rewarding task and Rebecca Cole was glad of it. She didn't want to think about anything else apart from rescuing the sea turtles before she moved on again – to another place, another country – until her mind had cleared. Life here had a pleasing simplicity. She was barefoot, dressed in a T-shirt and shorts, her hair sun-bleached from months travelling in far warmer climes than Britain. Rebecca carried the 'little dudes', as the Australian surfer guy next to her kept calling them, one at a time back across yards of white sandy beach, then lowered them gently just before the shallows and watched with satisfaction as they first crawled then swam out to sea.

She waved at the latest one. 'Good luck, mate,' she told him. 'I just saved your life. Don't mention it,' and the Aussie guy laughed at that. She turned and they locked eyes for a moment. He was cute and gave her the impression he liked what he'd seen and why not? Rebecca was tanned and had even lost weight from all the walking she had done on this trip. The Aussie guy had no idea how fucked up her life was, and Rebecca had no intention of enlightening him.

When guys asked her, she always gave them the same spiel about hitting her late twenties and wanting to quit the rat race for a while and kick back, resisting the temptation to add that she was trying to find herself, because as clichéd as it sounded, it was as authentic a description as any for her situation. In reality, she did feel lost.

Rebecca was in a mild enough mood for now, though, distracted by the sea turtles and their faulty internal satnavs, in no hurry to move on, taking each day at a time. She had barely thought about her own troubles today and that was unusual. Even when you supposedly left your worries thousands of miles behind you, you never did, not really. They stayed with you, like unwanted travel companions.

She felt lighter today than she had in a long time – but she should have known it wouldn't last. It was Polly who came looking for her. She had befriended the other English girl on the bus from the airport, in that no-consequences way fellow travellers have of coming together on the road, before drifting apart later when they've moved on. It had been nice to have someone to walk around with, then drink and talk together till the early hours, before crashing at the hostel. But the look on Polly's face provided few clues to the seriousness of the call Rebecca was about to take.

'It's your mum?' She made it a question, as if she wasn't sure that the woman on the other end of the line was actually telling the truth. 'Calling from New Zealand?' Again spoken as if she half expected Rebecca to answer, 'Don't be ridiculous.'

'OK,' was all she gave in reply, because Rebecca couldn't be bothered to explain that her parents divorced years ago, and her mother was remarried and living in Auckland with her second husband. Rebecca walked unhurriedly across the sand at first, until she realized the call might be costing her mother more than a few dollars, so there could actually be a serious reason for it. Also, she thought, why not just hang up when you learn I'm not there? Why wait on the line while someone goes down to the beach to find me?

The bloke on the reception desk pointed to the phone in the lobby, which was out of its cradle and lying on the table waiting for her. She took it and said, 'Mam?'

'Oh, Rebecca,' and that was all her mother managed before the tears came and Rebecca was left to repeatedly ask, 'What's happened? What's wrong? What's happened, Mam?' Her Northumbrian accent broadened when she was stressed and it was always *mam*, not mum.

'I'm sorry,' her mother said between sobs as she tried to compose herself, 'it's taken me ages to track you down.'

'I told you where I was staying,' Rebecca protested, and her exasperation came through. She was about to remind her mother of the detailed email, with all her ports of call listed in case of emergency, but before she could her mother finally took a deep breath and calmed down just enough to say, 'I'm sorry, Becky. It's your father.'

'Dad? What's wrong with Dad?'

'He's gone, darling. He's gone.'

Rebecca couldn't imagine a stranger time or place in which to receive the news. Moments earlier, she had been on that beautiful beach with the other volunteers, helping to guide sea turtles back towards the ocean. Now she was standing in the foyer of the hostel, rigid with shock. Her father was dead.

Her mother tried to articulate the details, but it was too much for Rebecca to take in. On one level, she knew her mother obviously wasn't making this up, so it had to be true and she would never see her dad again. Rebecca couldn't tally this undeniable fact with the way that the world outside their phone call seemed to be carrying on normally, as if nothing at all had happened. Rebecca became acutely aware of everything around her, as if her senses, struggling to deal with this, were trying to blot the awful news out by overdosing her with other details. Her mother's voice seemed fainter somehow and not because of the distance between them. The guy behind the reception desk was flirting with two girls in backpacks who were checking in and somewhere music was playing. It was a happy, life-affirming summer song she had heard in every bar and café for weeks. Rebecca realized that whenever she heard it again, it would always remind her of this moment.

'How?' she asked again weakly, her mouth bone dry.

Rebecca's mother managed an explanation of sorts but it mainly comprised of how little she actually knew.

'The police think it might have been his heart,' she told Rebecca. 'And he had a fall, I think.'

The police? Why were they involved?

There was going to be a post-mortem, her mother explained, and Rebecca couldn't bear that thought. They were going to cut him open and the idea made her feel nauseous, even though he was already dead and she knew he couldn't feel anything. She swayed slightly. *It's getting hotter in here*, she thought. For some reason the hotel, with its blinds and ceiling fan, was hotter than outside, and she felt as if she was burning up.

'Are you going to be all right?'

She looked towards the sound of a worried voice. It belonged to one of the girls who'd just checked in, her face a picture of concern, and her friend was also staring at her. Christ, what must she look like to prompt such a reaction from strangers? The guy behind the reception desk was frowning at her too but was that concern in his eyes or did he think Rebecca was just another drugged-up European about to collapse on his floor?

Rebecca didn't want them to help her but she wasn't going to be all right and she knew it.

*

A hastily purchased, last-minute flight took most of the rest of her money but Rebecca couldn't stay in Costa Rica now. With her mother living ten thousand miles away, she was her father's only remaining family. She couldn't bear the thought of never seeing him again or missing his funeral. She had to get home.

It was a four-hour bus ride from the coast back to the capital, San José, then on to Juan Santamaría International Airport to catch the plane to London, which took a little over ten hours. She spent much of that time thinking about her father, and though she felt a great sadness at his loss it still didn't feel quite real, as if this was all just a mistake somehow and he would be waiting for her when she returned, standing next to his old car at the railway station. He couldn't really be gone.

Rebecca's plane touched down at a rainy Gatwick Airport, which was at least ten degrees cooler than the tropical paradise she had left behind. She was tired and felt emotionally drained but still had a long way to go. Rebecca caught a train to St Pancras, to connect with a northbound service from Kings Cross to Newcastle, before waiting for a much smaller one to her home town of Eriston. The connecting train was, predictably, cancelled, and Rebecca had to hang around Newcastle Central waiting for the next one. She bought a tea in the little café on the main platform and read a newspaper while she waited. She hadn't seen a single person reading a physical copy of a paper since her train had pulled out of Kings Cross. Everyone was on their phones or tablets instead, surfing promiscuously from site to site, not knowing and maybe not caring whether they were reading legitimate news or batshit conspiracy theories invented to suit someone's political agenda. Her father, a former editor, would have been appalled. He'd been a newspaper man all his life and believed in their power to promote the truth. Rebecca had believed in that too once.

When it finally pulled apologetically into the station, the train to Eriston was small, old and decidedly rickety. It rattled along the ancient track and lurched quite violently as it went round corners, the driver applying his brakes when they were still some distance from each of the numerous stations scattered along the way between Newcastle and the Northumbrian coastline.

She looked out for the familiar landmark, which would signal that the end of her journey was close. The lighthouse stood proudly on the Point just outside Eriston – a promontory that jutted out from the coastline – a white sentinel that was long derelict but brought back fond memories for Rebecca whenever she saw it. Much of her childhood and teenage years had been spent there. Local children treated it like a castle to be played in and teenagers used to take it over in the evenings, before the place had been condemned as dangerous and fenced off. Now it reminded her of friends she had not seen in a long time and Alan, of course, her first boyfriend. She wondered if he would still be in Eriston after all this time. How would she react if she saw him again and how would he feel about her? Was any of that even important any more?

By the time she finally reached her home town, it was late, dark and there was hardly anyone left on the train, apart from a tiny handful of fellow passengers, late workers or weekday drinkers who wasted no time in heading home. Eriston had turned into a commuter town, its houses sold not to young local couples but city workers who were happy to turn a profit on a Quayside apartment in Newcastle and trade it in for walks on the coast with a dog, before bringing up their children by the seaside. Her father had accepted this as an inevitable consequence of the collapse of virtually every local business but had decried it nonetheless. 'Everyone used to know everyone in Eriston,' he'd remind her, during one of their periodic phone calls. 'It's not like that any more.'

Rebecca had planned to get a cab from the local firm, only to find the doors of its tiny premises by the station firmly shut. It was surely too early for them to be closed for the night and she was puzzled by this until she realized the closure was permanent. This local business, too, had failed.

With little option, Rebecca trudged out of the empty station, dragging her suitcase behind her on its wheels, one of which had worn down badly on her trip. Now it squeaked slightly, as if announcing her arrival, and she felt every bump in the road, making it more unwieldy. The journey was all uphill too; her father's house lay on the high ground overlooking the town and coast, a view he had always cherished and a major factor in his decision to buy it in the first place. His house was one of the 'Apostles'.

There was no one on the path she walked and no cars on the road either. The only signs of life came from lights in the windows of houses she passed, but their curtains were all drawn and she felt quite alone. It was starting to get colder too, thanks to the sea breeze, and one of Eriston's regular mists was beginning to obscure her view of the road ahead. *Great*, she thought, *perfect timing*, but she kept going, hoping the exertion would warm her. As Rebecca walked, she wondered how it would feel to let herself into her father's house for the first time without finding him there. Would she expect him to suddenly appear from an upstairs room and tell her off for not phoning, so he could pick her up from the station in his ancient Volvo, like he used to when she visited him for weekends? That was before her life became too busy and their time together less frequent, while she attempted to carve out a career as a newspaper journalist. Once again, she questioned why she had spent so much of her valuable time in a dying industry, destined to go the way of the mines and the steelworks.

No point in going over that again. Instead Rebecca focused on the steep climb ahead of her. It was then that she caught a flash of movement from the corner of her eye and she started. She turned sharply to follow an indistinguishable blur that had come from the far side of the bushes that separated a row of houses from the churchyard. Was somebody there? Was someone watching her? Or was her mind simply overwrought because she was tired from travelling and back on the dark and narrow streets of her home town? The mist didn't help. It always seemed to cling to Eriston like it couldn't bear to leave.

Rebecca stared into the bushes. She kept her gaze fixed on them but could see nothing lurking there now so, cautiously, she moved on up the hill, stopping more than once to turn and glance back the way she had come. No one there now, if there ever had been.

When she rounded the corner at the top of the hill, the Apostles loomed into view. Four large Victorian town houses made of dark grey stone, turned almost black from decades exposed to the sea air. They had been built together in one block, crumbling monuments from a different era and each one had a large letter carved into a space on the arch above its front door, clearly visible still, even in the light from a solitary street lamp.

M, M, L and *J.*

Matthew, Mark, Luke and John.

The Apostles.

Rebecca's father, Sean, lived in John, which was the house at the end of the block on the right. There were no lights on; not in his house or any of the others, which were all empty now, their owners having passed on or sold up. Her father used to have a next-door neighbour when she visited from college, but Mary Allen was old even then, and the state of her empty property told its own story. The front door looked as if it hadn't been opened in years, and the windows were covered in heavy net curtains so thick with dust you couldn't see inside. She must have died or moved into a nursing home, leaving her father as the last remaining resident of the Apostles. Now even he was gone.

The bulb on the street lamp kept flickering, as if it couldn't make up its mind whether it should be on or not. She hoped it wouldn't die before she was even through the door. Rebecca fished inside her jacket pocket for the key. She couldn't wait to get inside, out of the dark and the chill and into the familiarity of her father's house, even without him there. She was worn out and in need of a hot shower. Rebecca slid in the key and tried to turn it, but nothing happened. She took it out, examined it closely to ensure it was the right one, then tried it again but the door wouldn't open.

Rebecca scrutinized the lock. Only then did she realize it was new, with a different manufacturer's name on it. Why would her father change the locks? Had there been a break-in? He hadn't mentioned one. Maybe he had done it while she was away. She visited him so rarely these days he had probably never even given it a thought.

What could she do now? She didn't have a back-door key because she had never needed one and a locksmith wouldn't come out at this hour. She could hardly stay here on the doorstep all night, but where could she go?

Rebecca didn't know anyone in Eriston any more. She had lost touch with her friends years ago.

She had no choice but to walk back into town and hope somewhere was still open. Otherwise it would be a long, cold night at the train station, where even the waiting room would be locked. The last thing Rebecca wanted was a hotel bill, but she needed a roof over her head for the night. She trudged back down the road, pulling her case behind her. At least it was downhill this time but it was also dark, misty and very quiet, which made Rebecca feel isolated and more than a little nervy, particularly when she reached the churchyard again. She got a better look at it on the way down because the corner angled round and she could see the tombstones from the higher ground. That would be enough to spook some people at this hour, even if they didn't know the graveyard's history. People were still obsessed with the case even now, almost two decades on, and its ghoulish location had fascinated reporters and their readers. A twenty-one-year-old woman murdered in a graveyard captured the imagination. Her reasons for being there were equally intriguing. If you added in the quest to reveal the identity of her killer, you were left with a story that would run and run, long after Simon Kibbs had been arrested and sentenced to life imprisonment. Rose McIntyre had even acquired a tabloid nickname, the Eriston Rose.

Without Rebecca being conscious of it, her pace quickened as she passed the churchyard and increased further when she reached the spot where she had seen movement from behind the bushes on her way up the hill. There was nothing there this time but Rebecca still felt the presence of . . . something. This time she did not turn back.

4

I watched you from the hill tonight while you showered. I got to see all of you this time.

It was almost enough but not quite. I needed more and a thought started to form. You take long showers. Your unlocked garden gate beckoned me and I thought why not?

I know why not, of course, but for some reason I couldn't help myself. Am I getting worse? It's the longing that gets to me. I'd been thinking about this all day and I couldn't come up with a reason to deny myself.

I stepped out from the cover of the bushes and moved unobserved from the hill, till I reached your gate. I opened it silently and stepped through, but this time I did not linger in your garden. I knew it was risky but I quickly crossed the lawn and moved towards the back door. I took the handle in my gloved hand, slowly turned it and it opened.

I stepped inside and found myself in your home with you still in it and it was such a rush. No matter how many times I do this, it still gives me a thrill.

In the kitchen, the remnants of your evening meal were still visible. It was dinner for one naturally, because there's no one special in your life right now. I don't suppose I count.

I went through the kitchen, opened the door to the hallway, then looked up. The landing light was on and I could hear the shower. You were still in there and it was louder than I expected. You left the bathroom door open. Why not? You live alone, so there was no need for that extra layer of privacy.

The sound of running water abruptly ceased and was quickly followed by the scrape and swish of the shower curtain as it was pulled across, then I heard your feet step lightly down on to the bathroom floor. I couldn't move, mesmerized by the thought of you standing there naked.

All I had to do was walk up the stairs and we'd be face to face for the first time, with you at your most vulnerable.

I had to see you.

The proprietor of The Anchor did not look too pleased to see Rebecca. She had hoped he might be grateful for any business but he seemed to view her as an inconvenience from the moment she stepped up to a door he was in the process of locking.

'Can I help you, miss?'

'I was hoping for a room.'

He regarded her as if this was a most unusual request and she wondered if the place was no longer a hotel. Perhaps lack of demand had turned The Anchor back into a pub, which it had been for nigh on two hundred years until the seventies, when its stable block had been converted into extra rooms and the place re-advertised as a coaching inn.

'At this hour?'

'I'm locked out.' And she explained who she was and how she had been unable to get into her father's house.

He seemed to accept this, though warily, and let her in. 'We've got the Collingwood Suite, two king-size doubles and a queen, all with en-suite.'

'Do you have a single room?' She had seen the tariff on the wall behind him and didn't like the look of the prices.

'No,' he said, in a tone that made her feel like a time-waster, not a traveller on her own.

Left with no other choice, she told him, 'I'll take a queen-sized double then, please, just for one night.'

'Room fourteen,' he told her, as he handed over the key. 'Sea view,' he added proudly, like she could see anything at all from her window at this time of night, except dark sky above a black sea.

'Thank you.'

'I'll need your credit card,' he said brusquely, 'in case you want anything.' The bar and restaurant were all closed by now, so he really meant in case she stole something or left early in the morning without paying, but it made her realize she was hungry. The unexpected need for a room was already costing her, might as well see if she could make the most of it.

'Do you do room service?'

'Not usually this late. I suppose I could make you a sandwich. Ham or chicken?'

'Ham, thank you.'

'And something to drink?'

After the day she'd had? 'Yes, please. White wine would be perfect.'

She could tell by the look on his face that he had

meant tea or coffee. 'A glass,' he asked her disapprovingly, 'or a bottle?'

Rebecca was tempted to tell the judgemental git to bring her the whole bottle with a straw in it. She couldn't justify the cost, though, and didn't want to wake with a hangover in the morning. Instead she settled for the ham sandwich, a bag of crisps and a large glass of wine, which he brought up to her on a tray not long after she let herself into a coldly functional room, with Anaglypta wallpaper and a Velux window so high Rebecca would have had to stand on tiptoe to witness the promised sea view. She ate the sandwich and crisps seated at the dresser and took her wine to a more comfortable armchair in the corner of the room. She drank this while she ran a bath, which took an age because the water pressure from the ancient plumbing was so low.

This gave her time to reflect on her fruitless walk up the hill to the Apostles. On both legs of that frustrating journey, Rebecca had experienced the feeling she was being watched. On the way up, there had definitely been someone behind the bushes, at least for a moment. Teenagers? What would they be doing in the churchyard late at night? There were better places in Eriston to do the things teenagers wanted to do than a stark fifteenth-century church with a history of murder.

Who then, if not kids?

A thought flashed through Rebecca's mind then and she immediately dismissed it as stupid.

The Chameleon.

*

I took the first step and the bottom stair creaked in protest. Normally I'd have been in your house already, while you were at work, so I could prepare. I would have known about that creaking step and avoided it. I berated myself for being so rash and breaking my own strict rules.

Absolute silence from your bathroom. Did you hear that and freeze, straining to hear more? Were you imagining an intruder in your house? Did a shiver of ice just pass through you?

I stood completely still, with one foot on the bottom stair and one still in the hallway, hyper-conscious, listening for any sound or movement, ready to react to it. Were you already dismissing this as nothing and reaching for a comb, or looking for a makeshift weapon and wondering if you should call 999?

It would have been so easy to bring this forward, taking it to its natural conclusion. I decided then: I was coming up.

But no. I took another step and halted there. It was too soon and I wasn't fully prepared. When I acted on impulse and came silently through your back door, I told myself it would be all right. I was just going to take a look around and come back later. But I wasn't able to contain my excitement and I know now that I must.

I stepped gently backwards, making sure to avoid the offending stair. I banished the thought of your nakedness and vulnerability because they were too appealing.

Suddenly I heard your voice and it startled me. Were you calling out to me? Was there someone up there with you? How predictable. I got a pang of jealousy. Who were you talking to? Not talking, no, and, as you continued, I realized you were singing softly to yourself. Some silly song I keep hearing on the radio, another dirge about a stupid girl getting over a bad relationship. All thoughts of creaking stairs were out of your mind now.

Conflicted, I turned my back on you just as the hairdryer started and I knew I had a few moments, so I used the time well. I walked into the lounge and carefully scrutinized it, judging you on your taste in furniture, ornaments and books, of which there are a number. I approve. I like a well-read girl.

I went back through the hall and into the kitchen, reaching it just as the din of the hairdryer abruptly ceased. That was quick. Too quick. I heard the floorboards as you stepped out on to the landing, then started to come down the staircase. You were moving too fast! I knew you'd be downstairs any moment and might be heading for the kitchen. I almost froze, a part of me wanting to wait for you.

But not tonight. Not like this. Resist the urge, I told myself as I heard you coming down.

Abruptly I snapped out of it and headed for the back door and, without breaking stride, I reached into the laundry basket for a souvenir. I grabbed the underwear from the top of the pile and stuffed the pair of knickers into my pocket. I opened the back door then and stepped through, closing it behind me just before you entered the kitchen. Seconds later, I could see your shape through the frosted-glass window on the door. If you'd been a moment sooner, I'd have had no choice but to finish it, but I didn't want to do that. Not yet.

I retreated silently into the darkness, turning back when I reached the bushes. I waited then. It wasn't long before you walked back into the lounge. I could see you so clearly, dressed in your PJs, your hair still damp. You sat down on the sofa and watched TV while I gazed at you.

I felt exhilarated by the narrow escape but frustrated. I wanted to go back in there and join you, especially when my hand automatically moved inside my pocket to caress the soft material there. It has touched you intimately and so will I.

But not tonight.

This can wait. It has to.

But it's OK, because you're not going anywhere.

You'll keep.

5

She would have slept in, if it wasn't for two seagulls that chose to take each other on right outside her window. Their shrieks were like screams, which jolted Rebecca abruptly from her sleep. She experienced the disorientation of waking in an unfamiliar room, back in her home town after months abroad.

She blinked, let the room come into focus in the half-light of the post-dawn, then the seagulls let out another shriek and there was the speedy flutter of wings, as one or both of them beat a hasty retreat from her window ledge. Rebecca was still tired but once she was awake, that was it. There was no prospect of her nodding back off again.

She showered and joined the other residents for breakfast in a room that overlooked the harbour. There weren't many fellow diners that morning and she suspected Eriston was continuing to lose the tourist battle against more fashionable resorts like Seahouses and Tynemouth. Not many people came to Eriston for holidays any more, so businesses were just scraping by. With no surplus cash for improvements, the pubs, hotels and shops started to become run-down, making them even less appealing to tourists. It was a vicious circle and it had been going on for a long time now.

Breakfast was one of those help-yourself buffets. The coffee was lukewarm and tasted burnt from the percolator, the bacon was soggy and the sausages looked suspicious. Rebecca settled for fried eggs on toast as the least-worst option. She was surprised to be approached by the owner halfway through her breakfast.

'You said you were locked out?' he asked unsurely, as if he might have dreamt this part of their conversation from the previous night.

When she confirmed this, he told her, 'I can call the locksmith for you.' His tone was still brusque and she couldn't work out whether he wanted her to accept or decline this offer.

'Only if it's not too much trouble.'

'If it was too much trouble, I wouldn't offer,' he told her flatly. 'I know Gregg. We have a lot of locks,' and he walked away to make the call, leaving her feeling that once again she had somehow said the wrong thing. Rebecca was beginning to worry she might have changed too much after more than ten years away from here. Could she no longer read its people or respond to them in the way they expected? Just then, Eriston no longer felt like home.

She checked out and waited for the locksmith in the lobby. Gregg was a big man in late middle age. He told her they could ride up the hill together in his van.

'How did you know I live up the hill?'

'Your name, pet,' he said gently, and he nodded

towards the proprietor of the hotel who was checking out other residents. 'When he told me, I assumed you were Sean Cole's daughter?' When she did not contradict him, he said, 'I'm very sorry for your loss. Your father was a gentleman.'

'You knew my dad?'

In reply he simply nodded, then indicated she should follow him out to the car park to his little blue van and they set off.

'Do you think you'll be able to open the lock?'

'I should hope so,' he said. 'I installed it.'

Of course her father would have used the local guy. *Always choose the man who has to feed his kids and pay his bills even if it costs you a bit more.*

'Why did he change the locks?' she asked. 'Was there a break-in?'

It wouldn't have been a surprise if there had been. The house was isolated and neighbourless, set back at the top of the hill and if her father was out, a burglar would see it as a soft target.

'He didn't mention one.'

'What reason did he give then?'

'He just said something about securing the place. I think stuff was going missing.'

'Stuff? What stuff?'

'Dunno.'

She realized she was cross-examining him now and that might not be a good idea while he was helping her out.

When they reached the top of the hill, he parked

outside her father's house. The place seemed so much less imposing now but, if possible, the Apostles looked even more run-down in daylight.

They got out of the van and went to the front door. Gregg reached into his bag and took out a large leather wallet, which he unzipped and unfolded. Each half contained a row of tools that resembled surgical instruments. He selected one, peered at the lock, then set to work.

It didn't take him long. Soon the locksmith twisted his wrist and there was a satisfying click, as the tool turned in the lock and the door opened.

'You're in,' he said.

She went into the hall and was relieved to see a spare set of keys where he had always kept them, in a little wooden bowl next to the phone on a small console table.

She turned back to Gregg. 'Thank you so much,' and she started to reach for her purse to pay him.

He backed away then and put his hand up. 'No charge, pet.'

'Oh no, please.'

'It only took me a minute.' He turned towards his vehicle.

'But you came all the way up here.'

He was almost at his van now and he called back over his shoulder. 'Like I said, I knew your dad.' And that was all the explanation he seemed prepared to give her. He climbed into his van, then drove away, leaving Rebecca still holding her purse on the doorstep.

When he was gone, she closed the door and turned her attention to the house. The hallway looked exactly as it had done the last time she saw it. The coat rack had several jackets on it and a couple of scarves. He will never wear any of those again, she realized and suddenly she was choking back tears. For a moment Rebecca stood in the hallway and let the emotion hit her like a wave. There would be all manner of clothes and possessions she would have to sort through, because there was no one else to do it. Her father had been alone for a long while and had no other family. If he had friends who might have been able to help her, she was unaware of them. That was her fault because she hadn't been back to see him in a while. The task was going to be down to her then, but not today.

Rebecca took a breath, steeled herself and walked into the front room. There was no doubting or denying it now. The empty house confirmed what she already knew. Her father was gone and he wasn't coming back, but death had come to him swiftly and unexpectedly, so he had left his house that evening fully expecting to return to it later. Everything here spoke of a life interrupted. There was the sofa he rarely sat on, close to the armchair he favoured for reading and to watch the occasional documentary but never a soap opera or reality TV, because 'life is too short to waste time watching crap television'.

Life is too short. He was right about that.

Two large bookcases dominated the room and she noticed the books were mostly old. Was he trying to save money by not spending any on books, though he used to consider them one of life's essentials?

She went into the kitchen next. Whatever her father's last meal had been, he'd done the washing-up and left the plate to dry by the sink. To give herself something to do, she reached for the kettle, filled it and switched it on. She opened the fridge and found some milk, sniffed it and immediately poured it away. Black coffee then.

When the kettle had boiled, she began to pour some of its contents into a mug of instant coffee when a loud noise made her start. A thump and a bang came from within the house and she spilled a little of the boiling water on the worktop. The thump was a heavy object landing on the floor in the hallway and the bang caused by the taut springs of the metal letter box, which snapped back as the parcel fell through it.

'Jesus,' she hissed. Rebecca had been genuinely rattled by the sound and realized she was on edge. It was so quiet up here on the brow of the hill, and every sound was magnified.

Rebecca went to see what had dropped through the letterbox and it was only then that she realized her father had added another layer of security to the house, with two sturdy bolts on the front door. He really had been taking this seriously – but why?

On the doormat she found a slim cardboard box with a London postmark on it. She opened it and pulled out a book. It was a used copy and looked at least ten years old, judging by its condition and the leaflet that came with it. *Thousands of books!* it said. *Used, great condition, ex-library.* There would be a great many ex-library books around thanks to government cuts.

The book her father had ordered was called *Murdered – The Eriston Rose.*

Why was he still thinking about that?

6

PC Dominic Green was still waiting to speak. He'd been standing by the door for a while now. They had seen him but none of the four detectives had invited him to cross the threshold. Dominic had been told, more than once, never to darken the door of the major incident room again; yet here he was, darkening it. The man who had told him this still had his back to Dominic. DI Alex Hall was a large man with a short temper he could be relied upon to lose on a regular basis.

The sight of the uniformed officer standing there, patiently waiting for admission, proved too much for one of the other detectives. DC Fox did one of those fake coughs that are meant to alert other people to the presence of something faintly embarrassing. DI Hall turned, saw Dominic and the expression on his face soured. 'What the bloody hell . . . ?' he began, but Dominic interrupted him.

'I just need a quick word . . .' And, before he could continue, he himself was interrupted by the DI.

'No words,' he said firmly. 'Also, no leads, no half-baked hunches or outlandish conspiracy theories. Not from you. Ever. Understand? You're not a detective and you never will be, thankfully.'

One of the actual detectives, DC Carpenter, gave a

sycophantic laugh at that but the others couldn't be bothered.

Dominic shook his head. 'It's not that; it's –'

'No.' DI Hall put up a hand to stop him. 'It's *always* that. We don't want your ideas. I think I have made that very clear.'

'I know but –'

'No buts,' he said, 'unless a killer is sitting in the back of your car and you have a signed confession, I don't want to know.'

'It's –'

The DI actually shushed him then, as if he was a tiny child and he even raised a finger to his lips. The others were all looking at Dominic now. It was demeaning.

'Fine.'

'Fuck off then,' concluded Hall cheerfully and he waved his hand dismissively.

Dominic made as if to leave but, determined to deliver his news, he told the assembled room, 'Sean Cole's daughter is back in town. I just thought you ought to know.'

Rebecca spent some time wandering from room to room in her childhood home, at a loss as to what to do first and feeling overwhelmed, not even knowing what to think. The house seemed so empty without her father, but at the same time she still could not fully accept that he was gone and never coming back. Wasn't denial one of the recognized stages of grief? If so, she was struggling to move beyond it.

Every room in the house was messy, his bed unmade, books stacked on the bedside cabinets, clothes piled on chairs. *Maybe he got lazy living on his own*, thought Rebecca, *or perhaps he didn't care what the place looked like any more if no one came round to see it.*

His office, a small room on the top floor of the three-storey building, was the worst. There were papers on his desk, obscuring much of it, and other piles of paper on the floor, as well as the ubiquitous books. A small couch was completely covered with more papers and books and a waterproof jacket, as well as a pile of laundry he had obviously washed and aired but not got around to putting away. It seemed he was a man who was easily distracted. That was how she thought of her father, as a person who seemed to have the troubles of the world on his shoulders, always busy doing battle with problems from work at the expense of his family and his own free time. She hoped he had at least found a little calm in his final years but, on the evidence here, it seemed unlikely.

It had not always been like that, though. Rebecca's early memories were good ones. She sat down now in his ancient swivel desk chair, and began to move it from side to side and recalled her dad making it go all the way round at speed until she was giddy and squealed in delight.

There were other memories too, small things that had stuck in her mind and came back to her now: eating fish and chips with him on the jetty by the sea when Mum was out and he was too tired to cook; ice creams on the promenade; sitting in the front seat of his car while he drove, the seatbelt fitting loosely in all the wrong places. 'Don't tell your mum,' he'd say and wink at her. It struck her now that most of her memories of her father featured just the two of them, and her memories of her mother were similarly of them as a pair. Rarely did she think of the whole family together, as if they were already estranged somehow, long before the formal separation. Now her mother was living a different life, thousands of miles away, and Rebecca was left to sort through her father's possessions and find a home for all his things.

The doorbell snatched her from her thoughts and she trudged down the stairs, wondering if it was someone looking for her father, and she would have to break the bad news to them. She opened the front door to find a tall, thick-set man peering down at her. There were two other men behind him and they all wore suits. She waited for him to speak. When he did not, she said, 'Yes?'

'Rebecca Cole?' he asked in the formal manner of someone in authority, and she immediately pegged him as a police officer.

'Yes.'

'Detective Inspector Hall, Northumbria Police. Would you mind if we had a word?' He did not enlighten her any further.

'OK.'

She thought he meant from the doorstep but he

gestured with a palm to indicate that they wanted to come in. 'Can we, er . . . ?'

'Of course.' And she led them into the living room where they sat awkwardly. DI Hall had chosen her father's chair and that felt like an intrusion, which made her instantly and unfairly dislike him. He introduced his men as DC Fox and DC Carpenter. She did not offer them a cup of tea.

'First of all, I'd like to offer my condolences. I'm sorry for your loss.'

'Thank you.'

'Your father was a well-known figure in the community.'

She noted his use of 'well-known', as opposed to 'well-liked' or 'well-regarded' and she wondered if this detective had not been a fan of Sean Cole the newspaper editor, a man who could occasionally ruffle feathers with a fearless page lead or scathing editorial.

'I just wanted to let you know that we are continuing to look into the circumstances surrounding his death but that does not necessarily make them suspicious.'

Rebecca was startled by the use of that word. Suspicious? How could they be suspicious?

There was a pause while she waited for him to continue but it seemed he was not about to do that.

'My father died of a heart attack. That's what I was told.'

He shifted uneasily in his seat. 'That was the initial assumption, based on the available facts at the time.'

'What facts?'

'We learned your father had a heart condition.'

'He had to take tablets,' she told him.

'And his body was found in his old office in the newspaper building.'

'What was he doing there?'

'Removing the newspaper archives or so we understand.'

'Why now? The *Eriston Gazette* folded three years ago.'

'A developer bought the building. They're going to pull it down to build some apartments.'

Sooner or later it happened to every old building in town; the failing pubs and hotels, even the old Scout hut, had all been torn down and tall blocks of small flats with tiny balconies erected in their place. Under different circumstances, Rebecca might have been upset to learn that the old newsroom was about to join them, but she was entirely focused on the fate of her father now that it had been drawn into question.

'We thought he might have overexerted himself. Those big newspaper binders are heavy.'

'Where was he taking them?'

'We don't know. Here perhaps.'

That would be so like Dad, to try to store decades' worth of old copies of the *Eriston Gazette* in his own home to save them from the rubble.

'And you think his heart gave out,' she asked, 'or not?' She was unsure what he might be implying.

'It seemed a reasonable assumption. There was no

sign of forced entry or any kind of struggle, though the front door was left unlocked, so in theory someone could have joined him there.'

'Someone?' What was he getting at?

'An assailant,' he said.

'You think my father was attacked?'

'I'm not saying he was,' he said, 'but it is a possibility.'

Rebecca was reeling now. 'What makes you think it is a possibility?'

'The autopsy showed evidence of myocardial infarction. That's decreased blood flow, which can cause a section of the heart to die. A heart attack in other words. So it was reasonable to assume your father's heart had given out, but –' he paused for a moment, as if choosing his next words carefully – 'it also revealed a broken hyoid bone.'

Did he expect her to understand what this meant?

'I don't . . . I've never heard of that.'

The detective lifted up his chin and brought his hand up to a spot just below it at the top of his neck. 'It's here,' he told Rebecca.

'So,' she asked unsurely, 'what does that mean?'

'Well, it could have happened in the fall.'

'My mother mentioned a fall,' she recalled.

'We found your father's body at the bottom of the stairs.'

'You say it *could* have happened in a fall. Are you implying that he might have been pushed?'

He took a moment to reply. Was he stalling? 'We don't know,' he told her then, 'but we can't entirely rule it out at this stage.' Every word he uttered seemed forced, as if he was reluctant to say them.

'DI Hall, is there something you are not telling me?'

It seemed she would have to drag it out of him.

'Because of the nature of the injury, it's also possible that he was strangled.'

7

Rebecca ran. She was running hard now, as if someone was chasing her. Close to a flat-out sprint, she was covering ground quickly but it felt effortless, adrenaline powering her on, her mind racing, filled with conflicting thoughts.

When the detectives had left, after half an hour of answering, *deflecting* more like, Rebecca's questions about her father and the circumstances of his death, she had been at a loss over what to do with herself. At first she paced the living room liked a trapped animal, filled with impotent rage and feelings of helplessness that would not dissipate. So she went to her bag and pulled out an old T-shirt, shorts and trainers not specifically designed for running in, but they would do. Rebecca was an occasional runner, not an everyday Lycra-clad obsessive, but whenever she needed to think or clear her head, a run helped.

This time, though, it wasn't helping. DI Hall was not sure if her father had actually been killed or not and, if anything, seemed to think it was more likely to have been an unfortunate accident. When he asked her if her father had fallen out with anyone or had enemies, it felt half-hearted, as if he was simply going through the motions. When she was forced to admit she could not think of anyone who might have harboured a grudge strong enough to commit murder, this seemed to satisfy him.

He did concede, however, that around half of strangulation cases resulted in a broken hyoid bone, though in her father's case there were no other visible signs of strangulation. 'There were no marks left by a garrotte or any noticeable abrasions on the soft tissue of the neck. Perhaps he simply broke his hyoid bone in the fall down the stairs. There was no obvious motive for a break-in. The newspaper archive and old office furniture were valueless and there were no sightings of anyone else entering the building.'

Why would anyone want to kill her father? The detectives could not come up with a reason and neither could she, though he seemed to think she might, even though Rebecca and her dad had seen so little of each other in the past few years. Why was that? Hall had asked her and there was perhaps a hint of suspicion in his tone, as if she had somehow planned her father's murder in order to inherit his crumbling house. In truth, she didn't really know why, but distance had played a part. Before her travels, Rebecca had been working for a pop culture magazine in London that was launched, struggled, stuttered, then finally died, all in a matter of months. She had been three hundred miles from Eriston and couldn't just drop in on her father to see how he was doing.

Their phone calls had become shorter and less frequent too. He didn't have much to talk about and when he did tell her about his life there was a definite undercurrent of sadness, perhaps even bitterness in his words. Who could really blame him? His marriage had broken up, in part because of his preoccupation with a newspaper that had folded in the end anyway. He had even sent the last edition out with a black border round its edges, a final flourish from an editor who viewed this as the tragic death of a living, breathing thing. Did he think his life had been a waste?

It would explain his lack of enthusiasm or support for her chosen career. He seemed to take little pride in her accomplishments, perhaps because they did not come close to mirroring his at her age. Maybe he just didn't think she was all that good.

He had briefly regained his old spark when he informed Rebecca that he was writing a book. There was even a meeting in London with a literary agent, which had rekindled some hope in him that he might still have a writing career.

'A history of murder,' he had announced to her, between forkfuls of pasta eaten in the branch of a mediocre restaurant chain in Covent Garden, before he had to dash for his train home. 'Going back years. Eriston's murder rate has always been historically high. I'm going to write a book about it.'

Rebecca couldn't understand why he, of all people, who had been so personally caught up in the town's more recent tragedies, would want to explore them again, and when she frowned in disbelief at him, he quickly added, 'The historical ones, I mean, not the . . .' He didn't need to finish the sentence.

41

'Right . . .' she offered cautiously.

'Cases that happened decades and, in some cases, hundreds of years ago.' And he'd rhymed off familiar killings: 'The Mad Surgeon, the Fisherman's Son, the Keelman.' He made these real-life long-ago murders sound like harmless ghost stories.

'Sounds great, Dad.'

But perhaps he'd detected a lack of enthusiasm from her, because he quickly changed the subject. 'It'll probably come to nothing.'

And it did come to nothing. One publisher wanted it but asked for a very different book from the one her father was proposing. Less folklore and more true crime, not focusing so much on the old, long-forgotten tales of murder in and around Eriston. How about one that centred on the more recent, shocking crimes that her father knew about in his role as the local newspaper editor? The Eriston Rose case. And wasn't there another murder shortly afterwards? Hadn't one of his newspaper's own reporters been killed while investigating the case?

The shutters went down then and there was no more correspondence with that publisher. It must have planted a seed, though, judging by the book he'd had delivered and his interest in the old *Gazette* archives. As she ran now, Rebecca's mind went back to another time when she had run from something. As a little girl, not much more than eight years old, she and her father had walked through the woods at the back of their house together, as they used to do most mornings before school. It was their guaranteed time together in case he worked late and missed her in the evenings. There they discovered the blood-soaked body of Katherine Prentiss lying lifeless in the woods.

Don't think about that, Rebecca.

It was an instinctive response and one she had conditioned herself to give from a very early age, whenever her thoughts drifted back to that day and the slaughtered young journalist. Blotting it out had been her coping mechanism.

With a sudden clarity Rebecca stopped running so abruptly that another runner behind her had to swerve to avoid bumping into her. It dawned on Rebecca that if her father had, in fact, started to write this book, and had gone about it with his customary thoroughness and zeal, he might conceivably have discovered something new about the killings and this, in turn, may have even been the reason for his death.

Rebecca showered, then dried her hair while she thought more about this. So her dad was writing a book, possibly. What if, far from abandoning the idea as she had imagined, he had just got quietly on with it? If so, where was it? Rebecca realized that she hadn't seen his laptop anywhere. He used it to carve out a meagre living, writing articles that paid peanuts, with a sideline as a copy-editor and proofreader. Boring but necessary work that just about covered his bills.

Rebecca went to his office and stood by her father's desk. Definitely no laptop here. Had someone taken it?

He had told the locksmith things had been going missing. Could the person responsible for the missing laptop be the same someone who might have killed her father? Rebecca made a quick search of the office. She opened every drawer and found a jumble of papers, some old pens, a few ancient business cards and some envelopes, but there was no sign of his laptop. She searched the rest of the house but couldn't find it, so Rebecca was forced to give up the quest for now.

She didn't want to sit in the house doing nothing, though. It had been a while since Rebecca had walked around her old home town and she was curious to see how much of it had changed. If she was lucky, maybe she would run into someone who knew her father and might even know what he had been up to lately.

Rebecca was about to leave when the doorbell rang again and she was surprised to find a police officer standing on her doorstep. This one looked as if he was in his early forties and, unlike DI Hall, he was in uniform. Had there been a mix-up? Did he not realize she'd already had a visit from a detective? Momentarily confused by his earnest face, she waited for him to speak.

'Miss Cole? I'm Dominic Green,' he told her. 'I knew your father.'

'Oh,' was all she could think to say.

He took a breath. 'And I think I know who killed him.'

8

The police officer began with an admission that he was 'not here in an official capacity'. Senior officers were also unaware of his visit. He even admitted, 'I shouldn't have come in uniform.'

This would have been intriguing enough on its own, even without his insistence that he knew who had killed her father. Rebecca invited him in.

'I remember you,' he said, and smiled, 'from when you were just a little girl. We did community campaigns with the newspaper and I had meetings with your father. You used to sit outside his office and draw.'

'Sometimes,' she said, 'in the summer holidays.' If her mother was busy, her father would bring her in to his office and let her sit at an unused desk, but there were strict rules: best behaviour, only speak when spoken to and don't bother the journalists. Reading, drawing or writing were allowed until Mother returned to pick her up. It was never drawing, though, despite what the police officer thought. It was always writing, even then. Rebecca would invent whole new worlds full of characters but no princesses. 'Because they always have to be rescued by boys,' she had told her mother, 'and I don't like that.'

'Good for you,' her mother had said. 'And I'll let you

into a secret, Rebecca. In real life women nearly always have to rescue themselves.'

The policeman held a hand up to just above his waist height. 'You were about this high then.'

But Rebecca was not interested in his reminiscences. 'My father,' she reminded him, 'you said you know who killed him.'

'I think so, yes. You might want to sit down.' He didn't seem eager to come to the point and she wondered if he really did know anything about her father's death.

They sat opposite one another in the living room and he began cagily. 'I would get into trouble if anybody knew I was here.'

'Then I won't tell anyone.'

He seemed reassured by this. 'They don't like it when I tread on their toes.'

'Who doesn't?'

'CID,' he said.

'They were here earlier.' And she described DI Hall's visit.

'They don't appreciate it if you tell them something they don't want to hear.' He must have picked up on the look on her face and sensed her confusion. 'I'm not making myself very clear. I'm sorry . . . For some years now I have been –' he seemed to be trying to choose the right word and he settled on – '*interested* in the number of murders in the area and the people who just –' he spread his hands in a gesture that showed the suddenness of the act – 'disappear. I don't know if you are aware but for a town the size of Eriston and its surrounding area . . .'

'There's a fairly large number of unexplained deaths,' she offered.

'Usually they are explained away as an accident or a suicide; sometimes it's a domestic assault that went too far. In other cases blame falls on the victim's partner or their ex. The perpetrator is apprehended and jailed. In other cases he is never caught. The main thing is that we come up with explanations for all these deaths, even the unsolved ones. It's all to do with the stats, you see. CID are judged on clearance rates.'

'I don't . . .' She was frustrated that he was not coming to the point.

'Know what I am getting at?' And he sighed because he knew he wasn't being clear. 'Detectives are trained, maybe they train themselves, to look for the most obvious solution to a murder; it was the spurned boyfriend, the jealous lover, a controlling father, and they are right in the majority of instances, in most places. But Eriston isn't most places. Eriston is special. I reckon there is someone in Eriston who likes to kill people and he is getting away with it. I think that other people take the blame, because this person is very clever. Very clever indeed.'

Rebecca did not know what to think. Dominic Green didn't look or sound like a conspiracy theorist. He was well spoken and appeared intelligent. He was also a member of the police force, privy to information the public could not see, but his visit was, on his own admission, unsanctioned and his theory seemed far-fetched.

'This sounds like a bit of a leap,' she said.

'It sounds crazy,' he admitted. 'No one else in the Northumbria Police believes it. I suspect they all think I'm a bit mad, but do you know who did agree with me? Your father.'

Rebecca allowed Dominic to speak uninterrupted for long enough to explain how his path had recently crossed her father's again and what they had both hoped to achieve by sharing information.

'I'd known your dad for a long time. I think that's why he trusted me to help him in confidence.'

'Help him with what?'

'His research.'

'He *was* working on a book,' she conceded.

'You knew about that? I thought you might. It started out as a book. He was planning to write about the Eriston Rose killing and the murder of his reporter, Katherine Prentiss, but his research took him in an unexpected direction and that's why he came to see me.'

'He started to link their deaths with other killings?' she offered.

He smiled slightly at that. 'The apple doesn't fall far from the tree.'

That irritated Rebecca, because he assumed her powers of reasoning were simply inherited. 'You were explaining your theory about linked killings,' she said. 'It seemed a reasonable assumption.'

'Did he ever talk to you about his book, share any of his findings?' asked the policeman.

'Not really, no. He said he wanted to look into the Eriston Rose case again but never mentioned finding anything significant. I wasn't sure if he had even started the book.'

'That's a pity. I was hoping he might have told you something.'

'Do you think he found new evidence?'

'If his death was not an accident, then someone killed him and they had a reason for doing it. If we can discover what your father found out, we might be a step closer to finding his killer. I'm sorry, I know this must be difficult.'

'It is difficult but if there really is a killer out there then I want him caught, but I don't see how I can help you. My father didn't tell me anything. I haven't found any manuscripts or notebooks, no memory sticks or even his laptop.'

'He didn't have it with him in the newsroom,' Dominic confirmed, 'unless the killer took it, of course.'

'If he was clearing the newsroom, he wouldn't have taken it with him.'

'So where is it?'

'Apparently things had been going missing in the house. He even changed the locks.'

'You think someone stole it?'

'I don't know, but I'm thinking he probably changed the locks to prevent it from being stolen.' It seemed logical since it was probably the only thing in the house with any value. 'I'll keep looking,' she assured him because she was now as keen to read her father's book as he was.

'Like me to help?'

'No,' she said quickly. 'I'd rather go through his things on my own, if that's all right with you?'

And even if it isn't.

'Of course, sorry I . . . I didn't mean to intrude.' He must have realized the offer had made her uncomfortable. 'I'll leave you to it then.' He got to his feet. 'And I can't stress how sorry I am about your father. He was one of the good ones.'

'Thank you.'

'That's why I want to get the man who did this.'

'So do I.'

'If you do come across anything, then please let me know,' he said. 'Anything at all.'

'That's more or less what DI Hall said.'

'Yeah, well, he's not fully convinced your father was murdered.'

'But you are?'

'I'm afraid so, yes.'

'Then if I find anything, I'll be sure to let you know.'

'Same here,' he promised.

'Will you really?' she asked. 'I thought the police didn't like sharing information with members of the public.'

'That depends on the circumstances. Look, I'll level with you. I'm not always in the loop but I do hear things and I will keep on digging. If I hear something it would be useful to run it by you, to see what you think. If you don't mind?'

He took a pen and a notebook out of his pocket and wrote in it, then tore off the page and handed it to Rebecca. 'My number, so you can call me. If you would prefer to meet in person, I usually have my lunch at the old café near the harbour.'

'I know it.'

'Then maybe I'll see you there,' he said, before adding, 'when you're ready.'

9

After not one but two visits from the police in one morning, leaving her with much to think about, Rebecca felt the need to get out of the house and clear her head, so she walked down the hill into town. She had barely begun to accept her father's death and now it seemed he might have been murdered. It was scarcely believable but Dominic Green at least was convinced of it. The police officer even had a credible theory, a theory that she shared, having come to a similar conclusion herself that same morning. It made sense but was so hard to accept. Losing her father was one thing, the thought of him being taken from her violently only compounded her grief.

It was good to be out of the house at least. The sun was shining, which was far from guaranteed in Eriston, even in the summer, and the sea air felt fresh. Rebecca was suddenly hungry, having had no time for breakfast. She deliberately chose a café that had opened up since she left Eriston as a teenager. The owner wouldn't know her or feel obliged to offer her their condolences, a social nicety she was already struggling with. What could you say in reply other than a completely inadequate *thank you*?

She ordered a mug of English breakfast tea and

beans on toast; the cheapest items on the menu. Then she skimmed the newspaper she had bought on the way there. Everyone else in the café was glued to their phones, desperately liking their friends' Facebook posts and Instagram pictures no doubt.

When Rebecca had left London, she had also left social media and missed it even less than a city she had slowly but steadily fallen out of love with, as her career and personal life fell into a decline. She couldn't help but link the demise of both to her surroundings, even though they had nothing to do with the slow death of journalism or the inevitable failure of a relationship that had been in the doldrums for a long while. It wasn't that she resented all the good news she was bombarded with on Facebook, Instagram and Twitter, as her friends and former colleagues progressed, while her own life stalled, but she couldn't help but compare her own situation to their seemingly gilded lives. While they were being promoted, landing exciting new jobs or boyfriends, celebrating engagements or posting wedding photos and pictures of babies and toddlers, she felt she was in stasis. The edited highlights of their lives underlined the lack of real progress in hers. Rebecca felt as if she had been going nowhere for nearly a decade now and every life-affirming hashtag just rubbed it in.

#FeelingBlessed   #SoThankful   #LivingMyBestLife #KillingIt

Unlike me.

#ThisMan! #SoulMates #TodayIMarriedMyBestFriend Christ.

Her final post was a deliberately short and fake-breezy one, designed solely to explain her absence from the gush-fest that social media had become. A selfie at the airport, with a huge plane visible in the background through the window, then . . .

Going travelling! Off round the world. All the places I have ever dreamt of. So excited! Back in a year. See you all on the other side!

It was tempting to add *#NowPleaseLeaveMeAlone*.

She hoped that was breezy enough to stop everyone she knew from feeling sorry for her. Rebecca felt like a failure and the last thing she wanted was reminders that her life had not worked out the way she had hoped. All she wanted to do was run away. She didn't even check the replies before logging off for good.

Rebecca went back to reading *The Times* while she ate her toast. By the time she was done, the café had thinned out, as people returned to work or carried on with their sight-seeing. She knew that most of those actually staying in Eriston were there because accommodation was cheap but they would then get into their cars and head off to other parts of Northumbria, with less shabby high streets and nicer seafronts.

Rebecca was in no position to help her crumbling town, so she turned to more important matters closer to home. Had someone really killed her father or was the autopsy report wrong? The pathologist hadn't said for certain that this was a murder, just that it could have been. What if her father's heart had actually given out and he had fallen, then hit his neck on the way down the stairs, like DI Hall suggested? It might explain the broken bone but that seemed an even more outlandish theory than strangulation. No, she couldn't believe that. Her father was murdered. PC Dominic Green thought so and so did she.

Rebecca resolved that when she returned home that night she would scour the entire house again from top to bottom, search each room and open every drawer, until she found a manuscript, his laptop or a memory stick, something that could explain her father's theories on the local murders and then offer a clue about his own death.

'Becky?'

She was snapped from her thoughts by the sound of her name. Not many people called her Becky. It was spoken doubtfully by a man about her age, who had just turned away from the counter. He had a cup of tea in his hand and he was staring at Rebecca, as if he wasn't entirely convinced it was really her.

The newcomer had a strange look on an admittedly handsome face. His dark hair had been blown about by the sea breeze and he was harder to place because there was stubble on his chin.

Then he smiled. 'It *is* you.' And when she showed no sign of recognition, he added, 'Isn't it?'

'Yes,' she said and he finally moved closer so she could get a better look at him.

'Don't remember me, do you? Not a clue.' His brown eyes sparkled at this and he seemed to find it amusing. She looked at him closely then and it took a few seconds to place him. The passing of time and the changes the years had brought to his face, particularly the stubble which obscured part of it, meant it took longer than it should have. When it hit her, she found herself blushing. 'Oh God, Alan? Is it really you?'

'The same,' he confirmed. 'Have I changed that much?'

'Oh, I'm so sorry.' She was embarrassed now. 'And yes, you have, but for the better. You've . . .' She was lost for words now and waved a hand vaguely, before settling on 'grown up'.

'You mean I'm old?' he said, but he was smiling. 'Haggard? It's this place. The sea air. I should moisturize.'

And for some reason that made her laugh out loud. It even attracted some reproachful looks from other people who were making quiet, respectful conversation at other tables.

'Alan Miller,' she said quietly.

'The very same. We knew each other years back.'

'We did.' And they both stifled grins at that. Mindful of the looks they were getting from other tables she told him, 'Sit down. If you've got time.'

'I've got time.'

He placed his coffee and phone on the table, pulled out the chair and sat down opposite her. He looked serious then.

'I assumed you would be back. I was so sorry to hear about your father. I'll be at the funeral obviously. He helped me when I was starting out.' And when she didn't understand he explained. 'I renovate houses. He let me run some ads in the paper at less than the normal rate. A lot less. They got me going with my first jobs.'

'Did he?' She was genuinely surprised about that. Rebecca had always assumed her father hadn't liked Alan all that much.

'God,' he said abruptly. 'I can't believe it's you. How long has it been? Ten years? More? Must be.'

'Twelve, I think. I haven't seen you since we were sixteen.' *Not since I dumped you,* she thought, *because I had my GCSEs to sit and my dad somehow persuaded me that I had no time for a boyfriend and he was 'too young to become a grandfather',* a comment which had embarrassed her more than she let on at the time.

'You left town.'

'With my mam,' she confirmed.

'How is she?'

'OK, she's in New Zealand now. Remarried and happy.'

'Really? That's good to know. I liked your mam.'

And she liked you, thought Rebecca, *almost as much as I did, before Dad got involved and convinced me you were rough and unreliable.*

'How have you been?' she asked.

'I've been here mostly. Though I do work in other towns too. I'm OK, I s'pose. What about you?'

Was she OK? Clearly not, but she didn't really want to admit that to her ex. 'I'm good. I mean, apart from . . .' And she didn't have to complete the sentence.

When he probed further, she told him about her life after she had left Eriston – the jobs, the places – though she didn't mention the man she had lived with until relatively recently. It struck her that her most recent boyfriend didn't even make it on to the shortlist of her life's highlights now.

It was strange seeing Alan again after so many years but it felt nice, natural even. There didn't seem to be any bitterness or awkwardness between them, which she might have expected, but they were so young when they were going out and a lot of time had passed since then. Instead they talked openly and easily just like they used to.

He offered her another drink. 'Don't you have to get back to work?' she asked.

'I work for myself so . . .' He shrugged to indicate that he didn't have to answer to anyone.

They had another cup of coffee and spent time catching up on each other's lives, while he gave her updates on their childhood friends who were still in Eriston. It didn't take long as there weren't many. Rebecca was open about her own circumstances. 'You'll work something out,' he said when she told him she was unemployed. 'You always were the clever one.'

'Says the man with his own business.'

When they eventually couldn't face any more coffee, they decided to go for a walk down towards the harbourside. 'Don't you have to be heading back?' she asked after a while.

'Probably.' But he didn't seem to be in a hurry to leave her. 'I'll go in a bit.'

They heard a woman's voice then from behind them.

'Excuse me!' she called, and they turned to see the waitress from the café holding up a phone. 'Is this yours?'

'Shit,' said Alan. 'I'm always losing it. Thanks, pet. You're a star,' he told the waitress. She beamed at him and her face flushed. Did she fancy Rebecca's first love? It looked that way but Alan seemed oblivious. He was a good-looking man, though. She had to admit Alan had aged well.

The young woman left and they turned back towards the harbour, which was when Rebecca spotted a familiar figure on one of the boats. The man was tall, lean and looked to be in his early sixties but his face was well lined from working the sea for so long and being exposed to the elements every day.

'There's someone I need to see,' she told Alan.

They walked right up to the edge of the boat and she called, 'Hello.' But he did not even look up.

'Boat's full, love,' he said, because he assumed they wanted to board. 'We'll set out again in an hour.'

'That's OK,' she said. 'I only came over to say hi, Jack.'

He looked up and squinted at Rebecca. 'By God,' he said, 'little Becky Cole. Is that really you?'

'Didn't recognize me, did you?'

'Not my fault,' he assured her. 'Can't find me glasses.'

'They're on your head,' she said, 'as usual. Nothing changes round here, does it?'

He reached up, freed his glasses from a tangle of greying curly hair and pulled them down over his eyes. 'You're going to need them,' she pointed out, 'if you want to avoid the rocks.'

'You really think I need glasses to go round the Farnes?' He scoffed. 'Could do it blindfolded and one-handed, at night, in a storm, and you'd still be all right with me, as well you know.'

'I do,' she admitted.

When Rebecca was fourteen, she had trudged around Eriston looking for a part-time job to earn a little money but mostly to escape the rows at home. Work was scarce for adults, let alone teenagers, so she had no success in the shops and cafés. As a last resort, she had gone down to the harbour and asked the boat-men if they needed any help. They were a gruff lot and most sent her packing but Jack at least heard her out, even though he looked to be the most fierce. 'I'll give you a trial,' he told her. 'You sell tickets on the harbour, collect them when they board and flog souvenirs while I'm dodging the rocks. Let's see if you sell enough.'

The tickets had been easy. The selling of souvenirs, using a deep, home-made, wooden tray, with straps that hung over her shoulders, was trickier, especially as the boat lurched from side to side in the waves and she had to stand on a deck made slippery from sea-water. She hadn't thought to wear a coat because it had been sunny in town but it was cold and windy out at sea and she was freezing by the end of the trip. Rebecca endured all this, as much to prove to the older man that she could as anything else and he let her work the rest of the day. At the end he handed her the first money she had ever earned and Rebecca went home cold but happy, to find her father out and her mother sobbing upstairs in a bedroom. She had to make beans on toast for her tea. Rebecca went back the next day and worked for Jack whenever she could, during holidays and weekends, for the next two years.

She realized she had not introduced the two men. 'I'm sorry, Jack. This is Alan.'

'I've seen him around. Nice to meet you, son. You've got a lovely lass there, so make sure you treat her right or you'll have me and the rest of the boys to answer to.'

Alan laughed, and Rebecca said, 'Oh no, we're not . . . Alan is an old friend. We just bumped into each other. I'm back for –'

'I know why you're back, pet,' he said, 'and I was very sorry to hear it. I'm not one for funerals, so I'll not come but I don't mean anything by it. When you are gone you are gone and life is for the living.' Then he said, 'But there's not many like your fatha left now.' The word was never pronounced *father* round here by the older ones, or even Dad, always *fatha*. 'Everyone knows the price of everything but the value of nowt these days.' Then he changed the subject. 'Didn't you go off to become a reporter,' asked the old man, 'like your dad?'

'I did,' she admitted.

'He must have been proud.'

'No,' she said simply, 'he told me I was an idiot.'

Jack looked at Rebecca like he expected her to suddenly admit she was pulling his leg. When she didn't, he seemed a little uncomfortable. 'Anyhow,' he said, 'come back later and you can gan out for free –' he glanced at Alan – 'both of you.'

She smiled warmly at that. 'I might,' she said, 'but it won't really be free, will it?' When he frowned she said, 'You'll need someone to sell your ice creams, won't you?'

He chuckled at the thought of the grown woman doing what the young girl had once done. She turned away then and he watched them go but he couldn't resist calling out to her. 'Are you not married then, with bairns?'

She turned back and shook her head.

'Courting?' he persisted.

She walked backwards as she called, 'Nope.'

'Oh,' he said mischievously, 'I expect you're one of them lesbians then, are you? I hear they're all the rage these days.' She swore at him then and he laughed. 'See you later, bonny lass.'

She winked at the old man. 'Not if I see you first.'

When Rebecca returned home, she felt buoyed by her chance meeting with Alan and their encounter with Jack. It was remarkable how cheered she was by the familiarity of their faces and just a few moments of pleasant company. Jack was still the fierce curmudgeon she had worked for as a girl but she thought no less of him for that. Alan was . . . well, Alan was still Alan, and he retained the ability to make her laugh and distract her from the worst aspects of her life, even now. That was something he had been able to do when they were going out all those years back and it had been a blessed relief to spend time with him in the café and not to have to think about her father for a few precious moments.

She had wondered if he might suggest meeting again for a drink or a coffee but instead he had just said he would be at the funeral. She told herself it was probably for the best, because spending time with an old flame was generally a bad idea. *Never go back*, she thought. *He's probably got a girlfriend anyway. That waitress definitely liked him and she wouldn't be the only one.*

Once she was back in the house, Rebecca began another, more thorough search for her father's laptop. The kitchen held little more than the most basic utensils and plain, white crockery, along with some tinned food. The room screamed *single middle-aged male living on his own*.

The living room held no mysteries either; its chest of drawers contained no journals or notepads. Rebecca worked her way up the house and even checked her bedroom, which looked much as it had done when she had left it more than a decade ago, right down to the posters on the walls. Next, she checked the third floor, which housed the spare bedroom and her dad's office.

There wasn't even any bedding on the spare bed, just a mattress and no other furniture in that sad, little room. No one ever came to stay, she realized and Rebecca finally started to appreciate how lonely the last quarter of her father's life must have been, with no wife and an absentee daughter. It was a thought that filled her with sadness and a measure of guilt. She closed the door on that bare room and crossed the landing, which had an airing cupboard and a small door in the roof leading to the attic.

Was the chaos of his office indicative of a troubled state of mind? There was no sign of the laptop here and she was forced to admit defeat for now. She even wondered if he had sold it. No, he would have sold the house first before giving up on the one tool he still needed to ply his trade. If you took away Dad's writing there really was nothing left.

Rebecca went back to the kitchen and microwaved a spag bol she had bought from a corner shop, along with butter, milk, a small plastic jar of honey and a bottle of white wine. She poured a large glass of the wine and ate the spaghetti silently. When she was done, she washed up her solitary plate and cutlery and realized her father would have endured a lonely meal like this one every day for years.

She went into the living room and noticed she had left the light on in there. It was dark outside, so someone could look right in if they wanted to. She walked over to the curtains and drew them and, as she did so, she was sure she saw movement outside. Just like the night before when she had passed the churchyard; it was little more than a blur but she was certain someone was there. Were they peering into the house from across the way, their presence shielded by the darkness? There were other properties with mature gardens, housing trees and bushes, all the way up the hill. It would be easy to hide here if you wanted to. Rebecca parted the curtains again slightly and looked through a small gap between them. She couldn't see anyone but it spooked her sufficiently to go to the front door and lock the mortice and put the bolts in place.

Logically the blur that she had only partially seen could have been a cat or even a bird, whose sudden movement momentarily caught her eye. Even so, she went to the back door next to check that it was definitely locked, before taking the bottle of wine and her glass back into the living room, then putting on the kind of brain-rotting reality TV her father would have strongly disapproved of. It was a welcome and easy distraction and enabled her to pretend that she wasn't just drinking alone.

Eventually, when the bottle was two-thirds empty and her tired eyes were closing, she remembered there was no bedding on her bed and she would have to make it up. That was the last thing she needed when it was late and she was so tired but, even if Rebecca decided to sleep just on her father's large and comfortable couch, she would still have to cover herself with something. She walked up to the airing cupboard on the top floor and opened the door, hoping to locate an old eiderdown or duvet and a pillow. She was in luck. There was a single duvet and a cover to fit over it. She found two pillows and took them out, then rummaged under a collection of towels, duvet covers and sheets, looking for pillowcases. She found one and, as she felt for a second, her hand brushed against a cold metal object. It was such a familiar shape she instantly knew what it was.

'You're kidding me,' she said aloud, a combination of exasperation and relief, with incredulity thrown in, at the discovery of his laptop. Why would her father have chosen to hide it here unless he was afraid someone would take it? Why would he worry about that unless he had found something important and it was stored here on it?

That was close. You almost saw me tonight. I could tell by the way you froze as you pulled the curtains back, then, once I had ducked behind the treeline, I saw you part the curtains again. It was just enough so you could look out. You should have turned the light off if you didn't want me to notice. I have to remember you are new to this game, whereas I am an old hand.

Your naivety is really quite appealing. You think you are safe in your own home. Everyone does. While you were wandering the house, you left all the curtains open. I suspect you won't make that mistake again. Maybe I'll leave you alone for a while, until you relax and let your guard down. Women like you always do.

That's easier said than done. I don't have the restraint or willpower I used to possess. I've broken so many of my rules lately. Am I addicted to this and need it more, or is it the risk that makes it so thrilling? No point in overanalysing it. I'm no psychiatrist.

I'll linger for just a while and maybe I'll catch a glimpse of you while you are preparing for bed. I'm already feeling quite attached to you but I like to take my time getting to know a woman.

Don't worry, though, I'll definitely be back soon.

Until then, sleep well, Rebecca. Oh, and welcome home.

11

Rebecca woke the following morning feeling tired but restless, her night's sleep shortened by an inability to switch off following a fruitless hour spent trying to guess her father's password. Once she was up she immediately tried again, determined to break into the laptop, which allowed her three attempts each time, before locking her out for several minutes. She used the pen she always carried to write down every failed attempt and keep track of them. It was a Sheaffer Sagaris chrome ballpoint and the only really nice pen she had ever owned. Her father had bought it for her when she started her first journalism job, in an act that had surprised Rebecca, for both its spontaneity and because it was a rare sign of pride in her.

Rebecca tried a variety of passwords including his name, her name, her date of birth, his address, favourite football team and even the name of the newspaper, which was surely the one thing outside his family that he truly loved. When even variations of *Eriston* and *Gazette* failed, she snapped the laptop shut, placed it on the floor, lay down on the couch and almost instantly fell asleep.

There were probably many clever ways to hack into a laptop but Rebecca didn't know any of them, nor anyone else who might. She tried googling this on her phone but none of the answers were helpful. They either didn't work or were far too complicated for someone who wasn't a 'techie'.

Before leaving the house that morning, she tried more possible password variations, including *password* and *password123*, which predictably didn't work. She didn't think her dad would have come up with anything too complex, though. He would surely never be able to recall one of those passwords with a dozen characters, capital letters, numbers and symbols. He'd just forget it or would end up having to write it down, which would defeat the object.

Before she was locked out again, Rebecca tried variants of her name. Becky and Becks, which her friends sometimes called her, didn't work, so she reluctantly gave up and placed the laptop back in the airing cupboard for now. The more she thought about it, the more convinced she was that her father's death had something to do with the book he was writing. Why else would someone kill the editor of a newspaper that no longer existed?

Rebecca locked up the house and walked into town in an effort to at least start some of the formalities required before she could lay her father to rest, a process that would be delayed until the police formally released the body. She talked to his bank about freeing funds from his account to ensure the household bills would still be paid but they couldn't help her without a death certificate. She contacted the coroner's office, expecting to be told that nothing could be done, since the body had not been released yet. With a suspicion of murder she worried further tests might be needed, which could take some time. She was assured, however, that it was possible to get paperwork that would at least allow a funeral to go ahead and that was a relief. The death was still under investigation, she was told, but blood and microscopic samples had already been taken and sent for analysis. This meant, in effect, that they were done with her father's body and it could be released to the funeral director. An interim death certificate could also be provided, so she would be able to manage her late father's finances. At least her efforts that morning had been worth it.

By now it was lunchtime and, on a whim, Rebecca walked back down towards the harbour. She approached the old café with caution, so she could step back and change her mind if it didn't feel right. She wasn't certain if she really wanted to go ahead with this or not. The place hadn't changed since she was a girl, its familiarity helping her to take that step through its doors.

PC Dominic Green was sitting at a table to the rear of the café. She could see him through a large side window and he did not appear to have noticed her watching him from across the street. She wanted to quiz him some more on the circumstances of her father's death and he had promised to look into it more closely, but could she actually trust him? He wasn't on the murder squad but then they didn't seem to be treating her father's death seriously enough and she did not have much faith in DI Hall. Maybe Dominic was her only way into the investigation. She couldn't do this all on her own. She wouldn't tell him about finding the laptop, though, not until she had at least been able to get into it and had a look for herself. The police would almost certainly take it from her and she didn't trust them to go through its contents methodically enough. Whatever her father had found, she would keep it to herself.

Dominic looked up as she entered the café. 'Perfect timing.' He smiled. 'I've only just ordered. Are you hungry?' A harassed-looking waitress noticed her arrival and came over to take her order even before Rebecca had the chance to look at a menu.

'The all-day breakfast is very good,' Dominic told her.

Not wishing to delay things nor really caring what she ordered, Rebecca said, 'I'll have that then.'

'I wasn't sure if you'd come,' he said once the waitress was gone.

'I want to know the truth.'

He nodded slowly at that. 'You're absolutely sure you want to go over this?'

She understood his hesitation. They were about to discuss the details of her father's likely murder. Somehow she would have to coldly separate the man from the act, if she was to have any chance of objectively understanding what really happened to him.

Rebecca nodded quickly. 'What did you find out?'

'OK,' he said, then his tone changed, as he recounted the facts in a professional manner. 'The door leading up to the newsroom is not overlooked. They were hoping someone from the flats nearby might have seen somebody go in but no one did. There's no CCTV there because that part of town —'

'Is a dump. I know.'

'The door wasn't forced, so maybe he just left it open that night. He was clearing out the old newsroom and there was nothing of any monetary value on that first floor, so he may have thought it didn't matter whether he locked it or not.'

'Or he could have been meeting someone,' she said.

'Who?'

'I don't know,' she admitted.

'OK, well, we'll need to look into that but I don't think it's a lead they're currently following. The CID view is that if there was someone up there with your father and they did kill him, by accident or design, they are more likely to have been an opportunistic criminal disturbed in the act of a burglary.'

Rebecca didn't think so. 'The building has lain empty for almost three years. Anyone could have broken in during that period but no one bothered to. The odds are literally one in a thousand that they chose the same night my father was in there.'

'When you say it like that,' he conceded.

'Wouldn't there have been a light on too? Surely they would have noticed it from the street.'

'So you think your father arranged to meet somebody and that same person killed him? Why would he agree to meet someone he didn't trust?'

'He obviously did trust them.'

'Someone he knew then.' He seemed to mull that over.

She took a moment to gather her thoughts and put them in order. 'I think Dad uncovered something new in his research but I don't think it gave him the full picture. I don't believe he was confronting a possible killer there that night, all alone with no witnesses.'

'What if he didn't leave the door open? What if someone had a key?'

'Who?'

'The owner of the building?' he suggested. 'The letting agent, someone who used to work there with your father perhaps?' She realized it could be any one of a number of people. 'If someone had a key and knew your father was there, there is only one way in or out of that office. He'd have been cornered.'

Somehow that was worse. If the killer came up to the newsroom to confront her dad, he might have known he was about to die.

'Who would know he was there?' she asked.

'The agent who arranged for your father to clear out the place or anyone he or your father spoke to about it.'

'All we know is that *someone* killed him,' she admitted. 'And I don't understand how DI Hall could think otherwise.'

'He doesn't want it to be another murder,' explained Dominic. 'He's under enough pressure to clear his other cases. The major incident room in Eriston Town Hall is a permanent fixture, because we have so many unsolved cases. Hall can be a domineering personality.

He queried the pathologist's conclusion that a broken hyoid *must* mean strangulation. He got the man to admit that it can be caused by trauma, from a fall. Hall reckons your father could have collapsed because of his heart and fallen down the stairs.'

'Dad was just very unlucky? Is that it?'

Their food arrived then and they halted the conversation in front of the waitress, switching to small talk while she took an age to bring over their meals, drinks, cutlery, napkins and sauces. When Dominic learned she had been travelling he said, 'I haven't really been anywhere.' And she wondered if he meant that literally or if he was just not as well travelled as she was. 'Will you carry on?' he asked. 'When this is over?'

'I'll need to make some money first.' And in that moment she knew her round-the-world trip was definitely over. The realities of life, like dealing with her father's crumbling house and the need to earn a living, would have to be faced and soon.

He asked her a few questions about the places she had visited, then said, 'Eriston must seem very small to you.'

'It's still home,' she said.

They had nearly finished their meals when a shadow quite literally fell on their table. 'Working hard, I see.' They looked up to find a tall, stocky shape towering over them, blocking the light from the window. It was DI Hall and she immediately sensed he was not here for something to eat. He must have seen them through that big window and now he had something to say.

'I'm on my break,' said Dominic meekly.

74

'Out to lunch, eh?' sneered Hall.

'Rebecca, you've met Detective Inspector Hall,' said Dominic.

'When I offered my sympathies.' His tone was much softer with her than it had been with Dominic. 'Will you be heading home after the funeral?'

'I'm not sure about my plans.' Since the manner of her father's death was far from resolved she was in no hurry to leave and, in reality, she no longer had a home anywhere else.

'There isn't much round here for bright young things like you, is there, Dominic? Anyone with any brains left years ago.'

Dominic didn't respond. Instead he looked down at his plate, as if his answer might be written on it. He seemed cowed by the other man's presence.

'You two know each other of old, do you?' Hall asked her.

'No,' she said.

'Then why the cosy lunch?'

'I was hungry,' she said defiantly.

He gave her a look that said he knew she was being a smart-arse. 'Why are you eating *together*,' he asked slowly, 'if you don't know each other?'

'We do know each other,' she told him. 'You asked if we knew each other of old –' he blinked at her then – 'I didn't know Dominic when I lived here but he knew my dad. Like you, he expressed his sympathies.'

'Did he also offer to help you, by any chance? You might want to turn him down.'

75

Dominic closed his eyes, as if this was all a big embarrassing nightmare he was desperate to wake from.

'Have you told her?' asked the detective and, when Dominic did not respond, he demanded, 'Well, have you?'

'Why don't you stop?' asked Rebecca quietly.

'OK,' Hall said, sounding almost amiable now. Then he looked at Dominic and said, 'Every contact leaves a trace.' As if this had some significance Rebecca was unaware of. Then he walked away.

'I'm sorry about that,' Dominic mumbled when the detective had gone. 'He's a bastard.'

'That's OK,' she assured him, and Rebecca wondered if he would shed any further light on the DI's deliberately provocative comments, to defend himself at least. When he did not, she said, 'And if you ever want to talk about it, I'm –'

'I don't,' he said, cutting her off firmly, a warning look in his eyes.

'And that's OK too,' she said gently, because it was obvious he was trying hard to control his emotions. Whatever had just passed between the detective and Dominic, it had left the man in uniform feeling humiliated and there was real anger there too; she could sense it.

The waitress passed their table and Rebecca was grateful for the distraction. 'Excuse me,' she called after her. 'Could we get some more tea, please?'

'Not for me,' he said, 'I've got to be going.'

And that was it. Dominic rose from the table, leaving some of his meal unfinished. He hadn't taken a single bite since Hall had interrupted them. He took some money from his wallet and dropped it on the table.

'Oh no, let me get this,' she protested, because he had left more than enough to pay for both their meals.

'No arguments,' he said, brushing away her protests, and then he was gone.

'Was everything all right?' asked the waitress when she came back with the tea and observed his half-finished plate.

'Yes,' said Rebecca. 'He had to go.'

As Rebecca sipped her tea, she wondered how she would ever be able to find out the truth when the police who were supposed to be helping her were very obviously at each other's throats.

12

There was something vaguely comforting about being back in her old bedroom but it felt strange too, as if she'd regressed somehow into a person who was not quite her teenage former self but had not gone far beyond that state either. The familiar shape of the mattress accepted her grateful, exhausted form and Rebecca realized how mentally tired she was. Arrangements following a loved one's death were draining and she was dealing with all this on her own.

She supposed she should finish reading the book about the Eriston Rose murder that her father had ordered but so far there was nothing there that she didn't know already, just a rehash, using newspaper cuttings as its sources, with no fresh insights. Rebecca knew she'd be asleep almost as soon as her head hit the pillow so she lay down and closed her eyes.

Hours later, Rebecca opened them again suddenly, snatched from sleep and immediately aware of movement and a presence of some kind. She was hazily conscious that she was back in her childhood home again but, supposedly, the only one there. Whatever she was feeling, it didn't feel right, but it wasn't the benign supernatural appearance of her father. This felt human. This felt real.

It was pitch black outside and there were no lights on in her room so she could barely see anything, just opaque dark shapes against a black background.

While her eyes adjusted to the gloom, Rebecca lay quite still, trying to work out if it had just been a nightmare? She couldn't recall if she had dreamt at all, let alone what about. The darkness was not quite total now; a tiny shaft of moonlight outside was penetrating a slight gap between the thin curtains so she could just make out the wardrobe, a chair, the desk she used to do her homework on . . . and the new shape by the door that should not have been there at all.

Someone was in the room with her and she froze, her shocked brain trying to process if she was seeing something real or if this was a trick of the light – but it was clear enough to Rebecca that somebody was standing there, his back to the door, staring at her, unmoving.

What should she do, stay stock-still and hope that . . . what? Should she move, shout, scream, attack, punch, kick and claw at him, in the hope she could overpower or scare him off? Rebecca refused to believe this was happening to her. A man was in her room, but why wasn't he moving?

In one panicked move she shot to one side, grabbed at the lamp and pressed the switch but it wouldn't come on. Had the bulb gone or the fuse? She pressed it again and finally it flickered into life and illuminated the room.

Rebecca had never been so glad to feel foolish. The presence she had detected in her room was indeed an alien one, and no wonder its shape had frightened her. Her father had hung his long waxed coat, the one he wore for blustery walks along the Northumbrian coastline, on the peg on the back of the door, along with his cap. Its shape had looked exactly like a man.

She hadn't even noticed it when she went to bed and turned off the light. Rebecca checked the screen on her phone. It was two thirty a.m. She got out of bed and took the coat and cap down from the hook. She placed them on the desk chair instead, so they would cast no more frightening shadows, and climbed back into bed, then turned off the light.

As she lay there trying to get back off to sleep, she wondered what had woken her so suddenly. It couldn't have been the silent presence of the coat. Rebecca had a vague notion that it might have been a draught that stirred her, a cool feeling from air that was a little colder than the rest of the room but how could that happen when the window was tightly closed, unless the door she had instinctively looked towards had somehow moved and caused that draught to occur, but how could it do that unless it was stirred by movement somewhere else in the house? Another door opening and closing perhaps, causing the air to change and push against it.

This is ridiculous, she thought. *You know this old house has a life of its own. The floorboards creak in the night, the plumbing rattles even when the immersion is switched off and the old boiler makes thumping noises at all hours. The tree outside didn't help. When its branches were overgrown, they stretched towards the house, then swished in the wind and scraped against the spare bedroom window. You know all this, Rebecca*, she told herself. *You are just not used to it any more.*

Rebecca could remember how this house had the ability to terrify her when she was a small child, as every creak, hiss and thump convinced her there were monsters within the four walls – but she was no longer a child. She told herself there were no such things as monsters, and yet still she could not sleep.

She'd had several days of this now. Trying to think like her father. Attempting to unlock the mystery of the laptop password. She was convinced she could do this, if only she could focus. *Come on, Rebecca*, she urged herself. *You know Dad. It won't be something complicated.* He wasn't the kind of man to change passwords every two or three months. His mind would be on bigger things.

It would be simple, straightforward and something he cared about. But what did her father care about? Not her obviously, she thought. She told herself not to be so stupid then. He did care about his daughter. He just didn't have her at the very forefront of his mind when he had decided on a password, that's all.

What else mattered to him? Surely not his ex-wife. Their parting had been so lengthy and acrimonious, following such bitter rows but what if he was sentimental, nostalgic about a romantic past that predated their mutual hostility? With little expectation of success, Rebecca keyed in her mother's first name, *Judith*. Nothing. Then she tried *Judy* but again it didn't work. She tried the usual variations of it with a capital letter at the beginning and adding *123* at the end, then she was locked out again for another quarter of an hour.

Rebecca made a simple dinner and ate it alone at the kitchen table. As she ate, she wondered what else could have mattered to her father enough to become his password, which she had not already thought of and tried. Not her, not her mum, not even the *Eriston Gazette* or the town, not his car or the name and location of his house; its street name yielding nothing more than another lock-out. She tried the county, the region, the city of Newcastle and every place he'd ever liked to visit with her when she was younger: Tynemouth, Bamburgh, Seahouses, Cragside, Berwick, Durham . . . The list went on. She had a go at places further afield, destinations of childhood holidays, even places he had been to when he was a kid and drew the same blank stare back from the laptop.

Every sequence of password hacks she tried ended in the same way. Rebecca would have her three attempts then it would boot her out for fifteen minutes when she was allowed to try again. At one point she became so frustrated by a lock-out that she let out an exasperated cry that would have been loud enough to alert close neighbours if she had any.

Rebecca forced herself to calm down then and, instead of hurling the laptop across the room into the far wall, she told herself to count to ten. She went back into the kitchen, made some tea, then returned and drank it while she continued the mental joust with her late father.

What did you like? she asked him silently in her head,

and she pondered that question for minutes but did not come up with anything new.

What did you care about? Apart from everything I've already tried.

What did you want? She had even tried keying in the word *Jaguar*, because he always made appreciative noises whenever an old E-Type drove past them. He had wanted one once, long ago, before mere economic survival became the pinnacle of his dreams.

What did you love? Who did you love, apart from us?

It was a combination of things that led her to try it. Rebecca had been searching for something her father cared about enough to use as a password. At the same time her frustration was rising, because she had convinced herself the laptop held the answers she was looking for. The very personal book he was writing on the deaths of Rose and his young protégée, Katherine, might very well be the reason for his own murder.

The realization hit her so suddenly that she sat bolt upright and felt a surge of queasy excitement. Could it be? She thought for a brief second that she might be right but she didn't really want to be.

Rebecca scrambled for the laptop and hoped that enough time had elapsed to enable her to have another try. It let her in and the empty password box blinked on to the screen, waiting for her to fill it.

Rebecca took a breath and typed in the letters.

She had chosen the 'show password' option as a default setting, in case she wrote the correct one absent-mindedly then couldn't remember it.

She paused for a second after she had keyed in the word and surveyed what she had written.

Katherine.

It couldn't be, could it? She hit return.

No. Denied. That would have been too easy. She was about to give up on that line of enquiry when she decided to vary it slightly.

Katherine123.

Rebecca hit the return key and waited to be told that once again she had entered an incorrect password. Instead the laptop played a single triumphant note of musical affirmation, before the password box disappeared and it opened up into a home screen with programmes, apps, icons and folders all coming into view.

Finally she was in.

Katherine123.

Christ, Dad.

So that answered her question. What did her father love?

Katherine.

13

Rebecca opened up Word and scanned the contents of her father's document files. There were so many of them and she would have to go through them all to find what she was looking for. This she began to do, diligently and methodically. It was the only way, but she found it hard to fully concentrate. The breakthrough with the password was shocking enough in itself but it didn't begin to answer all her questions about Katherine and her father. They were the only ones who knew the truth about their relationship and both of them were now dead, but that didn't stop Rebecca wondering about it incessantly, as she continued to click on individual files to open them and scan their contents while she searched for his book.

There were folders containing articles written for submission to magazines, others containing proofreading jobs or copy-editing assignments. It wasn't clear from their titles what was in each file. Would she have to open every single one to check if there was a book in there somewhere? Every time she dismissed one, her thoughts returned to Katherine Prentiss. She knew how devastated her father had been after the murder of his young reporter, had seen it with her own eyes when they had found Katherine's body, but she had always assumed that the death of any young person you worked closely with was bound to be upsetting. It was only now, looking back on it with an adult's eyes, that she could begin to question whether their relationship might have been more than just a professional one. It would explain the rows with her mother. Was this what caused her family to fall apart? Was her father cheating on her mother and did he actually love this murdered young woman more than his wife, more even than his daughter? The thought made her sick.

Privately Rebecca had always attached a large amount of the blame for the break-up of her parents' marriage to her mother. Her father worked long, stressful hours at the newspaper to provide for them all, yet this seemed, perversely, to be the cause of much of her mother's resentment of him. What if there had been another reason for it? If her father had betrayed her mother, perhaps she had been blaming the wrong parent. Would her father have left them both back then for Katherine if she had not been killed? *Why weren't we enough, Dad?* she asked herself silently, and a familiar sense of hurt and abandonment hit her. *Didn't he love us at all?*

As she closed another article that had nothing to do with the Eriston Rose, she told herself to stop thinking so emotionally and to try to calmly evaluate the situation instead. Katherine's name was his password, but did her father really *love* his young protégée in *that* way or had it been an innocent infatuation, an unrequited, helpless and hopeless yearning of an older man for a fresh-faced, beautiful young woman? Or was it actually reciprocated? Was he sleeping with his reporter?

Sleeping with? Such a stupid expression when sleep has nothing to do with it.

Was her father one of those older men in positions of authority who took the younger women they worked with to bed? You read about men like that in the news. She shook her head, knowing she needed to stay detached if she was going to uncover the truth. She needed to view it from both her father's and Katherine's perspective.

Katherine had arrived in Eriston knowing no one, eager to make a mark, possessing skill and talent, along with ambition and drive, but she was raw, had no contacts and didn't know much about journalism. Her father used to say it can't really be taught in a classroom and you only actually pick up the skills when you start to work on a newspaper. He was good at what he did and would always help others, particularly the young reporters he demanded quality work from. He could have taught Katherine how to become the thing she most wanted to be. She would have been grateful for that and impressed by him, possibly even a little in awe of this older man. Did his attraction to her and her respect for him draw them naturally together till they began an affair?

He did work late, particularly on the evenings when he had to 'put the paper to bed', overseeing the publication of its final version and print run. Sometimes reporters stayed late and helped him. Did Katherine, new and keen after all, with nothing much to go home to, offer to do this and they ended up together afterwards; in the office, his car, her room? She didn't want to think about that, but people had affairs. It was naive to think it couldn't have happened. Rebecca had been hit on herself by enough lecturers, editors and fellow journalists to realize that opportunities were always there if you wanted to take them.

Christ, what did it really matter now anyway? It was all so long ago. Her father wouldn't be the first man to miss dinner with his wife and daughter to pursue an affair. Rebecca was an adult. She'd moved on. Hadn't she?

Except that it did matter. If you cared enough about something, you could never really move on. Her father's life and personality had altered for ever when they stumbled across Katherine's body. Everything changed that day. In a way it was the end of Rebecca's own innocence.

A bad man came to the town and did something terrible and that's why Daddy was so upset.

That's how her mother had explained it to Rebecca at the time. She spent years thinking her father had been so devastated simply because he knew the victim.

Her name was your bloody password, Dad.

More than that; her father's seeming obsession with Katherine Prentiss and the need to find her killer might have led him to his own death.

Eventually Rebecca had to force herself to stop thinking about it and instead made a conscious effort to focus fully on the task in hand, while she continued to search the laptop for clues to her father's murder.

She doubted there would be a single bombshell. She didn't expect to find the name of the killer here, but if she could find his book, read his own words, then try to follow in her father's footsteps, as he reinvestigated the murders, the truth of what happened all those years ago might eventually be revealed to her. Perhaps then she could finish the job he'd started.

She scrolled along the documents right to the end before realizing there was a separate folder that was simply labelled BOOK.

Rebecca clicked on it impatiently and opened it to find around two dozen separate files, some numbered and others bearing names or labelled as NOTES. She opened one entitled THE CHAMELEON and waited for the words to appear on the title page. This was it surely.

THE CHAMELEON

BY SEAN COLE

The Chameleon. That was the nickname a suspected murderer from our region acquired, simply because no one has ever seen him. In fact, nobody has even been able to prove he exists, yet he has become a local legend. The Chameleon is folklore here and even the subject of jokes. 'Be careful,' people tease one another, 'or the Chameleon will get you!'

Our murder rate is no laughing matter, though, at five times the national average. Some say it's just bad luck and others that there is something in the air in Eriston, as if the town is a singularly bleak and depressing place, likely to drive men mad. This seems to ignore the fact that many parts of the north of England or Scotland suffer from similarly long, dark winter nights and stormy weather, but the people there don't feel the need to murder one another.

There is another theory, popular among Eriston's older inhabitants, that the town is a lightning rod for the supernatural, and that the Chameleon has never been seen because he is not of this world. This might also explain how he gets into people's houses without breaking into them. Does he use unearthly powers to persuade his victims to open their doors? Most of the houses in Eriston are old and many said to be haunted, though why the Chameleon would choose to visit this town above others remains something of a mystery. More logical souls have pointed out that most of our killings and many of our disappearances have been solved. Men have gone to prison for the murder of strangers, family members or partners, bodies have washed up on the coast and suicide blamed. Those that vanished and never returned are written off with a shrug. People go missing all the time.

But what if the real story is far from as simple as the one portrayed and not everyone serving life is guilty of murder? Are the seemingly unrelated cases linked in some way and should we give more credit for our statistically high death rate to the mysterious Chameleon than those who joke about him in the pubs?

As the former editor of its newspaper, I had a disturbingly close and personal view of the harrowing events that made this town better known for murder than it ever was for tourism or fishing. I have spent the past year re-examining every suspicious case in as much detail as possible and have reached a disturbing conclusion. The truth is not what we think it is.

If what her father had written was accurate, then this was big, and it prompted an excited impatience in Rebecca. *What is that truth, Dad?* she asked silently, even though it was clear this was just the first draft of his introduction and he probably hadn't even arrived at the truth yet, at least not entirely.

It wasn't until Rebecca spotted the word count that she realized her father must have discovered something new and worth writing about. Why else would he have written 180,000 words? Rebecca was no expert but even she knew this was far too much for a book. Even if he was going to edit it down, he would have to lose half of it and that did not take into account all the other files here, which contained his notes.

If her instincts were correct, someone wanted to prevent this book from being finished and would rather kill her father to prevent its contents from being exposed. She would go over every word no matter how long it took her.

Rebecca turned to the next part, which was entitled SIMON.

The chapter's opening sentence made it clear where

her father now stood on the likely guilt or innocence of the man serving life for the murder of the Eriston Rose and he stated it with conviction.

Simon Kibbs did not kill either Rose McIntyre or Katherine Prentiss. I am certain of that now. He was wrongly convicted, following a botched police investigation, undertaken under great strain, in part caused by intense media scrutiny, which resulted in the thirst for a conviction overriding investigative best practices.

Simon being imprisoned for almost twenty years is one of the greatest miscarriages of justice in British legal history but even that is not the most chilling part of this story. In convicting the wrong man the police and Crown Prosecution Service have enabled the real murderer to escape justice; not only to live a life without consequences for his crimes but to strike again and again, leading to the deaths of more innocent victims.

This was powerful stuff. Rebecca knew that some people had doubts about the conviction of Simon Kibbs but few seemed entirely sure of the man's innocence. She herself had accepted that the right man had probably been convicted at the time. Her father was evidently certain of Simon's innocence, though. Next, he spoke of an appointment she knew nothing about and the casual way he revealed it shocked her.

I have met Simon Kibbs. I was the first visitor the man had had since his heartbroken mother passed away more than a decade ago, her life shortened considerably by the anguish of seeing her son rot in prison. In her own way Simon's mother was another victim.

I did not go to that meeting lightly but I tried to keep an open mind. I resolved to hear Simon out, because I already had my doubts about his guilt but I told myself that murderers can be clever and manipulative, extracting sympathy and understanding from the most unlikely people.

I was surprised to leave that prison building with the absolute conviction that Simon Kibbs could never have murdered anyone, let alone Rose or Katherine.

Let us examine the evidence against him.

Simon Kibbs is a man of little education, who was described by his teachers as 'slow'. At the time of the murders he was a gardener and apprentice handyman, whose main job was to maintain the church building and its grounds. The seventeen-year-old was found kneeling by Rose McIntyre's body, covered in her blood, which was on his hands, legs and chest. He told the police he had gone to help Rose while blood was still pumping from her wounds. He also swore he had seen another man leaving the scene but did not describe him in court. The police wondered if he was lying but they didn't arrest him, not at first.

They found the knife in the bushes, yards from the scene and there were no prints on it. This didn't help Simon because he was wearing gloves at the time for weeding and cutting back bushes. He could have thrown the murder weapon away once he had taken

Rose's life, the police reasoned, even though he lacked a motive for the killing.

No one else saw a man running from the church or even walking calmly from the scene. Simon was questioned repeatedly but stuck to his story. He didn't know the victim, had never seen her before and the first time he laid eyes on her she was lying on her side on the footpath at the back of the church, bleeding out.

Opinion was divided in the town. Some said this brutal killing was the work of the Chameleon or some other mystery man Simon caught a glimpse of as he fled. Others put the blame firmly on Simon. He had grown up in the town and most of its inhabitants knew him. He was a quiet boy and seemingly content to weed the graveyard and look after the church. The cause of his less than average intelligence was unknown but fantastical stories quickly did the rounds. He was dropped on his head as a boy; had been very smart until he was six when he fell out of a tree; he went to bed one night normal and woke the next day hardly able to speak or count numbers. All of this was rumour, most of it ridiculous, but it kept the townsfolk occupied during a worrying time, when they felt helpless because no killer had been apprehended.

Simon did not have a girlfriend but not every seventeen-year-old does. He did not always interact comfortably with females and there had been an incident of 'inappropriate touching' of a girl his own age when he was sixteen. They were alone together and he had reached for her breast. He was punished for this and apparently felt both remorse and shame. He said afterwards that he had wanted to be 'like the men in the films' who took control when they were with women. A lot was made of this during the trial. Simon had already shown what would happen when he couldn't control himself. No woman was safe. He had misread the situation with Rose too and killed her.

Regardless of the truth surrounding that first indecent assault, it was likely to have had an impact on the jury. I believe the police were heavily influenced by it too. When confronted with no other compelling theory in the murder of Rose, they looked to the closest suspect (literally), evaluated his character, then probed his past. They found a loner, who did not interact well with others, and he had already assaulted a young girl. In other words, he fitted the bill. He was first on the scene and found covered in the victim's blood, so they decided he must be the perpetrator. They never seemed to even seriously consider another suspect. Instead they went after him.

The young local reporter Katherine Prentiss, who worked for me at the *Eriston Gazette*, used contacts in the police to delve into the killing. She wrote a series of carefully worded stories about the events of that day and the victim. Katherine realized Rose didn't have an obvious reason for being at the churchyard. There were no close relatives buried there for her to visit. Katherine speculated she might have been meeting someone else there that day. She did not say it in the article but Rose was rumoured to have been seeing a married man, who has never been identified. If their assignation had been of a more innocent nature, then why not meet in a pub or café, instead of a secluded corner to the rear of a graveyard? Hardly the most romantic location. This gossip about Rose was largely forgotten when Katherine herself was found dead in the woods just days later.

Dead in the woods? Such an inadequate description, thought Rebecca. The young woman had been stabbed over and over during an attack of singular savagery, as if simply killing her was not sufficient. She wondered why her father had been so lacking in emotion and sparing in the detail? Because he did not want to sensationalize it perhaps or, more likely, could not bear to relive it, because he himself had seen the aftermath and so had Rebecca.

She had been a child then and they had been walking through the wood together. Her father had suddenly run on ahead to look at something he had spotted by the edge of the footpath that she could barely make out at first, until she moved closer and saw it too, just as her father let out a terrifying cry of pain and anguish.

He had come back towards her then with blood on his hands, looking deranged, shouting at her to run home as fast as she could. He hadn't wanted her to see the body, she understood that now, but back then she couldn't comprehend his reasoning and he unwittingly subjected her to the most traumatic moments of her young life. Rebecca could recall it even now, her heart pounding, running as hard as she could to get away from whoever it was that had caused the blood on her father's hands, all the while expecting them to leap out at Rebecca and kill her too.

Rebecca ran from the scene with a single image burned into her brain, the flash of a blood-soaked torso lying by the side of the path with one arm outstretched. Katherine's hand was so white in death it looked like it belonged to a shop-window mannequin, her fingers splayed, as if she had been holding on to something then suddenly let it go.

When her mother found Rebecca on the back doorstep, screaming and sobbing, she thought something terrible had happened to her husband. Rebecca had managed to tell her about the 'dead lady' in the park and her mother had been the one who had actually called the police.

Rebecca stopped reading and put down the laptop, her hands shaking. Her father's bland description of that awful day was still enough to trigger a vivid and painful memory that had long been suppressed and she found she could read no more.

14

Now that the memory had been triggered, it took a considerable effort of will to prevent herself from going over it again and again in her mind. She had to physically distance herself from the book and do other things for a while, as she told herself that nothing would be gained from reliving the episode. She had only been a child but Rebecca still bore the mental scars from that day. It was some time until she could force herself to pick the laptop back up and she had to take long, slow and deep breaths to calm herself before she could resume her reading.

Thankfully her father's book picked up during the aftermath of Katherine's brutal slaying, then he moved on.

This was too much to bear and the townsfolk became extremely vocal about its police and their inability to catch a double killer. Was anyone safe in Eriston any more?

At around the same time something truly damaging to Simon Kibbs was revealed. He did know Rose after all. Almost every day he went down to the little baker's in town and bought a ham or cheese roll, some crisps and a bar of chocolate for his lunch. Rose worked there and served him on many occasions. What really harmed him in the eyes of the jury was the testimony of her co-worker, who said there was definitely something odd about Simon. The way he looked at Rose wasn't right, she said. 'How did he look at her?' asked the prosecuting lawyer. She thought for a moment and said, 'With wonder.'

The police worked on the assumption that Simon Kibbs might well have become obsessed with Rose and that's why he had killed her. Simon was a little odd and he had denied knowing Rose, yet he bought his lunch from her. Simon said he hadn't known Rose McIntyre's name when the police told him who the murder victim was, but when he further stated he did not recognize her, even as she lay dying on the ground right in front of him, it was the clincher. They refused to believe he was innocent after that. The jury felt the same way.

He was questioned relentlessly by the police, without legal representation, something that would be unthinkable now but was more common back then. Whatever happened in that room, it was sufficient to lead Simon to eventually confess to the murder of Rose.

He retracted this confession but the judge ruled there was no evidence it had been beaten or forced out of him and he would let the jury make up their own minds about Simon, which they duly did. The fact that he was also assumed to be responsible for the death of Katherine Prentiss, just a fortnight after Rose's murder, didn't help him. Though he was never even brought to trial for that killing; one guilty verdict was enough to send him down for life with little prospect of ever being released.

Opinion on that verdict was divided. Most said it was good riddance to bad rubbish, others that Simon Kibbs might not be the real killer, just a simple soul who had stumbled across a dying woman and tried to help her, though no one could quite explain why he had not recognized Rose. The killings in Eriston and its surrounding area ceased, though, at least for a while, and that gave credence to the notion that the right man had been caught and put away.

When I visited Simon, I found a man who did not deviate at all from his original story, even after all these years. He told me he had come out of the church to do some work cutting back the bushes, saw a man moving quickly away from a shape on the ground at the back of the graveyard and went towards this to see what it was. Rose McIntyre was still alive but unable to say the name of the man who had attacked her and died as he tried to help her.

I then asked him the one question that had always bothered me during any discussion of his possible innocence. How had he not recognized Rose McIntyre when he had been served by her on countless occasions? He did not hesitate for a second and spoke with such calm assurance that I immediately believed him. 'It was the blood,' he said.

Simon explained that her face was incredibly pale and much of it obscured by her long hair, which was matted and thick with her own blood. More blood covered the rest of her face and hid her features from him.

I then asked Simon why he had not told this to the police and he replied, 'I did.'

When Rebecca woke the next morning her whole outlook on the Eriston murders had changed. According to her father, Simon Kibbs was serving life in prison for a murder he did not commit. Worse, it was the police who had ensured Simon was sent down for it by wilfully choosing to ignore aspects of his account. They had never seriously considered he was telling the truth when he described the presence of another man in the graveyard or tried to find that man. They had fixated on his inability to recognize a woman he saw every day, even though he claimed she was caked in blood, which was at least a possibility. They even bent facts to fit their theory that he was a murderer.

Rebecca had read her father's book until late into the night and had a lot more reading to do but for now she decided to take a break because there was something else she needed to do.

It was a crisp, clear, sunny morning as Rebecca made her way down to the harbour. The gulls were gliding around, attacking last night's rubbish. The discarded chip wrappers were of particular interest. She watched one of them peck through the paper, then break pieces from a half-portion of battered cod with its beak, which soon attracted other gulls, eager to share the spoils, and they fought over the remnants.

The harbourside was quiet at this hour but Jack was there, preparing for the first trip of the day.

'You want your old job back?' he joked.

He would have been surprised by how appealing that suggestion was to her. 'I can start on Monday,' she said earnestly. 'Is it still three quid an hour?'

He pretended to consider this. 'I may have to start you on less until you get the hang of it again.'

Then she said, 'I was thinking of coming out on your graveyard trip, if you don't mind?' He always called it that. Partly because the first excursion was never full but mainly because the tourists were older and closer to the grave.

He sniffed the air, as if that was how he told the time. 'The coffin-dodgers will be here soon,' he warned. 'You'll be the only one under sixty. If you want to make yourself useful, you can help me with the teas.'

So she did. Rebecca welcomed twelve people on board the boat and took the money for their tickets. They spaced themselves out on an uncovered deck, sitting in rows of bench seats that were bolted to it. Nearly everyone had white or silver hair and they were dressed in sturdy footwear with thick coats. They knew even a becalmed North Sea was cold.

Originally it had been Rebecca's idea to sell the tea and coffee. Before that, Jack had flogged nothing more than a few cheap souvenirs: ensign flags for the kids, fridge magnets with seals on them, bars of chocolate and bags of crisps, all of which they could buy in the high street. It was witnessing shivering passengers that made her suggest it. Jack considered the idea, then pointed out how impractical it would be. She explained that all he needed was plastic cups, tea bags, a large jar of instant coffee, some milk jiggers and sachets of sugar, along with an urn for the hot water that could be powered on the boat.

She didn't expect him to listen to a fourteen-year-old but he invested in a ten-litre water boiler, which paid for itself in less than a week and he gave her extra money from then on. In the summer they did ice creams, packing them in ice, inside the same boxes the fishermen used to keep their catch fresh.

'Still got your sea legs then,' he said approvingly once the teas had been handed out.

'I didn't spill a drop.'

'You never did, even when you were a kid. There might be a job for you after all, but I'll have to consult with the board of directors.' It was an old joke. Jack was always a one-man band and he liked it that way. 'I've no boss, no wife and no strife,' he used to say. As long as he could make the payments on the boat and pay for his fuel, the rest was a bonus and he got to live the life he enjoyed. It wasn't a bad philosophy.

Once they reached the Farnes, Jack had to fall into a gap in a line of smarter, fuller boats that had set off just after his from Seahouses, a more prosperous seaside town that had the benefit of being prettier and better known than Eriston and which lay closer to the islands and Bamburgh Castle.

Jack grabbed the mic with one hand then, as he expertly steered the boat, avoiding submerged rocks but getting in close enough for the tourists to see the huge number of birds that screeched and flapped above the rocky islands. 'We get up to fifty thousand of them in the nesting season,' he told his passengers, pointing out a few of interest, the puffins with their distinctive red beaks, cormorants, guillemots and Arctic terns, but these weren't the stars of the show. They rounded a bend for the main attraction and found a large number basking in the morning sun. Atlantic seals, dozens of them, were lying on the rocks or swimming lazily nearby and their presence energized the passengers, many of whom got to their feet and moved to one side of the boat, then reached for cameras to capture images of these grey-skinned, doe-eyed sea creatures. There was laughter as one of the seals stretched out a flipper, which made it look as if it was waving and not simply stretching following a nap.

Jack always made an unhurried trip round the islands before heading slowly back to the harbour. He gave them their money's worth.

Rebecca joined him in the tiny cabin at the front of the boat. They chatted about their lives in the intervening years, though his hadn't really changed; he still lived in the same small cottage close to the harbour and continued to maintain that he was 'saving up to get a girlfriend'. He asked her questions about London, a place he regarded with some suspicion, and newspapers, which he didn't seem to trust either.

'Are you back then?' he asked her. 'For good?'

'God, no,' she said abruptly, and realized how arrogant that sounded. He stiffened then. 'I mean, I have to get another job somewhere and we don't even have a local paper any more.'

'Aye, lass, you shouldn't linger. There's nowt in Eriston for anyone these days.'

She thought now might be a good time to bring up the subject she had been waiting to talk about. 'I always enjoyed the return journey when we had time for a chat. You used to tell me all the old stories about Eriston.'

'When the docks were full of fishing boats. Eriston cod used to fill bellies all over the north-east at one time. Not any more.'

'I liked the ghost stories best,' she said. 'Do you remember those?' He nodded slowly. 'The Flesh Market Witch?'

'She was no witch, just an old woman who made a few pence using herbs to cure people. She delivered babies an' all but was denounced by a jealous neighbour. This was in the 1600s and that was all it took back then. Margaret Apsley was hanged in the town square while everybody watched and with her dying breath she cursed the entire town.'

'She wished it terrible times,' Rebecca recalled.

'Then the curse obviously worked.'

The boat lurched upwards as a larger wave pushed against it. That was Jack's signal to glance up towards a sky whose clouds were turning grey. 'There's a storm coming,' he said with the authority gained from years at sea. Jack would be thinking about lost business now, if the sea turned too choppy when the rains came, but Rebecca wanted him to continue with his stories.

'Wasn't there a landlady too,' she recalled, 'who was killed by her own son?'

'He was found dressed in her clothes rambling about the devil possessing him. They didn't hang him; just locked him up in an asylum.'

'And a jilted bride who killed herself?' she reminded him.

'Left at the altar by a man who ran off to sea. More than likely with child; she knew she'd be ruined, so she hanged herself one night. Because it was suicide, she was denied a Christian burial. It was a crime against yourself, you see, and God. They buried her at the crossroads with a stake through her heart. People think that's for vampires but if someone committed suicide, they used to do that.'

'I remember all of them. You are quite possibly the reason I am a reporter.'

'That and the fact your father was the editor.'

'Oh, I never listened to him,' she joked.

'You always did like my stories, the grislier the better, but they never bothered you or you wouldn't have been able to sleep at night.'

'How do you mean?' The wind was picking up now; the sea air was colder and the sky had darkened. Jack was right about that storm.

'In the Apostles,' he said, as if that would shed enough light on it. 'They're haunted too. Your dad knew, didn't he tell you?'

'Given that I was a child, no.'

He snorted a laugh at that. 'I suppose he thought it best not to mention it.'

'You never told me this before,' she said suspiciously, sensing a wind-up.

'Given you were a child, no,' he said, turning her own words back at her.

'The house always did have a life of its own but I never met a ghost on the landing.'

'Your next-door neighbour did,' he said seriously, 'more than once.'

'Mary Allen saw ghosts?'

'And wasn't shy in telling folk about that restless spirit. Her home belonged to a fisherman by the name of Eli Lambton, the most feared man in the town. If you saw him coming you crossed the street, and that's the way he liked it. He beat his only son, Ethan, for just about anything and the lad grew up brutalized.'

'When was this?'

'It all came to a head in 1911. His father returned home from a night's drinking and took exception to something young Ethan had done, or not done, who knows? It was the lad's birthday but Eli gave him another beating just the same, which he took as usual. The father went off to bed and fell into a drunken slumber, not realizing that young Ethan had finally had enough. He picked up the poker from the fire, took it upstairs and brought it crashing down on his sleeping father's skull over and over again. He only stopped when his mother woke up and saw what was left of her husband's head on the pillow next to her. The police found young Ethan still standing there, covered in blood, next to his father's body, the head smashed to a pulp. He was still holding the poker and he was laughing, like it was the funniest thing he had ever seen.'

'So the father's ghost haunts the house next door to ours?'

Jack shook his head. 'Remember I said it was young Ethan's birthday. He was eighteen that very day. Old enough to hang for the murder, by one day, which he did because the facts of the matter were never in doubt. They say he went to the gallows still laughing but it is his tormented spirit that haunts the house next to yours.'

'And Mary Allen never left?'

He shrugged. 'Mary was born there and grew up in the house. She accepted his presence.'

'And claimed she actually saw him?'

'She heard noises coming from upstairs too. The sound of blows landing and, sometimes, laughing.'

Rebecca exhaled. 'It's a good story, Jack, but is it really true?'

'Ethan was hanged in Durham jail in 1911 and his body is buried there. Check if you don't believe me.'

'Well, I never saw him in our house. It seems he was happy enough living with Mary.'

'Not living exactly.' Jack scratched his chin thoughtfully. 'Mary's gone now, of course. I should imagine Ethan's quite lonely these days.' Then he added brightly, 'Maybe he'll pop in and see you.'

'Thanks for that, Jack, you bastard.'

He chuckled. 'I know you don't believe in ghosts.'

'I don't believe in God either, but I try not to upset him.'

And he laughed at that too. 'When you work on the North Sea you pray to God, whether you believe in him or not.'

'What was the other story you told me once, about that Keelman, the one who killed all those women?'

Even though it was a tale from long ago, he seemed to stiffen. 'He was a bad man, with no mercy at all.'

'He worked on the boats that carried coal to the collier ships, you said. Then in the night he'd prowl around the town, peering into windows, looking for girls, then he would break in.'

'Not break in,' he corrected her. 'He'd persuade them to let him in.'

'How did he do that?'

'He was a handsome devil, so the story goes. He'd whisper to them through their bedroom windows, until they opened up and he would climb in.'

'He must have been very convincing to get a girl to open her window.'

'They reckoned he was in league with the devil, who lent him persuasive words and the power to control young girls' minds. Whatever the legend, a Keelman did kill three young women back in the seventeenth century, before he was finally caught, tried and made an example of. He was put in a gibbet. That's a metal cage used to display the body of an executed man, but he was still alive when they put him in, so he died slow, of thirst and starvation.'

'But his spirit lived on?'

'He was blamed for the killing of many a young girl in the area for the next two hundred years.'

'We've always had that legend then?' she probed. 'People have talked about men, living or dead, roaming the town after dark and preying on young women?'

'The Chameleon, you mean?' He gave her a look as if he had expected better from her. 'That's a bunch of nonsense. I think the newspapers made that up back in the seventies or eighties.'

A thought struck her then. 'It could also be a distortion of the Keelman legend. Four hundred years ago he was called the Keelman, now we call him the Chameleon. They sound almost the same, don't they?'

'Bloody hell!' he said. 'You're right there, they do. I've never thought of that before.'

'You said the Keelman took the blame for murders for another couple of centuries.'

'Folks were more superstitious back then.'

'Pretty convenient if you can blame a killing on a long-dead villain and get away with it.'

'I suppose it was, but people have more sense nowadays.'

'Do they?'

'Do you think there's a ghost walking the streets of Eriston at night, persuading young lasses to let him in?'

She shook her head. 'No, but it's the kind of tale we tell to frighten people into locking their doors and windows at night. No one believes that sort of thing any more, so we are always looking for a more rational answer that makes more sense. We can't believe it's a ghost and we don't think it could be just one man doing it all, so when a woman is found dead, the police almost automatically assume it's her partner or former boyfriend and that's who they go after. Do you see what I mean?'

'There might be something in that.'

She was surprised he agreed so readily. 'You think? You're not one of those people who say that Simon Kibbs definitely killed Rose?'

'I never believed Emily Kibbs's boy was a killer.'

'I was too young to know him,' she said. 'But I have trouble believing that he suddenly stabbed a woman he knew because she walked into the churchyard where he was working.'

'Simon was just a bit slow and he used to get his words mixed up when he talked to you. The coppers tied him up in knots.' So her father was not the only one who doubted they had got the right man. 'I don't see how he could have killed Katherine either.'

'Did you know her?'

'She did a feature on the Farnes and came out on the boat to write about the seals and whatnot. She was a bonny lass, clever too. A bit like you, really.' Rebecca did not welcome the comparison but he didn't seem to mean anything by it. 'You'd see her in the pubs sometimes with blokes from the paper too.' This interested her more.

'Which blokes?'

'I don't know their names but the reporters, you know.'

'Jason or Graham?'

'Aye, if you say so,' he said.

'Which one?'

'Well, both I think. Maybe not at the same time but she'd come in with one and then another day with another.'

'Did you get the impression she was seeing one of them?'

'I don't know. Maybe, or perhaps she was just having a drink after work. I wouldn't blame either of them for trying, though. Why do you want to know about her?'

'Not just her,' she said quickly. 'I'm looking into both murders.'

'To write about?'

She was glad he had jumped to that conclusion. 'Perhaps a feature, yes.'

He seemed to accept this. 'I doubt there is anything that hasn't already been written about them.'

'There's always a new angle. I understand there was a bit of gossip about Rose possibly having an affair with a married man.'

'Gossip, aye,' he said. 'But that's all it was. No one ever proved it.'

They were close to land again now and he was slowing the boat then steering it towards the harbour side. She wouldn't have much longer for her questions.

'So,' she said as nonchalantly as possible, 'you saw Katherine about, in the pubs?'

'Sometimes.'

'Did she ever go in them with my father at all?'

There was the merest moment of hesitation from Jack, as if he sensed a trap, and she noted his hands gripped the steering wheel a little tighter than before.

'Sometimes,' he said lightly, 'aye.'

Rebecca spent much of the rest of that day reading her father's book, hoping to find information she could take to the police to help them unmask his killer. The bombshell chapter on Simon Kibbs's innocence did not immediately lead to further revelations. Instead he had written a long factual account of both murders. This could form the basis of a good book but Rebecca was feeling increasingly frustrated because it didn't tell her much that she did not already know.

She was about to take a break when she reached a chapter that renewed her interest. This one was simply called KATHERINE.

KATHERINE

For the sake of full disclosure it is hard for me to write in detail about the second murder that occurred that year in Eriston because I was close to the victim.

Yes, Dad, but how close?

Rebecca read on, as her father described the bright, talented young reporter he had guided through her first job in journalism. How he could see her talent even in the earliest days and knew she would have gone far, if her life had not been cut short. All that potential had been destroyed in one violent act. He even admitted he had been the one to find her body while out walking early one morning. Jarringly he did not mention Rebecca. Why had he written her out of the moment?

Was he trying to protect Rebecca in some way, by excluding her from the account or had he forgotten she was even there?

She called me on the night she was killed. I was surprised because she had only left the office an hour or so before, while I was 'putting the paper to bed' as we called it. She knew I would still be there and I think she just wanted to talk to someone, though there was precious little information for me in that call. I was a little preoccupied but we spoke for a while and she said she had theories about the murder in the churchyard. I already knew she thought Rose was having an affair with someone, so this must have been something else, but she declined to shed more light on them. Katherine told me they were only half baked and I foolishly replied, 'Then why don't you tell me about them when they're fully baked?' She promised she would.

Katherine was on to something. I'm sure of that now but I have no idea what she found out. I did not feel the need to press her, because I assumed I would see her in the office again in the morning. Her final words to me were, 'There's no need to hold the front page,' and I said, 'That's good, because I've already sent it.' I didn't realize then that the next time I wrote a front-page story Katherine would be its subject. We were all devastated when we found out she was gone.

I think about that last conversation every day and how I should have pressed her for answers. Maybe if I had, Katherine would never have been murdered and Simon Kibbs wouldn't have spent twenty years in prison. I will regret that failing for the rest of my life.

The page ended there and there was no more on Katherine. He must have put that chapter to one side and left it unfinished. Perhaps it took too much out of him. Rebecca was affected by the emotion he obviously felt and the deep sadness of his regret. Had he really thought about it every day for twenty years? She believed he had.

Rebecca was about to stop reading and settle down for the night, because it was the funeral tomorrow and she had a long day ahead of her, when she noticed her father had written another sentence under it. It appeared to be a note to himself, a prompt or reminder.

Go and see Simon Kibbs again. Ask him what he really saw.

Wouldn't her father have already asked Simon what he had seen that day? Why the need for a second visit and why underline the word *really* like that? Was Simon hiding something even now after all these years?

15

The funeral was a surreal experience. Rebecca felt as if she went through the whole thing in a daze. She heard someone close by tell the person next to them that it was 'a good turnout', as if that made everything all right somehow.

The church was half full and she took in the rows of predominantly male mourners, in their dark suits and ties, recognizing some familiar or half-familiar faces altered by age. Did they feel obliged to be here or were they genuinely drawn by the need to say a final goodbye to Sean Cole? She wondered if some of the older people knew her father well or if they liked to attend funerals because it got them out of the house, a suspicion heightened by a cynical comment from the caterer. 'You'd best think of a number and double it. There'll be a few who are only there for the buffet.'

DI Hall was in attendance, along with his two subordinates, Fox and Carpenter. Were they quietly observing the congregation in case the killer was among them? Did murderers come to funerals to gloat or pray to assuage their guilt, if they felt any? Rebecca scanned the faces. What does a killer look like? How easily can they mask their guilt?

The door at the back of the church opened again just

before the service started. Dominic Green walked in then, dressed in his police uniform, presumably on duty but keen to pay his respects. He took a seat at the back of the church. She wondered if rumours surrounding the manner of her father's death had reached the general population of Eriston. Gossip was always a valuable commodity in a town where there wasn't much else going on to distract people from their daily grind.

Rebecca had tried to write some words about her father and fully intended to read them out in church but the more she thought about that, the less she liked the idea, preferring to leave the vicar to sum up the man's life, with her assistance. If she became too emotional in front of everyone it would have been excruciating and, if she did not, would they wonder if she cared about her father at all, while questioning why she so rarely returned to his door? Rebecca told herself she did not care what other people thought about her, while already knowing this to be untrue.

In the end the vicar got most of it right, though it was a bit of a stretch to describe her father as 'a family man'. More accurately he cared deeply about the state of the world that he was part of. His was 'a life well lived' in the pursuit of truth, and Sean Cole was a dedicated servant of his community. *Well done, vicar. Not bad, not bad at all.*

Rebecca experienced the disjointed emotion of the atheist when called upon to sing hymns and pray, but she went through the motions anyway. All too quickly the service was over and her father sent on his final journey.

There was a line-up then, like the ones they have in weddings. She knew families stood to one side to meet and shake hands with the mourners to receive their sympathy. Being the only family member there, she stood alone. Rebecca wished she could have had her mother by her side to support her but she was thousands of miles away. Rebecca lost track of how many people said the same thing: 'I'm sorry for your loss.' And all she managed to say in reply was 'Thank you.'

Gregg, the locksmith, told her to 'Take care, pet.' He was followed by some men her father's age that she did not recognize. One of them said a little sheepishly, 'We knew your dad from the pub, like.'

'Which one?'

'The Lion.'

So he drank in the Lion often enough for some of its regulars to attend his funeral? He had clearly changed a lot in the last few years, but was it drink that had drawn him there or loneliness?

Next in line was a face she recognized. As a teenager, she'd had a bit of a crush on Jason, until she understood he was the kind of man every girl liked the look of and he knew it. He had been one of the two other reporters working for her father when Katherine was murdered and had stayed with him for years afterwards. He must have been a young man then and was now into his forties. 'It's good to see you again, Rebecca.' He must have realized how that sounded.

'Sorry it had to be under these circumstances. Your father was . . . a great editor. He taught me a lot.'

Why the pause between *was* and *a great editor*? Was he struggling to find something good to say about him?

His fellow reporter was Graham, who seemed just as awkward as he had been as a young man. When he arrived, he had spotted Jason and they had blanked one another. She wouldn't have noticed, if Graham hadn't made a point of leaving the pew he'd chosen when he noticed Jason was already sitting there. Jason had shaken his head in mock disbelief at this pettiness. What could have caused a rift between two guys who had worked together for more than twenty years at the *Eriston Gazette*, that was so serious they wouldn't sit together at a man's funeral?

Rebecca was keen to find out but she was even more interested in what they knew about her father's final days. They had both worked with Katherine, so might know what was going on between the young reporter and her father or have some idea of what she was looking into before her death, though now was not the time for those conversations.

Graham opened his mouth but did not manage to say a word to her. He just took her hand limply in his to shake, then gave her a look that conveyed his sadness and bewilderment, so she thanked him for coming.

Rebecca could have done with someone at her side during the wake; even her ex-boyfriend would have done, if she could have had him back for just an afternoon to offer moral support and make her feel less like a failure. She had to banish the notion that afterwards everyone was going to be talking about Sean Cole's unemployed single daughter turning up to his funeral on her own.

The small talk and platitudes were draining, even though she was sympathetic because she knew they were all probably at a loss as to what to say to her.

Rebecca used her empty glass as an excuse to break away from one elderly lady who regaled her with tales from the parish council and how her father had published most of its concerns, not that anything could be done about many of them, even with the support of the editor of the local paper.

As the barman poured her another glass of white wine, a man appeared at her side. Her first image of him was of a hand setting down a pint of lager on the bar very close to hers, the expensive material of the sleeve of his dark suit and a large gold signet ring on his finger. She got an overpowering whiff of aftershave and instinctively wanted to recoil from it.

'Hello, Rebecca. It's nice to see you again,' he said as she took her drink, before quickly adding, 'Sorry it had to be like this.'

The man appeared to be in his mid-forties. He knew her but she did not recognize him at all. He must have detected this. 'Connor,' he told her, 'Connor Owen.'

'I'm sorry, I . . .' she began and immediately regretted not simply saying 'of course'. Why couldn't she just lie about these things? He looked disappointed, then rallied slightly. 'I've lost a lot of weight.' He seemed both proud and self-conscious about that and she tried and failed to recall the chubby man he must have been. 'We did quite a bit of advertising with your father.' He said that archly as if it was a clue she should somehow pick up on. Why couldn't he just tell her who he was?

'Right.'

'I'm an Owen,' he reminded her, as if she was unaware of the most basic things. 'We own quite a bit of Eriston.'

Finally the penny belatedly dropped. He assumed she must recall him walking around the town like he owned it, because, in truth, his family did, or at least a fair portion of it. Everybody knew the Owens; it was a surname that was synonymous with greed. 'The landlords?'

He didn't like that description. 'Property developers,' he corrected her before conceding, 'these days.' Then he added, 'I took over the business when my own father passed away.'

'I'm sorry to hear that.'

'It's not as fresh as your loss.'

'It's been a difficult day,' she admitted, because she couldn't think of anything else to say to him.

He reached into his wallet and produced a business card, then handed it over to her.

'I'm not sure why . . .'

'My card,' he said, as if she was blind. 'I've been in discussions with your father for some time.' He was all business now, a man in a hurry.

'About what?'

'The house,' he said, as if it was obvious.

'Why?'

'I was looking to buy it,' he told her, 'and I think it's fair to say he was beginning to warm to the idea.'

'He never mentioned it.'

'Didn't he?'

'No.'

'I'm surprised to hear that. I already own the other three Apostles and I'd like to renovate them all together. It would make more sense.' Then he reached into the inside jacket pocket again and, with a flourish, drew out a gold pen, took the card back out of her hand, turned it over and placed it on the bar, so that the blank side was facing up, then he wrote down a figure. Once he was done, he put the pen back in his pocket and handed the card over to her. Rebecca glanced at it. He had actually written down a number with a pound sign. Clearly it was the price Owen was willing to pay for her father's house. Rebecca was taken aback. Not by the amount he was offering but the fact that he was trying to buy it from her here at the wake. It was a sizeable amount but not a breathtaking sum and she had nothing to compare it to.

'It's a good offer,' he said as if he recognized she had little knowledge of the Eriston property market, 'and you'll not get a better one.' Then he added, in a tone a benevolent vicar might use, 'This will help you to move on.'

'I haven't even thought about whether I *am* moving on,' she said, without really thinking that through. She had not looked beyond her father's funeral or given his estate much, if any, thought, other than being vaguely aware that she was now his sole heir. He had divorced her mother years ago and bought her out of her share of his house. It was now Rebecca's but she hadn't considered selling it or contemplated the practicalities of keeping it.

'I just assumed that, as a woman, you wouldn't want to be up there in that old house on the hill, all on your own.'

'Well, Connor, *as a woman*, I've just travelled around six countries on my own.'

'I didn't mean . . .'

'What did you mean?'

'It's just an expression. I wouldn't want to live there on my own, as a man, so I figured you'd probably feel the same way.'

Connor Owen seemed to be waiting for her to speak, possibly even to agree to sell the place, so she could quit the town. Maybe she would have, if she actually *had* a life outside of Eriston.

Instead she told him, 'Perhaps this isn't the best time.'

'No,' a new male voice said, 'it isn't,' and the tone was reproachful. 'Show some respect, Connor. She's only just come from the funeral.'

It was Alan, who must have slipped into the back of the church unnoticed, and he did not look happy. There was anger in Connor Owen's eyes too, as he turned to confront the newcomer behind him, but he must have thought better of that when he saw who it was, or maybe he realized how unseemly an argument at a wake would be.

'Of course,' he told Alan. 'I just wanted to make sure that Rebecca had all the information she needed to spare her from worry. It's a big house and that can be a burden.'

'Or an asset.' Alan was glaring at Connor now.

The sharp-suited man stared back at Alan, who was also in a suit with a white shirt and black tie. 'Well, home ownership is a double-edged sword,' said Connor, 'there are bills to pay and, of course, that place will need a lot of work.' He turned back to her. 'And there are not many jobs round here.' He looked as if he was about to continue until he received another frown from Alan. 'But I'll leave you to think it over. There's no rush, but don't leave it too long, will you? I can't wait for ever. My sympathies again.' And with that he left the bar and the wake.

Rebecca turned her attention to the man who had sent him on his way. The top button of Alan's shirt was undone, as if he was unused to dressing like that and couldn't wait to loosen it on the way out of the church.

'Sorry, I should have rescued you sooner.'

'I didn't need rescuing,' she told him coolly.

'My mistake then.'

At least he had her interests at heart and he had seen off the property developer, who had taken the cloud of aftershave with him. 'But thank you anyway.'

'Sorry about Connor,' he said, as if the man was his responsibility. 'He's always been a cock.'

'How do you know him?'

'I do some work for him.' That surprised her. He hadn't shown the respect normally reserved for a client. 'I do up the old houses he buys and sells on; new kitchens, bathrooms, that sort of thing.'

It seemed he may have put his livelihood at risk. 'Won't he be mad at you now? I hope you won't lose any work.'

Her former boyfriend shrugged. 'Sod him. He thinks he can do what he likes. It's not on. Anyway, he needs me to turn his run-down properties into something he can sell. There's no one else round here who can do that for him.' He didn't say it boastfully but there was a measure of self-confidence in the words.

At that point Rebecca received a delegation in the form of three men who solemnly explained they were town councillors who knew her father. Alan retreated so as not to monopolize her and Rebecca immediately felt disappointment.

Then he said, 'Call me. If you fancy another coffee or just a chat.'

'I will,' she told him, and meant it.

16

She felt emotionally drained after the funeral but she couldn't sleep. Every sound in the house made her imagine an intruder. This was ridiculous. Rebecca reminded herself that the old house always made noises. It used to scare her as a child, particularly when she was very small. Almost every night she would run into her parents' bedroom because of the monsters she heard in the attic.

'There are no monsters in the attic,' her mother explained with slightly less patience each time she did this. 'It's just a creaky old house, that's all, darling.'

Her father's words on the subject had not helped. 'This house has a life of its own,' he'd said.

The house was alive!

'Now go back to bed!' he'd ordered.

Things improved as she got older and could rationalize every creak and moan the house made. It helped that monsters never did appear and there was reassurance that her parents were only across the hall. But being here alone, even as an adult, was different and her feelings alternated between fear and foolishness.

Rebecca slept fitfully and woke with a start at four o'clock in the morning when there was an almighty crack from the rooms above her on the third floor. It sounded like an explosion and her overwrought imagination concluded that the boiler must have blown up at the very least. Then she heard the howling wind outside and the sound of trees being battered by one of the coastal storms that could descend on this part of the world with little notice. That must have been the cause but what could have come loose so violently inside the house?

Tentatively Rebecca climbed out of bed and eased the door open, ready to jump back if someone was there, but the landing was empty. She turned on the lights, which made her feel a little better and slowly climbed the stairs, looking upwards until she could trace the origin of the sound. The loft door had come loose, thanks to the wind that she could now hear whistling through tiny gaps in the timbers of the attic. It had blown open and crashed down with such force it had struck the wall behind it.

Thankful for a rational explanation but numb with tiredness, Rebecca trudged downstairs to find something she could use to close it. In the cupboard under the stairs she found the stepladder. She went back up to the top floor, climbed the ladder and pushed the door upwards. It took a couple of attempts but eventually it fitted snugly back into place, and the mechanism on the loft door engaged and it clicked shut. Exhausted, Rebecca went back to bed, fell asleep instantly and did not wake again until it was light outside.

*

That day she chose not to see anyone. Being forced to speak to so many people at the funeral had left Rebecca feeling overwhelmed and she wanted to be on her own to rest and to grieve for her father.

She spent some of her time reading his book but could sense his growing frustration when he could not find the real culprit. Because of this his book had no ending. She decided to stop reading and take a break from it. She recalled how her father had written that note about going to see Simon Kibbs again, to *ask him what he really saw*. He never got the chance but maybe she would. It was something she could do to try to move things forward, so she decided to act on the impulse.

In a letter Rebecca explained she was Sean Cole's daughter and that her father had recently died. She kept it simple, setting out the facts, which included her father's belief in Simon's innocence and her need to come and see him to ask some questions, just like her father had done. She did not want to overcomplicate matters for a man with a lower than average mental age. All Rebecca could do was hope that he would reply and grant her request, though the thought of visiting a convicted murderer in prison was a daunting one, even if she was becoming convinced of his innocence.

When her letter was done, she found herself at a loose end once again and, without giving it too much thought, she reached for her phone. She had already added Alan's number to it and she wrote out a quick message. *Fancy a coffee tomorrow?*

It took Alan nearly an hour to answer her text and

she had begun to wonder if he wasn't too bothered about meeting up again after all but when he did come back there was a reassuring lack of game-playing. He just wrote, *Great. Let me know time and place and I'll work round it.*

She spent the afternoon going through her father's things, filling black sacks with his clothes and old books for donations. She kept a few sentimental items and photographs but tried to be ruthless. There was no point in keeping all this stuff when others could benefit from it.

Rebecca had been keeping in touch with her mother, sending her emails for the most part, so she could explain the arrangements for the funeral, but there was a distant feeling to it all. It struck Rebecca that at one time her father was the most important person in her mother's life. They had met, started seeing one another, then fallen in love and married. That love might have been tested but it lasted right up to the point when Rebecca was born and throughout the early years of her life when she continued to feel that they were a loving family. It was only later when it all fell apart that the gap between her mother and father had widened until it was a chasm.

First came the arguments, then the eventual admission that their marriage was a failure, followed by separation and a divorce so acrimonious her mother chose to leave town, taking her daughter with her and uprooting Rebecca in the process. Those years away from Eriston, when Rebecca had lived alone with her mother before leaving for college, now seemed a brief and barely noteworthy interlude.

Eventually her mother met the man who would become her second husband, more years passed and she joined him in New Zealand. Rebecca's mother had moved on through several different chapters in her life. Her father, conspicuously, had not. He remained in the town, stayed in their house and continued in the same job. He hadn't even contemplated selling up and embarking on a new life, even after the *Gazette* closed down. Why could he not bring himself to leave?

Rebecca FaceTimed her mother in the evening, timing it to the start of the day in Auckland. They talked awkwardly about her father and who had bothered to turn up for the funeral until her mother blurted, 'I would have come, Becky. If we had still been in the UK.'

'I know.' Rebecca knew it was unreasonable to hope her mother might have flown over ten thousand miles to attend her ex-husband's funeral.

'I don't want you to think . . .' Her words tailed away, so Rebecca completed the sentence for her.

'I know you cared, Mam.'

That seemed to pacify her. 'I realize it has been difficult for you, Becky, handling everything there on your own.'

'I'm not exactly busy these days.' And that led to a well-meaning enquiry about job prospects in the area and whether Rebecca had managed to have any thoughts about her future. 'I've not really had time to think about anything, Mam.'

'You'll be able to do that once you've sorted out the estate.'

Rebecca half laughed. 'You make it sound like Downton Abbey, not a crumbling old house in the arse-end of the north-east.'

On the screen Rebecca noticed the expression on her mother's face change, to reveal her true feelings. 'I always hated that place.'

'Then why did you buy it?'

'I didn't want to, but you know how persuasive your father could be once he got an idea into his head. I suppose I gave in.' Then she added, 'I used to do that back then.'

'So you don't care what happens to the house now?'

'It's yours, Rebecca. Your dad bought me out years ago and you're his only family. Do what you like with it. I'd sell the place to anyone daft enough to live there.'

Rebecca didn't really want to think about selling her father's home yet, so abruptly changed the subject. 'I saw Alan,' she practically blurted.

'Alan?' Then the penny dropped, 'Oh, Alan. *That* Alan? I remember him.' And she was surprised there was such warmth in her mother's voice. 'Your first love.'

'I wouldn't go that far.' Though she didn't really know why she was denying it.

'Oh, he was. You were smitten. We hardly saw you that summer.'

'Dad didn't like him.' She expected her mother to attack her former husband for that.

'No one would have been good enough for you in

your father's eyes, darling. You were only sixteen and he loved you.'

She hadn't thought of it like that before. Looking back, she had resented her father for giving her the hard word on Alan, but really, with the benefit of hindsight, she was more disappointed with herself for not standing up to him or finding a way to carry on seeing the boy in secret. Now she realized that even her mother, who had cause to denigrate her father, thought of it as an expression of her father's love, albeit the overprotective kind.

'How is Alan? Married?' The interest in her mother's voice was almost comical.

'No, but you are.'

'I wasn't asking on my behalf. Is he seeing anyone?'

'I didn't really ask.'

'Mmmm.'

'What does that mean?'

'Nothing, darling.'

To keep her mother from dwelling too much on Alan's romantic life, Rebecca told her about his business working on the numerous properties being renovated in Eriston.

'I always knew he would do well,' she said.

'Husband material, obviously,' Rebecca deadpanned.

'I didn't say that.' Her mother sounded flustered. 'Anyway. How are you? Are you eating properly?'

This led to a lecture on the importance of a nutritious breakfast and how vital it was to get a good night's sleep. Rebecca endured her mother's advice before she found the courage for the question she really wanted to ask.

'I've been looking at some of Dad's papers . . . He was writing a book actually –' she took a deep breath – 'which incidentally is about the murders in Eriston and –' her mother visibly straightened and her body stiffened – 'I might even look at seeing if I can complete it, you know, for Dad or maybe if not a book, a podcast and . . .'

'Oh, Rebecca, are you sure about that?'

'Don't you think I can do it?'

'I think you can do anything, darling, but . . .'

'But what? I think it might bring me closer to Dad if I tried to finish his work.'

'Do you really want to rake over it all and become obsessed with it like . . .'

'He did?'

There was a pause and Rebecca wondered if her mother would deny this.

'Yes.'

'I won't get obsessed, Mam.'

Her mother sighed. 'All right, fine.' She held up her palms defensively. 'Do what you want to do. You always do.'

'What's that supposed to mean?'

'It means you remind me of him.' And her mother sounded huffy now.

'Look, I haven't made up my mind yet, not fully. I just . . .' How could she put this? 'There was something I wanted to ask you, because I think it's relevant to everything that happened back then and that's why I need to just come out with it.'

'What?'

There was no going back now. 'When you and Dad started having . . . problems, was he . . . Did you ever suspect he might be having an affair?' And when her mother's face fell, she added, 'With Katherine Prentiss?'

'Oh, Rebecca. Please, don't go there.'

'Why not? I'm trying to put together the pieces of a very complicated puzzle and I don't know all the facts, let alone what they mean.' Her mother looked uncomfortable. 'I can understand why the question might upset you, even after all these years,' Rebecca conceded, 'and I'm sorry, but I need to know what happened.'

Her mother appeared to contemplate this for a moment before answering. Rebecca felt sure she would refuse to discuss it further but instead she seemed to want to provide an explanation that went back even further. 'In the early days we were good together,' she began, 'and then when you came along we both loved you so much. Your father was working his way up as a journalist: first reporter, then senior reporter, chief reporter and finally editor, the youngest in the newspaper group's history. He did so well, Rebecca, and he was proud of that – so was I. He worked longer hours, especially in the run-up to deadline day and I saw less of him, but I was busy bringing you up and there always seemed to be something that needed fixing in that house. If I left it for your dad, it would never get done.' Rebecca listened impatiently, hoping she would jump forward a few years and she obliged. 'Then the paper started to struggle financially and the hours at the newsroom got longer. They wanted him to cover a wider area beyond Eriston and there weren't enough reporters.' Rebecca let her mother talk uninterrupted. She sensed she was building up to something important and wanted to tell the story in her own time. 'His days were getting longer and longer. Some weeks he barely saw us.'

'I remember,' Rebecca confirmed.

'I never thought there was anything else keeping him from us, though, not for a long while.' Her mother glanced off to one side then, as if she was distracted by something, but Rebecca sensed she didn't really want to look her daughter in the eye. 'Then *she* came.' *She* was Katherine Prentiss. 'I never once felt threatened by this new arrival,' she said. 'Until I finally met her.

'It was at the summer fête and the whole team was down there, taking photos, interviewing the Carnival Queen. It almost felt like a day off for them, so I thought I'd go with you and surprise him. We came round the corner and he was standing there talking to her. He seemed so animated and happy and he hadn't been like that at home for a long time. Then he saw me and I wouldn't say he looked guilty but he *was* surprised. I saw her face for the first time too and . . . I can't explain it but I just knew.'

'You knew what? That he was seeing her?'

'That I had no chance,' she said instead. 'If this girl wanted your dad, then she would get him. She was so beautiful and the way she carried herself, with total confidence, I felt so plain by comparison. He introduced us but I could tell she had no interest in me. I wanted to leave right then, but I'd promised you an hour there. When you were done, I couldn't get away quick enough.'

'But was he actually seeing her?' The full truth remained tantalizingly out of Rebecca's reach and she needed to hear it from her mother.

'I wondered that myself, every day. I even phoned him at work to check he was still there but it was easy for him to explain when he wasn't because of a story.'

'What made you think she was interested in him?'

'He was her editor and he knew things. She was ambitious and he could help her. Your dad could be inspiring company and he was attractive. I mean, *I* fell for him.'

'But did she?'

Her mother either did not hear or chose to ignore the question. Instead she said, 'When she was killed and he found her, it broke him. I think he was in shock for quite a while but he insisted on attending every day of that boy's trial, even though he was the newspaper's editor, not a reporter. I think he thought he owed it to her. He started drinking in the evenings too, which he had never done till then. He was under immense strain and I was just trying to keep our family together.'

'So you never asked him about her?'

'Not for a long time, then I asked him outright whether he loved her. This was years later when we were arguing all the time.'

'What did he say?'

'It doesn't matter.'

'It might,' Rebecca probed.

'No, Rebecca. That was what he said to me. *It doesn't matter*. We were over by then and we both knew it. You and I left not long after.'

'So he never admitted it?'

'No.'

'But you believe they were having an affair?' She wanted to hear her mother say it now. Rebecca needed her suspicions to be confirmed. Maybe then she would have something to blame for the bitterness of her life being derailed back then, or someone. Was it all Katherine's fault?

'Yes.'

'How can you be sure?'

'Because our marriage was doomed the day Katherine died. I saw your father mourn both his parents but that was nothing like this. He was never the same again.'

Though she had no proof of her husband's adultery, Rebecca was sure her mother was right about that. Her father's life and his whole outlook had changed then. Maybe their family died that day too, or perhaps Sean Cole's marriage had been over the day Katherine Prentiss first walked into his newsroom.

17

I can't help it. I'm fooling no one, not even myself. It has to be tonight. I can't stay away from you any longer. I tell myself I should but I need this like a junkie needs a fix.

I still need to plan. There can't be any mistakes and I get a surge of excitement when I think about how this will go. I'm trying to decide if you look like a struggler. It won't make any difference. There won't be time for you to call out and people don't come running anyway. That's a myth. They hear something and wonder what it was, but if there are no more screams they rationalize it in their own minds. They didn't really hear anything or it was just a stupid teenager out way too late or a cat fighting another and they go back to sleep.

The easiest one left her downstairs front sash window open because of the heat, then closed her curtains and forgot all about it. Later, she went to bed. I watched in disbelief when she turned the downstairs light off but forgot to close, let alone lock, the window. She might as well have left the front door open for me.

I continued to watch as the downstairs lights went off and the upstairs ones blinked on: landing, bathroom, bedroom. I waited till they were extinguished and gave it another hour before I walked up to that open window and climbed inside.

She was a smart, independent woman living on her own in a starter home ten miles from town, right on the corner of her street, not overlooked. I'm guessing she liked the privacy but that's double-edged.

She had been working such long hours and being tired can make the best of us careless. We swear we've done something and it turns out we haven't. We leave cars unlocked or a bag on the back seat all night. Sunglasses, phones, wallets and purses are left behind on restaurant tables because we are distracted when we leave, but the most it usually costs us is money and a little inconvenience. We curse our carelessness but forget it within days. No harm done.

But if I take an interest in you, your carelessness will cost you everything.

She woke that night to find me standing at the side of her bed looking down at her, then I covered her mouth with my hand.

I wonder if she realized how I got in before it was all over. Did she recognize her stupidity or die wondering how I had managed to get so close without her hearing a thing?

Having jumped at every sound lately and let her mind run riot each night before she went off to sleep, Rebecca decided to keep her bedroom door partly open this time. It was her way of ensuring that muffled sounds were not exaggerated by her imagination. Rebecca reasoned that stress, fatigue and a maelstrom of emotions had pushed her unconscious mind to breaking point and now she was hearing footsteps on the landing, creaking floorboards and movements in the attic, and all because she was quite obviously exhausted.

Tonight, it would be different. She would tackle the issue of her irrational fears head-on. Surprisingly it did not take long for her to fall into a deep sleep.

Her dreams were confused but there was a common

theme. Rebecca was in peril, being chased through the woods. She had to run into town to get help but there was no one in the streets. All the doors she tried were locked and nobody would answer no matter how hard she banged on them. She had to move quickly from place to place because she could sense that whoever was after her was not far behind but she couldn't get off the streets or find anywhere safe. Why was no one in Eriston willing to help her? She woke, panicked and may have even let out a small cry.

There was a man standing in her room, watching her from the doorway but that had to be a dream too, or was she half awake now? The rational part of her brain told her she was still dreaming and this was just an extension of her nightmare; the fact that she was back in her bed did not make sense but then dreams were disjointed. She allowed her half-open eyes to look directly at the door, which was still partially open. Rebecca realized with sudden clarity that it was not a dream; she was almost fully awake now and, this time, there really was a man standing in the doorway staring at her.

18

Rebecca jumped up and screamed. The man jumped too and she kicked the bedsheets away from her so she could roll out of the bed and reach for something, anything, to use as a weapon; it was still dark but there was enough moonlight to make out shapes in her room. She reached to one side and grabbed the lamp so she could swing it at him if he went for her, forgetting it was plugged into the wall and not much use for fending off an attacker. Her loud, panicked cries did not sound like her but they must have had an effect because, instead of launching himself at her, the intruder turned and fled.

Rebecca half scrambled, half fell from the bed, landing with a bump on the floor but never taking her eyes from the gap in the door. No sign of the man but he had definitely been there, she was sure of it, even as she warned herself that he may have been a fragment from her dream or a shape she'd misrecognized, like her father's coat on the back of the door. No! Not this time. It was too vivid, too real. Rebecca could still see his face and unkempt beard as well as his shoulder-length hair; she could describe the clothes he wore and, somehow, he was in her house. If there was any doubt left in her mind, it vanished as she heard the man running up the stairs.

He was going up not down. She was sure of this but

why? If he was a burglar trying to escape, then surely running downstairs was the only option. Was he about to grab something and come back to hit her with it? She had to protect herself and quickly. She closed the door, then frantically dragged the heavy chest of drawers across it to make a barricade. Would that hold him if he tried to get back in? It would certainly delay him.

She grabbed her phone and hit the first number that came up. It was Alan's, from when she messaged him for a coffee, and her first instinct was to get him here. Why not the police? She could have dialled 999, but the response time in the middle of the night, for what would be classed as a burglary, didn't bear thinking about. Rebecca had a direct line to the one man who might have taken her seriously but Dominic Green's card was inside her bag in the hallway. No way was she going down there to get it. She knew Alan would be quicker; if she could just get him to pick up.

As the phone rang out, she thought she heard a scrambling sound from above.

'I've got a knife!' Rebecca shouted. 'I'll stab you through the fucking heart!' and she hoped that sounded convincing.

The phone was still ringing.

Pick up, for God's sake, pick up.

Please pick up.

Alan answered with a grunt, as if woken from a deep sleep.

'Alan,' she told him, 'there's someone in my house.'

*

He couldn't have made it round there much faster. While he was on his way, Rebecca had stood behind the chest of drawers and listened but she heard no further sound from beyond the door. She hoped her instincts were correct and that the strange ragged-looking man had been as alarmed by her presence as she had been by his and that he had turned on his heel and fled. She recalled the sound of his footsteps running up the stairs and could not understand how he could have escaped. Was he still up there somewhere on the top floor?

What if he came down again and attacked her and Alan? Why hadn't she just called the police? It had been an instinctive move. Would they believe she had woken from a bad dream to find a man in her room, with no evidence that he had ever been there? Perhaps she should call them now. Before she could think about it any further, her doorbell rang and this was accompanied by a loud and urgent banging on her front door. She had to get to it to let Alan in.

Rebecca pulled then dragged the dresser away from the door and opened it carefully, half expecting to find a crazy man standing there waiting for her. The landing was dark but empty. She walked out on to it and flicked on the light, while the impatient banging from the door continued and the sound of Alan's voice reached her as he called her name. The familiar voice lent her the courage to run down the stairs and unlock then open the door. She found Alan standing on her doorstep with a torch in one hand and a hammer in the other. He had a determined look on his face.

'Show me,' he said.

Now that he was here her fears calmed a little but she knew the man might still be in the house. Rebecca quickly explained and Alan took it all in without comment. She worried that he might not believe her but she needn't have done. He promised he would check every room, holding the torch out in front of him and readying the hammer to swing at anyone who might leap out at them. He checked the lounge first and she switched on the light. They found it empty.

Rebecca followed him into the kitchen and when she turned on the lights, what she saw banished any lingering thoughts that she might have imagined this. There was a carrier bag on the worktop and half a dozen items had been taken from the cupboards: cans of soup and beans, some slices lifted from the loaf of bread, a bottle of water. If this was a burglar, he wasn't greedy and wanted only the most basic items. It looked like this guy was trying to survive but did that make him less or more dangerous?

Alan looked at her. 'Not me,' she told him.

They turned on every light in the house and checked each room as they went higher. There was no one on the next floor and when they started towards the top floor she warned him to be careful. He went up slowly, the hammer ready. Rebecca followed. The first thing they noticed was the attic door. It was open again and hanging down on its hinges but the wind wasn't the cause this time. Someone had used this door to leave the house somehow, but it was high up and there was no ladder. More importantly it only led to the attic.

They both looked around and she saw Alan glance at the top of the high bannister, which was scuffed and a little worn. They both must have been thinking the same thing. It was possible to stand on the edge of the bannister and jump the remaining distance. If you were tall and agile enough, reasoned Rebecca, you could probably reach the entrance to the attic and haul yourself up there but only if it was already open, so this must have been the way he had gained entry, as well as providing his exit, but how?

They checked her father's office and the room opposite, which was still empty, then they went back and peered up at the open attic door. 'This is how he got in,' agreed Alan, 'somehow. Do you have a ladder?'

'Don't go up there,' she cautioned.

'He's probably long gone,' he said with a confidence she did not share, 'but I need to make sure.'

Rebecca left Alan on guard as she brought the stepladder back up to the top floor, then she waited on the landing while he cautiously climbed it.

'There's a light somewhere,' she said. 'A switch just inside the door.'

Gingerly he put his head through the gap, ready to duck back down again if he had to, but when no attack came he reached inside and found the switch, flicking it on and illuminating the attic. He quickly looked into every corner. 'It's fine,' he reassured her. 'He's gone.'

He climbed up into the attic then and a moment later she heard him say, 'Jesus Christ.'

'What?'

His muffled voice came down to her. 'You need to see this.'

19

Alan extended an arm to help her into the attic and, with some trepidation, Rebecca allowed him to pull her up there.

At the far end of the loft there was a sizeable hole in the wall that quite obviously led to the attic next door. The four houses had been built together in one block and were separated by thick walls but Rebecca realized the attic space must have originally been a single large area, which was then subdivided by less sturdy dividing walls. Judging by the condition of this wall, they must have weakened over time, which was how her intruder had been able to burrow through this one so easily. He had taken advantage of the empty house next door and the poor state of the brickwork, to make a space large enough to climb through. If he had done this while her father was out for the day, there would have been no one left in the block to hear him. He had the run of the house. He could move around it freely and take what he wanted. What had the locksmith said to her about her father commenting on things going missing? This would account for it.

Rebecca had thought someone had been watching her, was convinced she had seen someone behind the bushes that first night back in Eriston, then seen movement in the darkness outside the house later when she had been preparing for bed. It would also explain why she thought she had heard sounds in the middle of the night. The truly terrifying part was that they had turned out to be real. Only now did she understand how vulnerable she had been. She had put every creak and groan down to the house's age but it was likely that at least some of those noises had been caused by this intruder.

When she had woken earlier, Rebecca had seen him standing in the frame of the doorway staring at her. When she thought about that now, she felt violated. Had he noticed her for the first time because her door was partially open? Was he shocked to discover someone sleeping in the previously empty room? What would he have done if she had not abruptly sat up and screamed, scaring him away?

They approached the wall and shone Alan's torch through the gap. They could see the route the intruder had taken. The attic of the house next door was empty and its door open. He had to have made his escape into it, might even have been living as a squatter in the empty property, while invading her house to steal supplies. Rebecca had no desire to explore it now in darkness.

'I'll brick this up for you,' Alan promised her, but she knew that would need daylight, materials and time.

'I don't want to stay here,' she told him.

'You don't have to.'

'I want to go now.'

'We should call the police,' he said.

'And how long will it take them to get here only to find that he's gone. Hours probably and they won't care. They'll say he's just a burglar. He didn't attack me. I just woke up to find him looking down at me.' And even saying that aloud made her feel sick.

'Bloody hell.'

'He was probably as surprised to see me as I was to see him. I hope.'

'He could still be down there.' He meant inside the empty house next door. 'But I doubt it. I could try to block this off now, somehow.' He meant in case the man did return tonight.

Rebecca shook her head. 'There's nothing worth stealing here.' *Except the laptop*, she thought, and she could take that with her, along with her rucksack. That would only take two minutes to pack and she just wanted to get out of there.

Rebecca dressed, then packed her own belongings and picked up her father's laptop. Before they left, Alan turned on all the lights in the house, then switched on her father's radio and placed it in the hall. It was the Radio 4 World Service and would be on all night. Two men were in earnest discussion about the state of the world and Alan said, 'Just in case.' He meant that their voices might fool the man into thinking someone was in the house, if he really was foolish or crazy enough to attempt to make his way back into it.

149

When they left, Rebecca turned back to look at the house, which was illuminated by the lights Alan had turned on, then she glanced at the house next door, which was dark and appeared lifeless. Was there a crazy man lurking inside? 'Let's go,' she said firmly.

Rebecca had promised Alan she would call the police in the morning and report the intruder. They climbed into his pick-up truck and set off down the hill. It was three o'clock in the morning and no hotel would take her at this hour. It was as if he had read her mind.

'Come back to mine,' he told her.

'But you've got work in the morning.'

'I'll be fine,' he told her, 'and you look like you need some sleep.'

Rebecca did not really have an alternative and was too tired to argue with him by then. He drove her to his home, a small old cottage set back from the main road at the edge of town, with a little cut along one side that he drove down, before parking his pick-up out of sight to the rear of the building. He opened the back door of the cottage to let them in and walked her straight to his room. Alan insisted on making her some tea to help her get to sleep but Rebecca was convinced that would be impossible after the night she'd had.

She was surprised to wake hours later in Alan's bed to find it was the middle of the morning. Rebecca was momentarily disorientated, then a little relieved to find she was alone. Her life was already difficult enough without complicating it any further. She had a vague recollection of a polite argument in the early hours about who should have the bed and which one of them should take the couch. When Alan had insisted Rebecca should sleep in his room and showed her the large comfortable bed, she had blurted, 'It's a double; we could share.' Then she'd made things even more awkward by adding, 'To sleep in.'

My God, how quickly this man made her regress to the awkward teenager he had once known. What was wrong with her?

'You take it,' he said simply, and she hadn't argued further.

It was half past ten. He must have left her sleeping and by now would be industriously installing a kitchen somewhere. If it felt strange to be padding around her ex-boyfriend's house in her underwear and the baggy T-shirt she had slept in, how must it have felt for him to be summoned by a crazy woman in the middle of the night because he was the first person she had thought of in her moment of panic?

The house was small but nice and he kept it neat and tidy, in direct contrast to her ex. She walked into the kitchen and jumped. He was standing there by the kettle, which was just coming to the boil. 'Morning, Shortbread,' he said lightly, and the use of her teenage nickname would have made her smile if she hadn't felt self-consciously underdressed.

'I heard you moving around. Tea?'

'Please. I assumed you were at work.'

'I thought you might like someone with you when you go back to the house.'

'Thanks. I'll, er . . . just get dressed.'

'Take your time,' he said. 'I'll make us some breakfast.'

They drove back to her father's house and Rebecca called Dominic on the way but the police officer's phone went straight to voicemail, so she left him a message.

As they entered the house, she immediately sensed it was empty and hoped her instincts were correct. The prospect of sitting around there waiting for Dominic to respond was not an appealing one.

'Why don't we take a look?' she asked, and her eyes went heavenwards so he knew she meant the attic.

'Do you think we should,' he asked, 'before the police get here?'

'Something tells me this won't be their highest priority.'

He couldn't dispute that, so they went up to the top floor, climbed the ladder into the attic, turned on the light and surveyed the scene. Rebecca found the large hole in the wall deeply unsettling and was thoroughly spooked by the thought of a man climbing into her home whenever he wanted and roaming the house while she slept.

Alan climbed through the gap and she followed. They were now in the attic of the house next door and technically trespassing but, since no one lived there officially, what did it matter? Alan had brought the hammer again and he kept it by his side as he looked down through the open attic door of the neighbouring property to ensure no one was waiting there. The opposite wall of the attic was untouched, so it was clear he had been using this house to move into Rebecca's.

When he was sure no one was on the landing below, Alan eased his legs through the gap, bent lower until his fingers could grip the edge of the loft hatch, then lowered himself through the hole and dangled there for a moment, before letting go and dropping to the landing.

Rebecca followed him and, as she gripped the frame of the hatch and lowered herself, she felt his hands on her hips take some of her weight, then gently cushion her drop to the floor. There was an awkward moment as he kept hold of her for a second more than was needed and they exchanged a look before he let go.

The rooms on that floor were both empty, so Alan and Rebecca went down the stairs with him leading the way, his hammer at the ready.

They didn't really expect to find anyone and a quick search of the old house confirmed their suspicion that the man was long gone. They guessed he had cleared out as soon as Rebecca had screamed at him. He had obviously departed in a hurry, because he had left behind the only evidence that he had been there at all; a tatty old sleeping bag and a battered night light in a first-floor bedroom. There were items of food in the kitchen along with a carrier bag he was using to keep rubbish in, which was full of old tins and an empty bottle of the cheapest wine you could buy.

The back door had a wooden frame with two large glass panels. The lowest one was smashed where he had forced entry, shielded by the backyard wall.

'Well, he's not here,' said Alan. 'When the police have gone, I'll brick up the gap in the attic. I'll call Connor and tell him he's got squatters in the Apostles. I guarantee he'll have metal shutters put up on every door and window.'

'Thank you, Alan.'

'You have to be able to sleep easily in your bed,' he said, then there was a pause until he added, 'but you're welcome to stay at mine again tonight, of course.'

'No,' she said quickly, 'I'll be all right and you need your bed.' She was grateful he didn't push it. In truth, she would have quite liked the idea of spending more time with him but she was wary. Waking up in a less isolated part of town was an appealing prospect but there was a danger they might sleepwalk into resuming a relationship that probably should have been restricted to flirty reminiscences.

They left the house through the gap in the back door, then walked round to Rebecca's front door and into her house. When a police car finally pulled up outside, it was Dominic. 'I'm sorry for the delay.' He seemed genuinely apologetic but he also looked stressed and on edge. 'Another woman has gone missing.'

20

Rebecca could hardly argue that her situation was more serious than a missing woman.

'What happened?'

'She lives over the way.' Dominic pointed at the cliff opposite the Apostles. 'In the High Houses. She's a solicitor and didn't show up for work so they called her and got no response. It's very uncharacteristic behaviour so they reported it. CID sent someone round. I think they were worried they'd find a body. She wasn't in her home but her car is still there. She lives on her own and wasn't in a relationship, as far as we know. Everyone is keen to locate her as soon as possible so we can rule out a worst-case scenario.'

'I hope you find her and I appreciate you coming round at all under the circumstances,' said Rebecca.

She invited him inside, then introduced Alan to him and the two men eyed each other warily.

For someone who was worried about a missing woman and claimed to be obsessed with catching a killer that preyed on them, Dominic Green didn't seem too troubled by Rebecca's story. He did briefly express concern when they showed him the hole in the attic wall. Once he was satisfied it had been caused by a rough sleeper and not a serial killer, his interest seemed to wane, though Alan reminded him that the man could be both. By then, Dominic had already convinced himself the intruder would most likely have moved on to a different town by now.

'I'd do a house-to-house but the other houses are all empty,' he told Rebecca before asking, 'He didn't actually assault you then?'

'No,' she admitted. 'But he was in my room.'

'Standing by the doorway? So he didn't *enter* the room?'

Before she could confirm this, Alan said, 'You don't seem to be taking this very seriously.'

'Oh, I am taking it seriously,' he assured them. 'And we will find him.'

Rebecca was surprised by his confidence. Everything he had said so far seemed to indicate that he did not think this was a big deal.

'You sure about that?' asked Alan doubtfully.

'How far can he get realistically?' asked Dominic. 'He has no vehicle presumably, no money and no food or shelter. He has to show his face eventually.'

Alan did not seem reassured by this. 'What about getting some prints?'

'We only get usable prints from one in ten cases and he's probably not even on our database.'

'Well, he might be,' said Alan a little indignantly.

'Yes,' conceded Dominic, 'he might be.'

Rebecca decided to intervene. 'Look, I don't want everyone spending ages looking for a vagrant, if that's all he is, particularly when you are searching for a missing woman,' she said. 'This guy might not be a threat to anyone but I would like to know for sure.'

'We'll get him,' Dominic said with conviction.

Alan and Rebecca exchanged looks that revealed they did not share the policeman's confidence.

Dominic continued, 'Someone will report seeing him sooner or later. I don't think this man is a killer,' he told her. 'His first reaction on seeing you was to run. He didn't attack you.' Then he added, 'Thankfully.' It was almost an afterthought. 'He probably figured the place was empty, otherwise he wouldn't have opened the door and walked in on you. Don't get me wrong, it must have been pretty terrifying for you –'

'It was.'

'But I don't think you were in any actual danger.'

Easy for you to say. You weren't there.

She had to admit he was probably right, though it galled Rebecca to think that her terror might have been misplaced, even though she had no way of knowing it at the time.

'Leave it with me, Rebecca,' he told her.

An hour after his departure, workmen showed up to put metal shutters on every possible point of entry to the empty houses next to hers. They were thorough and Rebecca surveyed the results of their work with approval. Alan disappeared for a while to get materials to brick up the attic wall for her and returned just as they were leaving.

By the time he was finished the day was almost over.

He wouldn't entertain the idea of being paid for his time but Rebecca insisted on buying him dinner as a thank-you. He had lost a day's work after all and eventually he relented.

'I'll have to get cleaned up first,' he said, and they agreed to meet later at a pub he knew that served good food and overlooked the sea.

Now that the house was secure Rebecca felt safer and she spent her time reading more of her father's book. She began it sitting on a chair, then lay down on the couch, with the laptop perched on a cushion that was balanced a little precariously on her stomach. She read until her eyes started to feel sore and heavy, the stress of the previous twenty-four hours having completely exhausted her. Without meaning to Rebecca closed them and dozed for a while until she opened them again with a start and realized what time it was. Christ, she was going to be late.

21

She *was* late. Alan had been waiting in the pub for fifteen minutes by the time she arrived but he didn't seem to mind. 'I had a pint,' he said. 'You look nice by the way.'

'Thanks.' This was surely a lie. She had quickly showered, hurriedly tied her hair back, then pulled on the only dress she could find that wasn't horribly creased, before almost running down the hill to meet him.

'You've had quite a day.'

'It could have been worse,' she reminded him. 'A woman is missing. All I had to contend with was someone breaking in for food.'

'You don't think it's linked in any way?'

'My intruder has been living next door for who knows how long. I doubt he'd venture all the way across to the opposite cliff, abduct a woman, then come back for me,' she said. 'Or do it the other way round.'

'She might not be missing. She could just have gone off somewhere I suppose.' But he said this half-heartedly.

'She is a solicitor. They're usually pretty reliable, aren't they? Anyway, time will tell. Let's hope they find her.'

'Do you feel happier now your house is secure?' he asked.

'Thanks to you, yes, and I am sorry I called you in the middle of the night. I don't know how you got to me so quickly.' He had managed to get from one side of the town to the other in moments, and she still couldn't work out how he'd done it.

'I may have broken a few speed limits,' he admitted. 'Anyway, you probably didn't need me. I only came round to make sure you didn't kill the guy.' She laughed at that and sheepishly recounted her shouted threat to stab the intruder through the heart. 'That sounds like the girl I used to know,' he said dryly.

'I am *not* scary,' she mock scolded him.

'Well,' he said doubtfully, 'maybe just a little.'

'Careful,' she warned him. 'There will be knives on our dinner table.'

'Then I'll change the subject quickly.' But when he did he was still referring to the intruder. 'You were right about calling the police,' he said. 'Not interested.'

'You weren't impressed by PC Green then?' she asked.

'Were you?'

Rebecca had been disappointed Dominic seemed so underwhelmed by what she had experienced but perhaps he knew what he was doing. 'He did have other things on his mind, but I'll reserve judgement. Let's see if he catches my intruder.'

'He won't.' It was Alan's turn to speak with conviction.

'You seem very sure about that.' She frowned. 'Do you know him?'

'Everyone knows him. He's been our local copper for years. His father was a horrible git who used to run the chemist shop. Don't you remember them?'

'Not really,' she admitted.

'But then you were never in trouble.'

'Nor were you,' she reminded him, 'unless you went off the rails later.'

'You broke my heart,' he said, deadpan, 'so I turned to crime.'

'Your only crime was a bit of underage drinking, as I recall.'

'You did that too, though you never got drunk.'

'I have a reassuringly high tolerance for alcohol.' It was true. Rebecca was rarely drunk and her metabolism seemed to be able to cope with most things. Even the rare forays into drugs during her college years left her unimpressed. When everyone else was getting stoned on weed it seemed to have little or no effect on her.

'I was never arrested,' continued Alan, 'but anyone who spent their late teens on the streets of Eriston will remember Dominic. He was always there to move you along. Eriston must be the only town in Northumbria that still has a beat bobby. I have no idea why.' Then he said, 'Don't you remember the time we all had to run away from the lighthouse because Tony lit that fire?'

That did ring the vaguest of bells. 'Was that him?' She distantly recalled a police car pulling up by the edge of the field and a policeman getting out to break up their gathering. She'd have been sixteen then and going out with Alan. His best mate Tony had decided it would be a good idea to make a bonfire out of an old wooden pallet, only it must have been coated with something because it had started to smoke badly and the fumes were acrid. Her last memory of that incident was of them running from the burning pallet and across the field as fast as they could to get away from the policeman.

'Yeah, that was him. You couldn't get away with anything round here back then.'

'Except murder,' she said. 'He thinks someone has been getting away with that.'

At that point the guy behind the bar came over to tell them their table was ready. Only when they were reseated and the barman had left was Alan able to lean forward and quietly ask, 'Murder?'

Rebecca decided to tell Alan everything then, including the suspicion that her father might have been murdered. She could tell he was shocked. It was written all over his face. When he had heard her out, he said, 'That's terrible, Rebecca. I am so sorry. Who does he think might have killed your dad?'

'He doesn't know. He said he did but he doesn't really. He just meant that it might be all down to one man.'

To her surprise Alan then said, 'The Chameleon? People round here have been talking for years about a killer that no one can see.'

'How is that possible exactly?'

He answered her question with another. 'How is it possible for so many people to die and the cases are either unsolved or everyone is left doubting the verdicts when they are?'

'You're talking about Simon Kibbs?' she asked.

'Him and others. Look, I'm not saying that the gossip is right. I'm just telling you that there *is* gossip.'

'Then tell me more.'

Even for a date that wasn't really a date, the evening was still an unusual one. While they ate, they spent the first part of it talking about the mysterious, reputedly supernatural killer blamed by many for a number of suspicious deaths in the region. Like her, Alan had a healthy cynicism about it but he couldn't explain it away either.

Eventually they turned their attention back to Rebecca's house and whether she would really be OK sleeping in it alone. 'Of course I will,' she lied, because she didn't want him to have to offer his bed again. When he reminded her that a woman was missing, she said, 'The houses next door are boarded up and you bricked up the attic, so I'll be good. My uninvited guest can't be a supernatural killer or he wouldn't need to break through walls.'

'Or steal cans of soup,' he agreed.

She was weary of the topic and eager to finally put it out of her mind. 'Let's talk about something else.'

'OK.'

There was a pause while they both waited for the other to speak.

'So you're not married then,' he blurted. 'Or so you told Jack, and you're not wearing a ring. Women generally do.'

'I'm not married.'

'And no boyfriend?'

'There was one, until a few months back.'

'What happened? Not that it's any of my business.'

She didn't want to go into that either. 'It petered out. What about you? I'm guessing you're not married or you wouldn't be having dinner with an old flame. She probably wouldn't like that. Your wife, I mean.'

'I told her I was out with the lads and she's busy with the kids.'

'Really –' she mock frowned – 'I didn't see her or the kids while I was staying at your house.'

'They're away,' he said, keeping up the pretence. 'Visiting the grandparents.'

'How many have you got?'

'Five.' His brow furrowed then. 'Or is it six? No, I'm pretty sure it's just five.'

'You've been busy.' Then she dropped the joke. '*Are* you seeing anyone, Alan?' She tried to make the topic sound natural, just a catch-up between friends, with nothing at all at stake.

He opened his mouth to answer, just as the waiter appeared to check that everything had been all right with their main courses, then he swept their empty plates away. At that point Connor Owen walked into the restaurant, spotted them both, did a double take and came over to their table. His first words were urgent. 'Have they sorted it?'

'Evening, Connor,' said Alan to remind the property developer that he hadn't begun with a greeting. 'If you mean the shutters? Yes.'

Connor was visibly relieved. 'Good. Fucking squatters. That's all I need.'

'Rebecca didn't need them either,' said Alan. 'Especially when one of them appeared in her bedroom in the middle of the night.'

'No, of course not,' he demurred, then he asked her, without much concern, 'Are you all right?'

'I will be.'

'I guess it's just another reason to get shot of the place,' he said. It was clearly the only thing on his mind. 'I was wondering actually, if you'd had time to think over my offer?'

'Jesus, her feet have barely touched the ground, Connor,' said Alan.

Rebecca held up a hand. 'It's OK.' She knew Alan meant well but was determined to fight her own battles, even the unwinnable ones. 'I haven't decided what I want to do with the house yet.'

'You'll not get a better price,' he assured her. 'There's no one else in Eriston with the clout or the cash to match it.'

'Well, I haven't tested the market yet.'

'You can try but no one will want it.'

'What makes you say that?'

'The condition of the place for one,' he told her, 'and I own the three adjacent properties, which are scheduled for redevelopment. Do you think anyone will buy a house under those circumstances, and do you really want to live on a building site for months?'

Rebecca was at a loss for how to deflect that argument.

Annoyingly he was right. *She* wouldn't buy a house under those circumstances. No one would.

Alan intervened then. 'Those three houses aren't worth much without the fourth one, though, are they, Connor? Which makes this a seller's market.' She could tell the developer didn't like this but Alan wasn't done. 'You don't really want to redevelop them. You want to tear them down and start again. You'll cram in far more flats that way but you won't get planning permission to demolish three houses if they're still attached to Rebecca's and you know it.'

Connor Owen's face fell. 'Then it seems we are at an impasse,' he managed.

'Not really,' said Alan, 'you just need to sharpen your pencil and come up with a better offer for Rebecca, a *much* better offer. If you do that, at least she has a choice.'

'What choice?'

'Accepting your offer or doing the place up and selling it to one of those commuters.' Then he turned to Rebecca and said, 'You've got a prime location at the top of the hill there. I told you I'll renovate the kitchen and bathroom; maybe add an en-suite to the master bedroom. You can pay me after you sell the place. There's no hurry.'

He made it sound like a serious offer they'd already discussed in detail, even though he'd never mentioned it before. 'You did say that,' she lied, 'and I'm seriously considering it.'

'And Connor will tell you, I'm very reasonable, aren't I, Connor?'

The property developer looked sick then and he turned on the other man. 'Don't bite the hand that feeds, Alan.' That was his last word on the subject and then he was gone, not quite storming out of the place but as good as, thought Rebecca.

She turned to Alan, wide-eyed and, as one, they laughed.

'Did he just flounce?' she asked.

'I think he did,' agreed Alan, his smile not dampened by the implied threat from Connor, 'but he'll be back. He can't just sit on those properties. You're tying up his cash. He'll come back with a better offer before the end of the week.'

Rebecca wished she shared his confidence. It was easy for Alan to be so blasé but the house was her only asset these days. Connor Owen was far from likeable but he might be the only buyer she could get. 'You don't know what he offered,' she said, 'so how do you know he will come back with a better one?'

He smiled. 'I know Connor. He'll always offer the bare minimum. He'll make a small fortune turning those four houses into apartments. Perhaps you can put a little dent in that fortune if you hold your nerve.'

You're not in.

How disappointing.

I had been so looking forward to seeing you again. Now I find the house dark and the curtains drawn. I can't even look inside. I could get in easily, of course, but what would be the point?

It was a wasted night. Not the first and it won't be the last. If this world has taught me anything, it's patience. You have to wait for the right moment.

I waited a long time to make a move on Amanda but it was worth it. Now she is done but I'll always have the memory of our time together.

Now I am ready to move on, but where are you? What are you doing?

No one stays out till this hour on their own.

I have to admit I'm a little jealous, Rebecca.

Is he kissing you right now, touching you, undressing you or watching you undress? Will you show him everything?

Women do that these days with very little thought. It's not like it used to be. Virtue has no value any more. Not in this world and that's a shame.

I suppose I'd better be going then. No point in waiting around here for no reason.

Until next time, Rebecca.

22

When they emerged from the pub, he said, 'I'll take you back.' Then he looked around as if the idea had only just struck him. 'Unless you fancy going for a drive? It's a nice night.'

Was that why he hardly drank anything? Had he always intended to take her for a drive afterwards?

'Where should we go?'

'Along the coast road?'

They drove through the town and out the other side while Rebecca took in her surroundings. Two miles along the coast road, she spotted a familiar landmark; its white walls reflecting the moonlight. The lighthouse.

'We used to hang out there all the time,' he said, 'in a group . . . and just the two of us.'

'I remember.'

The lighthouse had always been part of her childhood. Rebecca and her friends had played there, oblivious to the dangers of the occasional falling stone from the dilapidated stairwell and its crumbling brickwork. As she grew older it became a place in which to experiment; Rebecca's first furtive cigarette had been smoked there and alcohol shared illicitly with friends. Her long walks with Alan on summer evenings always seemed to end up at the lighthouse. She told herself that definitely wasn't the reason he decided to pull the car over now. The wire fence that surrounded the whole site and the darkness beyond it prevented them from taking a closer look anyway.

'I'm surprised Connor Owen hasn't bought the lighthouse and turned it into apartments.'

'Oh, he tried.' And when she looked disbelieving he said, 'He really did but it's listed.'

'It's *listing*,' she said, because the lighthouse did appear to have a slight lean to one side.

'It's Grade One, which means it can't be demolished, extended or altered, much to Connor's frustration.'

They gazed at its walls through the car window. 'It was the one place where we could escape the prying eyes of the adults,' she said. 'I used to hate the way everyone knew everybody in Eriston.'

'I quite like it,' he said, 'though it was a bit inconvenient when you were looking for somewhere private to cop off with your girlfriend.'

'You make everything sound so romantic. I'm surprised you're single.' She was fishing to see if he actually was but infuriatingly he didn't answer.

Instead he pointed. 'That's where we used to get in.' There was a low gap in the stone wall a few yards before the wire fence. She knew that beyond it was a well-worn footpath that took you right up to a piece of high land that jutted out into the sea. That was where the lighthouse stood. Everyone called it the Point.

'It's all fenced off now, though. I feel for the kids of today. They're all stuck indoors on their iPads instead of hanging out with their mates outdoors like we did.'

'In a dangerous lighthouse,' he said dryly, 'drinking and setting fire to things.'

'When you say it like that,' she conceded, and she looked back the way they had come. 'We used to get bags of chips and eat them on the walk up here. It's further from the town than I remember.'

'That's because we weren't in a hurry. Kids never are. Someone would get hold of a bottle of something, cider or wine? We all had to pretend to like it.'

'Yes, we did.'

'We used to play that game from America,' he said, 'what was it called, Seven something?'

She remembered. 'Seven minutes in heaven?'

'That was it.'

'That was Ellen's idea,' said Rebecca. 'Remember that poor American girl we used to hang out with?'

'She ended up in Eriston because her dad managed a plant outside of town.'

She was still remembering the game. 'That was a great idea,' she said wryly. 'Force two awkward teenagers to go into a scary lighthouse together. Make them decide whether they should kiss each other or just stand there for seven very awkward minutes.'

'It wasn't such a bad idea,' he said significantly. 'That's how we got together.'

She deflected again, by pointing to the lighthouse. 'It's taller than I remember.'

Rebecca got out of the car then and he followed.

They surveyed the huge semicircular wire fence that had been put up to cut off the Point and keep the latest generation of teenagers away. There were warning signs stating there was a DANGER OF DEATH, which sounded both ominous and grammatically incorrect to Rebecca.

The lighthouse was a little over ninety feet tall. Its roof had rotted away and its upper floor was windowless and exposed to the stars; not that anyone had been up there in years, because the rest of the building was almost hollow. The lower decks had collapsed under their own weight. All that remained were the remnants of the stone staircase that clung to the inside of its walls.

The Eriston Lighthouse had been built on the promontory that jutted out into the sea, its foundations laid in 1820 and the rest of the building built out of stone and timber; its upper deck had been equipped with the latest available system of lamps as well as a Fresnel lens, which was considered a technological wonder at the time. But within two decades the lighthouse was rendered obsolete by one built further out to sea on the Farne Islands. When the old lighthouse keeper finally died of natural causes it was decided it wasn't worth the cost of employing a successor. The lighthouse was locked up and abandoned until it gradually fell into a state of disrepair. The timbers had all rotted away, leaving a building that now resembled a hollow chimney. Only a fool would ever try to climb the stone staircase, which had crumbled and fallen from the walls until much of it had collapsed into rubble that littered the sandy floor below.

Rebecca and Alan were standing side by side, just looking at the lighthouse behind its wire perimeter and neither of them spoke for a time, while they both recalled their own private memories of the place.

'God, I was nervous when I asked you out,' he told her suddenly.

'You didn't seem it. You just walked up to me, in front of my friends as I remember, which was quite impressive, and I think you said something romantic like "Wanna gan out?" ' She acted out the reaction of a shy and embarrassed girl who could not look him in the eye. 'And I was, like, "Yeah".'

'I had a way with words. It's no wonder you fell for me.'

'What girl wouldn't?'

'I'm surprised your mates didn't warn you off.'

'They tried.'

'Really?'

'Of course not. You were the school bad boy, so obviously they thought you were lush.'

'I wasn't that bad.'

'It's all relative. Eriston is a small place and my date with you was all they talked about for a week.'

'Did you have to report back to them afterwards?'

'In detail.'

'Oh God. What did they want to know?'

'*Did you snog him*, obviously, and was he any good at it?'

173

'I hope you gave me a decent review.'

'Well, I went out with you again, didn't I?'

'Can you remember where we went?'

'Can't you? I'm appalled. You took me to the cinema. I was incredibly nervous and worried that if you tried to hold my hand, you'd realize my palms were sweaty.'

'I do remember.'

'No, you don't.'

'I took you to see *Pirates of the Caribbean: At World's End*.'

'Because you had a thing for Keira Knightley.'

'Because I had a thing for you. I barely glanced at Keira all evening.'

'Liar.'

'I mean it. I only watched the film at all because I was trying to pluck up the courage to kiss you.'

'I knew it was coming. You took me into the back row.'

'That's what happens when you go on a date with the school bad boy.'

'Happy memories,' she said, 'but a very long time ago.'

'I was surprised you remembered me at all.'

'Really? Of course I did. It's special at that age.'

'It was.' Then he smiled. 'Until you dumped me ruthlessly.'

'I'm sorry. You were lovely but I just couldn't handle the pressure.'

'Pressure? From me?'

'At home. My parents were rowing constantly and,

174

when they weren't doing that, they were fretting about my future. Exams were looming. My dad said you were a distraction, which of course you were but not necessarily in a bad way. I don't even know why I caved but I think even then I knew I wouldn't be staying in Eriston much longer. I suppose I thought it would be easier to break it off before we got too involved.'

'And then you left.'

'Mam left,' she corrected him, 'and took me with her.'

'That broke my heart,' he said, 'or at least dented it.'

'Bet you were out with a different girl the following week.'

'Nope. Even Keira Knightley could not have consoled me. I was gutted.'

'What can I say? I'm a ruthless heartbreaker.'

'You certainly were.'

Neither of them spoke for a moment. It was as if they had taken the teasing about their former relationship and its messy break-up as far as it could go without something significant being said about it. Rebecca did not want that. Perhaps he didn't either.

Then he looked at his watch. 'I've got an early start tomorrow. Got to fit one of Connor's kitchens in a day, so . . .' He shrugged to explain his need to get going.

'OK, then.' And she felt a surge of disappointment that they were not able to reminisce a little longer about their teenage courtship.

He leaned in then and she realized it was for a kiss and, without thinking about it for once, she let him but confusingly it landed on her cheek. Had the memory of their break-up ruined the moment?

They got back into his truck and she said, 'I suppose I'll see you around.'

'Yeah.' And then he asked, 'Are you doing anything at the weekend?'

She smiled. 'I *was* planning on washing my hair.'

'Wanna gan out?'

She laughed at the words and the nervous tone he had used and she wondered if that was entirely fake. Her reply mimicked the excited wide-eyed teenager she had once been.

'Yeah.'

23

Even with shutters on the doors and windows of the neighbouring houses and the attic safely walled up, Rebecca retained a feeling of nervousness as she prepared for bed. She was alone again now and the memory of seeing a man standing in her bedroom was still fresh. It was not an experience she wanted to repeat. Rationally, Rebecca knew that was unlikely to happen but when you are on your own in a big old house and it's dark outside, irrational thoughts often win out. She reminded herself the man was long gone and not likely to try to break in again, though she still felt vulnerable here at the top of the hill, as the sole resident of the Apostles.

Rebecca made a point of double-checking the doors were locked and securely bolted, and she left the landing light on when she went to her room. She even took a large kitchen knife upstairs with her for protection. She read for a while in bed but there were no more breakthroughs and she found it hard to concentrate, so she put down her father's laptop and lay for a while thinking about her evening with Alan. It had been nice and he had turned out well. If she had met Alan for the first time in a place with more promise than Eriston, she might even have thought there could be a prospect of . . . *something* developing, but it didn't seem very rational to prolong this.

'Stop being so sensible,' she told herself quietly, because that had never really got her anywhere but back here again in Eriston. She would go on that next sort-of-date with Alan because she enjoyed his company and deserved something nice in her life right now and that was the end of it. Having made her decision, she rolled over and promptly fell asleep.

Rebecca was in the shower when the call came and she missed it. It was Dominic and she wondered if he had news about her intruder. His voicemail suggested they talk in a café at lunchtime but she noticed he chose a different venue from the one where they had been interrupted by DI Hall. This one overlooked what passed for Eriston's beachfront, a lump of sand and seaweed that stretched for a mile to one side of the harbour, before ending abruptly at a pile of large rocks. The sand contained shell fragments and shingle, so it wasn't the easiest surface to walk on in bare feet. Yet another reason why Eriston failed to compete with the larger, sandier beaches.

Rebecca killed some time in the town before heading to the café early and selecting a table to the rear. When Dominic arrived, there were two rows of empty tables between them and the nearest other diners, a pair of pensioners taking advantage of the venue's special offer of 'half-cod and chips' for OAPs.

'Have you got him?' she asked as he reached her table.

'Your intruder? No, not yet,' he admitted. 'But we will.'

'And the missing woman?'

He shook his head to denote the lack of progress.

Dominic looked a little uncomfortable then. 'Listen, I'm sorry about walking out on you that time.' He meant the day he had left his lunch half finished in the café. She had seen Dominic since then at her house but he must not have felt comfortable apologizing to her while Alan was there. 'It's Hall,' he explained. 'He always gets to me.'

'What's his problem?' She meant it in a general sense but he must have thought she wanted specific answers about his relationship with Hall and he shot her a look. 'I'm not prying,' she said quickly. 'I just didn't like his attitude.'

'I don't mean to be defensive. It's just –' he seemed to be hunting for the right words – 'I got the blame for something years ago and he never lets me forget it.'

He clearly didn't want to tell her more, so she asked a different question. 'Does Hall always investigate the serious crimes around here?'

'He covers the whole region, so yeah. Him and his team.'

'Does he usually catch someone?'

'Pretty much.'

'But you don't think he always gets the right man, do you?'

Dominic seemed reluctant to get into this here. He looked behind him to check that no one had walked in since he had arrived. 'He is sometimes reluctant to look beyond the more obvious suspects.'

Her father had written something along those lines in his book. Rebecca recalled his scepticism at the likelihood of Simon Kibbs being a killer. Were there others like him? She decided to just come out with it. 'Who else is in jail that shouldn't be, apart from Simon Kibbs?'

He obviously wasn't expecting her to make that jump or to be so direct but he said, 'What makes you think Simon shouldn't be in prison?'

She took a leap of faith then and told him. 'I found my father's laptop and read his book.' She went on to explain everything she had learned about the Eriston Rose case and the subsequent murder of Katherine Prentiss.

He immediately wanted to know if her father had made a breakthrough that might identify the real killer. Rebecca assured him that all he had really managed to do before he died was seriously question the guilty verdict against Simon Kibbs and the police methods used to reach it.

'I suppose you are going to tell me I should hand over the laptop to DI Hall, even though he won't take a word of my father's book seriously, especially since it portrays CID in a bad light.'

He considered this for a moment, then said, 'Obviously if you were to tell me you had found it, I would be duty bound to instruct you to hand it over or at least inform DI Hall that you have it, even though he never listens to a word I say.'

'Right.'

'So it's just as well that you haven't told me that you found it,' he said. 'Isn't it?'

Their eyes met for a moment and she realized they were about to enter into a conspiracy of sorts and one that involved a considerable amount of risk to Dominic if it were ever exposed.

'Found what?' she asked, and he nodded slowly and approvingly at this answer.

'You know what?' he said. 'Everything you have learned so far is shocking but none of it surprising, sadly, and it backs up what I have been saying for years. I told you your father believed me.'

'You did.'

'There have been a number of suspicious deaths in the area. Some in the town, others in the surrounding villages and beyond them. All women, all found dead, but we don't know if they're linked or if they're . . .' He shrugged helplessly. 'Frankly we don't know what they are. In some cases a body has been found in the woods months after death, then there were others where it was floating in the sea or washed up on the coast. When they've been in the water for a while it's hard to know what you are dealing with: murder, accident, suicide.'

'So they might not be suspicious at all?'

'I'll tell you what is suspicious,' he went on, 'and it isn't just the murder rate. The suicide rate is also "statistically anomalous". We have more accidents leading to death, and incidents of domestic violence are several times more likely than normal to result in serious injury or a fatality. In short, living in or around Eriston is bloody dangerous,' he concluded.

'And no one is talking about this?' she marvelled.

'Oh, people talk about it . . . behind closed doors. Mainly they look for explanations other than the obvious.'

'Which is?'

'That there is a killer living among us.'

'And another woman has gone missing,' she reflected.

'From the High Houses.' He was looking at her intently now. 'I even thought maybe we could take a look.'

'At what?'

'Her home. The outside of it at least.'

'Why?'

'Perhaps we'll see something the others didn't.' When it became apparent that she still did not understand him he said, 'Maybe you will then. Look, I'm on my own here and I feel like I'm pissing in the wind. We share a common goal. We want to know what happened to your father and prevent it from happening again. Shouldn't we try to do that together?'

'But I'm not a police officer. Won't you get into trouble?'

'I will if you tell anyone.'

'I won't.'

'Then let's do this.'

24

The High Houses were at the northernmost tip of the town, situated on the hills directly opposite Rebecca's family home. The gap that stretched between them housed the rest of the town. It had started as a fishing village hundreds of years ago and gradually expanded until every bit of space at sea level was filled with houses. By the Victorian era there was no space left to build on except the hills that overlooked them.

The area where Rebecca's father had lived had been called Inglenook Top, because as far back as Tudor times, the hill had been used as the site of a beacon to warn of hostile ships or alert the townsfolk if a vessel had gone aground. An ingle was a fire but more of a domestic one, the kind you associated with a hearth and it was meant to convey a sense of cosy gentility in a more civilized age. Everyone in Eriston just called it the Nook. The High Houses also had a fancier name when they were first offered for sale to the town's more prosperous residents, but this had been long forgotten and everyone simply called them the High Houses. This was not entirely due to their location. There was an intimation that if you could afford to buy one, you were looking down on the rest of the town, in every sense of the word.

'Amanda Mayhew works in Newcastle and trains it home in the evening,' Dominic explained as he drove them up the hill.

'Has she always lived on her own?'

'With someone to begin with but the relationship ended. When he left, she stayed on. They're trying to trace him, to see if he has had any contact with her recently.' Then he muttered, 'He'll be the first person CID blame if she turns up dead.'

'What's Hall's view?'

'He is, quote, *keeping an open mind*. They are making enquiries but there is no evidence of foul play.'

'He thinks what? That she just ran away?'

'People do,' he conceded. 'Every day. Almost a quarter of a million people a year jack it in and disappear because the pressure suddenly gets to them. Most come back in the end but not all of them.'

'But you don't share that view, obviously.'

'Amanda has been at the same company for six years. They think highly of her and she was not working extreme hours or under any particular performance-related pressure. Her mother backs that up. She liked her job, enjoyed her life seemingly, though she was looking for a new relationship. Other than that, she was perfectly happy and her mother is worried. She can think of no reason why her daughter might want to run away.'

'Looking for a new relationship,' she repeated. 'She was dating?'

'She uses one of those apps where they claim they will find you a perfect match. They're looking into that too, to see if she had any dates recently, but it is just one avenue.'

'But Hall doesn't think there is a crime here, just like he is reluctant to admit that my dad was killed?'

'His team are already struggling. He badly needs this to be a story about a woman who cracked under pressure and ran away.'

'It's usually men who do that,' she observed.

'Statistically you are correct. Men are far more likely to run away than women.' He then said dryly, 'Hall reckons that's because lots of women have kids and don't want to leave them. This woman does not have kids, therefore she is more likely to have run away.'

'He's a relic of a bygone era, isn't he?'

'The last of a dying breed.'

'How come you're not a detective, Dominic? You think like one. Have you never thought of transferring out of uniform?'

'If I did that, they'd post me somewhere else and I'd have to leave Eriston. I don't want to do that.'

'Why not?'

'Because it's my town,' he told her firmly, 'and I want to keep it safe.'

From anyone else that could have sounded absurdly old-fashioned but Dominic said it with such resolution Rebecca couldn't help but respect him for it.

They were almost at the top of the hill now and Rebecca glanced out of the window. From here she could make out the rows of houses on the opposite hill, which included hers. If anything, the Apostles looked even bleaker and more foreboding from here. From a distance they resembled a tombstone in a dark corner of an old graveyard.

The road narrowed before reaching a dead end at the top of the hill, so Dominic parked up to one side and they walked the rest of the way. The house they were heading for was set back from others on the slope with tall hedges round its front garden.

'No one can see you,' she observed. 'You could stand by the front door and wouldn't be spotted by neighbours.'

'You can get round the back too.' He indicated a cut down the side of the house and they went along it together. The path had the gable end of the house on one side with a wooden fence beyond it, which marked the perimeter of the back garden. Trees bordered the other side of the cut.

Rebecca heard a faint sound then and she stopped.

'Do you hear music?' They both halted and listened for a moment but the sound she thought she'd heard eluded her now. Rebecca could have sworn she had picked up the faintest traces of music coming from beyond the fence, towards the rear of the house. Perhaps the missing woman had returned, unaware of the furore caused by her sudden disappearance.

They stood in silence and, though Rebecca was convinced her hearing had always been very sharp, she did not hear the sound again. She was about to dismiss it and even started to say, 'I thought I heard . . .' when she caught a tiny tinkling once more.

Dominic answered her confused look with, 'Wind chimes.'

That would account for the intermittent nature of the sound, which would only ever reach them on a breeze. He had said it with such certainty but Rebecca still couldn't make it out clearly. 'Are you sure they're wind chimes?'

He didn't answer straight away but looked thoughtful for a moment, then said, 'I read in Hall's report that she had some.'

'Why would Hall bother to mention wind chimes in his report?'

'He's very thorough. His reports are like *War and Peace*.'

Rebecca imagined Hall using his reports as evidence that he had seen and fully examined every minor detail of the crime scene, before rebutting any theory that did not tally with his own.

They walked down to the gate and Dominic pulled out a pair of disposable gloves and put them on, reached for the door handle and turned it. It wasn't locked and it moved silently and easily open. They exchanged looks that told them they were both thinking the same thing. The house was secluded and the rear of the property unsecured.

'She was burgled once too. A year or so ago. You'd think she would have secured this at least.' He meant the gate. 'I told her to.'

They stepped inside and surveyed the back of the house. Rebecca asked, 'So you met her then?' He hadn't mentioned that.

'Only to take a statement,' he said. 'After the burglary.'

'Did you catch the culprit?'

'Not this time.' And she wondered if the police ever caught burglars these days.

'But you gave her some advice, which she seems to have ignored.'

'She changed the locks.'

'How do you know?'

'Because I got Gregg Poole up to do the job. He's the local locksmith.'

'I know,' she said. 'He changed the locks on my dad's house.' Unnecessarily as it turned out, because the intruder was coming in from the attic not the front door.

Their eyes were drawn to the wind chimes then as a slight wind disturbed them. They were hanging between the conservatory and the back door, which led to the kitchen.

'You can see right in there,' said Rebecca. 'Through the conservatory and into the lounge.'

'And if she left her back door open, he could walk straight in. Anyone could get in here without being seen or heard.'

'She lived alone,' observed Rebecca, 'but how would he know that? Was he watching her?'

'If he was, it would be easy.' And they both looked around the garden with its bushes and mature trees that would make perfect vantage points, particularly at night. Rebecca thought of the woman sitting in her home with the lights on, which would make it almost impossible for her to see if someone was lurking in her back garden after dark.

'But for all he knew she could have a partner who is away or at work,' she said.

'Maybe he watches them for a while, until he can be sure.'

'Maybe, but would he want to waste the time?'

'What are you getting at?'

'Perhaps he knows them in advance,' she suggested.

'You think he knows them already?'

'I think he knows *of* them,' she said. 'Even if he's never met them before. Perhaps he's seen her on the train home. Maybe he knows her socially or from the dating app and he wouldn't necessarily have to have gone out on a date with her. He could have just seen her on there,' she said.

'So, maybe he has worked out she is single and lives alone,' he offered. 'We don't know exactly how yet but he knows it.'

'Yeah.'

'But he watches her anyway,' said Dominic.

'Why?'

'Because he enjoys that part.'

25

Rebecca might have been alarmed by how easily Dominic placed himself inside the killer's head, if he hadn't quickly added, 'It's behavioural profiling. Think about it. He builds up a picture. He must do. There's planning here. He is meticulous and could conceal himself here. It also explains why I've never seen anyone when I drive around and neither has anyone else.'

'It would,' she agreed. 'The way the town is laid out doesn't help. These hills with all the homes cut into sloping sides at strange angles, and down in the town it's all narrow dark streets and ancient houses with small windows.'

'And those bloody mists we get coming in from the sea,' he added.

'It all works to his advantage,' she agreed.

'That and the fact that nobody really believes he is out there.'

'Not quite,' she said. 'We do.'

They drove back down the hill towards the town, an unlikely, unofficial partnership – this downtrodden policeman and the unemployed journalist – but both felt they were in a position to at least try to help each other when no one else seemed to want to do anything about it. DI Hall had not been back in contact with Rebecca and she had received no answer to the letter she had sent to Simon Kibbs requesting a prison visit and she had felt as if she was getting nowhere.

When Dominic and Rebecca parted company that day, with a pledge to meet up again soon to share whatever information they uncovered in the meantime, it felt to Rebecca as if she had at least done something positive that might steer her closer to the truth.

So when Dominic went back to doing whatever it was that a 'beat bobby' did in the twenty-first century, Rebecca decided to go for a long walk along the seafront. It was possible to walk all the way to Seahouses and back in a day from here but she wasn't looking for anything that arduous, just a chance to think and she was able to do that, despite the constant squawking of the gulls.

The question that still remained largely unanswered was how could she help to solve the mystery of her father's death, if even the local CID wanted it to be an accident? A lot had happened to Rebecca since the funeral. This had kept her from focusing on her main aim of finding out more about her father's life and what he had been up to in the weeks before he died. Graham seemed like a good person to begin with. Rebecca remembered the reporter as the gentle, shy one at the newspaper, not good-looking like Jason but approachable enough, even when she was a child. He didn't say a lot, so he would be a hard one to get to know but it was clear that her father rated him as a journalist. He would complete a job well enough and on time. Graham was dependable, so perhaps she could depend upon him too.

This prompted her to open up her father's email account when she got home. Having located a routine email from Graham, she copied the address. She wrote a short but polite message asking for a meeting and suggested the Red Lion pub.

Graham replied within five minutes, agreeing to meet her.

When the reporter was late, she wondered if he would show up. Was he the forgetful type or one of those people who agrees to something to avoid conflict, even though he has no intention of actually doing it? She had just decided to give him five more minutes before leaving, when he walked in.

'Thanks for meeting me, Graham,' she told the reporter.

'No problem.' He didn't apologize for his lateness but, like everyone else, he offered Rebecca his condolences, which she accepted. She bought him a drink and steered him to her table by the window.

'I used to meet your dad here,' he said.

'Did you see him regularly?'

'I'd call in on my way home sometimes and he'd usually be sitting here.'

'Doesn't sound like Dad,' she said. 'Drinking alone.'

'Maybe he had no one else to drink with.' There was no edge to his words but they still hit home. Rebecca always thought of her dad as a well-known and respected man in Eriston but the newspaper had taken up so much of his time. Perhaps he didn't have enough left to make many friends, other than a few regulars who called into the same pub every day.

'I hadn't seen Dad for a while. I have a few questions to ask you about him, if that's OK?'

'Of course.'

'Were you with the paper right up until it closed?'

'No, I left. Didn't he tell you?' Graham seemed a little aggrieved that his departure had not warranted a mention from his editor.

'We didn't have as much contact as I would have liked.' And she felt that jolt of guilt again. Christ, how often had she even phoned him during the last year? 'Was Jason his last reporter then?'

'He left too in the end. There was another reporter after him but she quit.'

'Why?'

'Your dad never said and I didn't like to ask but she didn't stay long.'

'What was her name?'

'Leah . . . something . . . Palmer, I think. I never met her, just saw her byline in the paper.'

'Where is she now?'

'Still in Eriston, working for the town council, I think.'

Dad's reporters usually stayed with him for years but not this one and Rebecca wanted to know why.

'What made you finally leave after all that time?'

'I got an offer,' he said. 'Chief reporter. Better pay on a bigger newspaper with more job security.' He seemed a little embarrassed. 'We had a bit of a falling-out over it actually.'

'How come?' Surely her father would understand if a better job came along.

'He said he would try to get us more money and asked if I would stay. I thought there was no chance of that, so I said yes because I didn't want to hurt his feelings.' He sighed. 'Somehow he managed to get pay increases approved so he expected me to change my mind.'

'But you left anyway?' she asked. 'And he got mad.'

'He got *really* mad. Told me he'd gone out on a limb for us and that I had wasted his time.'

'What did you say?'

He looked guilty then. 'I told him I'd been wasting my time for the past twenty-odd years.' And he raised his hands with the palms forward in a defensive gesture. 'Obviously I didn't mean that. He told me to clear my desk and just leave, and I said *fine*.'

'Was that all there was to it?'

'Your dad could be pretty stubborn and we both went too far to back down.'

'You worked for him for twenty-odd years, though.'

'And I really wanted a change, Rebecca. You know what it's like on regional newspapers. You write the same stories every year and it's never anything big.'

'Except in Eriston,' she countered, 'where you get murders.'

'Oh, we didn't write them.' And when she questioned this with a look, he said, 'Sean wouldn't let us.'

Rebecca didn't understand. 'He wouldn't let you write about the killings?'

'The *Eriston Gazette* reported them,' he replied, 'but Jason and I didn't write the stories.'

It took a moment for her to understand his meaning. 'My dad wrote them?' She realized there was disbelief in her voice.

'He said it was because he had the best police contacts.'

'And you accepted that?'

'We weren't happy about it, obviously, but he was the editor and wasn't going to change his mind. I think he took the whole thing very personally.'

For someone who made his living imparting information, Graham didn't always make himself very clear and Rebecca found herself having to guess at his meaning. 'By whole thing do you mean Katherine's death?'

'We were all devastated but Sean took it particularly hard. I think he felt responsible, being her editor. Whenever there was a suspicious death he would go into his office and close the door.'

'And do what?'

'He'd be on the phone to people, reading stuff and he made reams of notes but he never discussed any of it with us.'

A middle-aged couple walked into the pub then and they had to wait till they sat down before resuming. Rebecca lowered her voice. 'How did you get back on good terms with him, Graham? He wasn't the most forgiving person.'

'A year or so after I left, I heard the paper was closing down. I dropped him a line to say I was sad about it. He replied and said he was glad I got out when I could. We sort of picked up again from there.'

'What about Jason?'

'What about him?'

'At the funeral, you were about to sit down when you realized he was in the same pew, so you moved.'

'I don't really want to discuss Jason.'

'Why not?' Rebecca wanted to know Graham's real opinion of his closest former colleague.

'I thought you wanted to talk about Sean.'

'I do,' she replied. 'And anyone who might have had contact with him lately, including Jason. Graham, I'll be honest with you, I'm trying to piece together the last few weeks of my father's life.'

'Why?'

'Because he might have been murdered.'

Graham looked genuinely stunned. 'Oh my God,' then he added several more *Oh-my-Gods* for good measure before composing himself enough to ask, 'But who . . .?'

'That's what I'm trying to find out.'

'Are the police looking for someone?' he asked, as if this might all just be a product of her imagination.

'Yes, but so far they have no leads.' This was her assumption, as Rebecca still hadn't had any contact from DI Hall, since he had belittled Dominic in the café. If he had made any progress, he was keeping it to himself. Rebecca explained the findings of the pathologist's report to the shocked reporter so he knew she was serious. 'That's why I want to talk to the people who knew him best. You and Jason.'

'I don't know anyone who might have wanted to murder your father.'

'Not even Jason?'

'God no!'

'And yet you wouldn't sit with him at Dad's funeral.'

'That was a different thing altogether.'

'What was your problem with him then? Was it because of Katherine or did it come much later?'

'Katherine's death was years ago. She had nothing to do with it.'

She had only mentioned Katherine to see if he would offer up the real reason, but he didn't enlighten her.

'So you both had a positive opinion of her?' she asked.

'We both loved Katherine.' And the ambiguity of that comment was not lost on Rebecca.

'How long did you work with her?'

'Eight months.'

'Not so very long then? She must have made quite an impression.'

'She did,' he admitted. 'Katherine was going places. It would have been Newcastle next, then London for one of the nationals.'

'She had it all mapped out?'

'We had lunch together every day. She told me her plans,' he explained.

'You were friends?'

'Yes.'

'But not more than friends? She was a very attractive girl.'

'No.' He looked down then.

'You wanted more, though?' She knew she was pushing it and waited for him to tell her to mind her own business, but he actually seemed a little shy.

'Everyone wanted to be more than just friends with Katherine.'

'Ever ask her out?'

'No.'

'Why not?'

'Because guys like me don't get girls like Katherine. She didn't see me that way.'

'Was she seeing anyone?'

Rebecca watched Graham intently to see if he knew whether her father and Katherine had been intimate but he didn't show any sign of discomfort.

'Katherine was quite a private person. She never said anything to me about seeing anyone.'

'What about Jason? He ever try?' She was deliberately steering him back to his old colleague.

'She was a woman,' he said archly, 'so, yeah, he tried.'

'And?'

'Didn't get very far.' He seemed happy about that.

'What did Katherine think of him?'

'She said he was transparent. It was obvious what he wanted.'

'Not a relationship then?'

'He's never really had one of those. I don't think he likes women, other than for the obvious.'

'How did Jason react when Katherine was found?'

'He was very upset too, obviously. We didn't fall out over Katherine. Do you think I'd have endured five minutes more of his company if he had disrespected her? No, it was . . .'

'What?'

'Something else.' She could tell he wasn't planning to reveal more.

'That's a little unusual, Graham, if you don't mind me saying so. You work with a guy for years and then, all of a sudden, you have a massive falling-out.'

He must have realized she was not going to let this go. 'It took me a long while to see it but Jason is not a nice guy. He's basically a sociopath.'

'Based on what?'

'You don't really know someone if you only ever see them at work,' he said. 'I was renting a place and the landlord wanted to sell it. I found another flat but it wasn't ready. Jason said I could crash on his couch for a bit. I was grateful but then I got to live in Jason-world.'

'What was that like?'

'Dark,' he told her. 'And cold. Jason and his flatmate were out every night and I do mean every night.'

'On a local reporter's pay?' This seemed unlikely.

'The other guy was minted. I don't know if it was his job or family money but he pretty much picked up the tab for everything and was happy to do so. He needed Jason.'

'Why did he need him?'

'Girls. They'd go into Newcastle and Jason would pick one up then the other guy would get her friend. He called Jason his "wingman"; told me he had never had so much *action*. It wasn't nice. They'd get the girls really drunk and bring them back to the flat. They treated them like shit and boasted about it afterwards. I finally saw him for what he was.'

'A misogynist?'

'Based on the way he treats women and talks about them, I'd say he hates them, yes.'

'How does he talk about them?'

'If he liked a woman . . . or sometimes if he didn't like a woman . . . he would say she needs a good . . . you know . . . shagging, and he would make jokes about tying them up and raping them.'

'He said that to you in the office?'

'When it was just the two of us. If a female sales rep came in to see Sean, he would wait till the office door was shut and say stuff then.'

'Did he realize it made you uncomfortable?'

'I think that's why he did it.'

'To torment you then, not necessarily because he hated women?'

'Both.'

'You think he has a dark side?'

'The man was dark all right and then there was all the Nazi shit.'

'What Nazi shit?'

'He had loads of books on Hitler and the Third Reich, the SS and the concentration camps.'

'You think he has Nazi sympathies?'

'Well, what do you think?'

'Did you ever challenge him about it?'

'I was working with the guy and sleeping on his couch, Rebecca. I had nowhere else to go. You think I am suddenly going to ask, "Hey, Jason, how long have you been a Nazi?" Of course I didn't challenge him, but as soon as my new flat became vacant I left.'

'Was that when you stopped being friends?'

'It's hard to stay friends with a man who thinks and acts like he does. I stopped talking to him after that.'

'There were only two of you in the newsroom, apart from my dad. That must have been awkward.'

'It was and he didn't like it.'

'What did he do?'

'It was more what he said. Mean things, about me not having a girlfriend, joking that I was queer or weird and the comments about women never stopped.'

Rebecca considered this for a moment. 'Some men say terrible things about attacking women but don't mean them. Did Jason mean it?'

Graham regarded her closely for a time before finally saying, 'You're asking if Jason is capable of hurting a woman? I don't know, but I couldn't stand up in a court of law and swear that he wasn't.'

26

Graham excused himself and went to the gents. He was gone for a while and when he came back and sat down Rebecca noticed that the front of his hair was a little wet. Had he splashed some water on his face and, if so, why? Was he disturbed by the memories she had dredged up for him or was it the shock of hearing that her father, like Katherine, had been murdered?

'When you last saw Dad, did he say anything out of the ordinary?'

'I saw him the week before he died but he didn't say anything strange.'

'Was he worried about anything?'

'We mostly just talked about the paper.' He took a sip of his drink and avoided eye contact. Was there something he wasn't telling her?

'He didn't tell you he was writing a book then?'

The answer was a mumble. 'He did mention some-thing about that.' And he shifted uneasily in his seat.

'And you thought it was a bad idea?' He gave her a questioning look then. 'Your body language,' she explained. 'And I think most people would question the sanity of writing about something that had wrecked their life.'

He didn't contradict that. Perhaps Graham could

also trace the slow downfall of her father right back to the death of his young reporter. 'I don't think he wanted to hear that it might be a bad idea.'

'He was re-examining the murders. I think that might be the reason he was killed.'

'Christ, well, if he did find something, he didn't tell me what.'

'But he must have told you his reasons for writing it?'

'He thought Simon Kibbs was innocent. He didn't believe a seventeen-year-old boy would suddenly snap in broad daylight and stab a woman to death in the churchyard he worked in, making him the obvious suspect.'

'What did you think?'

'I agreed it was unlikely but disturbed people do strange things. Honestly, Rebecca, I didn't know if Simon was guilty or innocent and I still don't.'

'Did he say anything else?'

He took a moment to answer. Finally, in a low voice that was almost a whisper, he said, 'He thought the police had covered it up.'

'Covered what up?' Simon's claim about the blood on Rose McIntyre's face rendering her unrecognizable perhaps?

'Simon said he saw someone else that day.'

'But nobody believed him.'

'Everyone assumed he was making it up to save his own skin.'

'But Dad didn't think so?'

He looked to one side to ensure the other couple

weren't listening to their conversation, then he leaned closer and lowered his voice again. 'He told me the police knew who Rose was meant to be meeting that day.'

'The man she was supposed to be having an affair with?'

'Yes.'

'Who was it?'

'He wouldn't say. I am not sure if he actually even knew who it was but he was sure that they knew. He told me that was what they were covering up.'

'How could he know that?'

'I don't know but he had his contacts.'

'In the police?'

'And other places. Your dad knew a lot of people, going back years. He heard things.'

'Do you have any idea who his contacts were?'

'The trouble with having confidential sources, Rebecca, is you have to keep them confidential. He never asked me to identify mine. I wouldn't have asked him to name his.'

'Is that everything, Graham?'

'That's it. Honestly, Rebecca, we didn't talk about the murders all that much. I think he knew it was something I didn't want to go over.'

'So you just talked about your time at the newspaper together? Nothing else?'

'We talked about other things: politics, news . . . stuff,' he finished vaguely.

'Stuff? What stuff?'

'You know.'

'No, I don't.'

'Families.' He sounded flustered. 'You.'

'Me? You talked about me?' This felt like an intrusion, even though her father had every right to discuss his daughter with an old colleague. 'What did he say?'

'He was worried about you.'

'What was he worried about?'

'Keeping a job in the current climate. I think he thought . . .' He hesitated and that was enough for Rebecca.

'That I wasn't good enough.' Graham looked at her in shock. Would he be the one to finally admit the truth after all these years? 'That *is* what he thought, isn't it?'

Graham's face contorted into an expression she could not translate; was it confusion, anger, sympathy? 'Oh, Rebecca . . .' he began but she interrupted him.

'It's all right, Graham. Deep down, I've always known.'

'He *never* said that.'

'But he thought it.'

'He was –' again there was a long, thoughtful pause and she wanted to slap him to speed things up until he said decisively – '*so* proud of you.'

She wasn't expecting that.

'He talked about you all the time, how clever you were and such a great writer.'

'Graham, if you are making this up . . .' Rebecca felt so choked with emotion she could barely get the words out.

'He said you were far better than he was at your age. I remember that specifically. We were sitting right here when he said it. I'm surprised he didn't tell you.'

'Well, he didn't.' And she immediately wondered why, because it would have made all the difference in the world if he had.

They're all still looking for Amanda but they'll never find her. They won't even be able to prove anything bad happened to her. She'll just stay missing for ever.

Nobody saw me. No one ever does.

This town is perfect for me. It could have been designed for a man with my interests. Steep hills on three sides and nothing but the sea on the other and narrow, twisting, dimly lit streets packed together. It's hard to see what's going on here, even in the daylight. After dark, you can get away with anything.

The cold winter nights are the best, when everyone closes and bolts their doors and locks their windows against those biting North Sea winds. Locked up in their own homes, with their curtains drawn, they mind their own business and leave me to mine. I don't think I would get away with my activities anywhere else but here.

Amanda didn't hear me at all and only awoke when I was standing over her. I took her away with me in the middle of the night. It was almost too easy but the excitement of the time we had together afterwards more than made up for it. I prefer it when I can take my time.

You almost jumped the queue but I'd been watching Amanda for a long time and I didn't want to keep her waiting any longer. Her unexplained departure will just add to the mythology. Name me another place in the country with more murder and madness in its past. I can't think of one. There is definitely something in the air in Eriston. They have a history of dark deeds. Did this town make me, I wonder, or do I just fit in so well here?

They never see me coming, Rebecca, and neither will you.

27

Rebecca found Jason the same way she found Graham, by searching for the former journalist's name in her father's email account. He worked in PR now. Her dad had messaged Jason wishing him good luck in his new role but it looked as if he had not bothered to reply.

She emailed asking to meet and suggested the same pub where she had met Graham. Jason agreed but offered his apartment instead because it was 'cosier'. Thanks to Graham, she was wary of Jason but didn't feel as if she was in a position to impose conditions in case he turned her down. She reminded herself that Graham's opinion was just that, an opinion and not necessarily a true reflection of Jason's character. Her father had trusted the man and worked with him for years without a falling-out, which could not be said for Graham. Also, she felt in little danger from a man who had known her since she was a small child.

'Rebecca,' he said, eyeing her up and down on the doorstep, without even bothering to disguise the fact, 'and you're all grown up now.' Maybe this had not been such a good idea after all.

He offered her tea and she accepted. When he disappeared into the kitchen to make it, Rebecca went into the lounge and took the opportunity to scan his book-shelves from top to bottom. It was conventional stuff to begin with, mostly thrillers, some famous names and some she had not heard of but nothing out of the ordinary. Then, lower down, the titles with a Second World War connection started, until she reached the bottom shelves and saw what Graham meant. Every book there had something to do with Hitler or the Nazis. There were histories of the Third Reich, books about the Holocaust, a memoir from an SS officer who had fought on the Russian front and several biographies about senior members of Hitler's inner circle. Rebecca resolved to challenge him about this but not until she had asked more pressing questions about her father in case he clammed up.

He brought the tea in and set the mugs down on a table by the sofa. Were they supposed to sit there together at either end of it? She chose the armchair instead. When they were seated, she said, 'I didn't see you at the wake.'

'I wanted to come over but you were with someone. I couldn't stay long but I did want to pay my respects.'

'Thank you.'

'Your message said you had questions about Sean?'

When Rebecca explained the reasons for those questions, his reaction was markedly different from Graham's. There was no shock, just disbelief, particularly about the details of the pathologist's report. 'Are they serious? Surely that kind of injury could happen accidentally?'

'It can,' she admitted.

'Well then,' he said, as if that concluded the matter.

'I know my father was murdered,' she said, and she was surprised by her own conviction. 'I don't know who did it but I'm going to find out.'

'Then I wish you well, but please be careful, Rebecca. If someone is capable of murder, then who knows what they will be prepared to do to cover their tracks.' Even this seemingly well-meaning warning sounded a little menacing when he put it like that. 'Anyway, you had questions for me.' Then he snorted. 'I hope I'm not a suspect.'

His tone rankled. It was as if he wasn't taking Rebecca or her claims seriously and even trivializing her father's death. 'Someone got close enough to my father to kill him,' she told Jason. 'Everyone who knew him is a suspect.'

'Even me?' Again, the disbelief.

'Even you.'

'Wow, Rebecca. Should I get a lawyer?' He gave her a look that conveyed how absurd this seemed to him. 'I never had a grievance with your father.'

'Did you know he was writing a book about the Eriston murders?'

'No, I didn't.' He thought for a while before saying, 'You think that had something to do with his death?' It was as if she had suggested her dad had been killed by aliens.

'It's possible, if he got too close to the truth.'

'The truth is that Rose and Katherine were both

killed by Simon Kibbs. The most obvious suspect usually turns out to be the one that did it. If your father was murdered, it could have been for an entirely different reason. Some people will kill a man for the contents of his wallet.'

'They didn't take his wallet,' she told him.

'Some other reason then?' he suggested but did not offer one.

'And you got on all right with him?'

'Sean was my editor for a long while, and we were fine.'

'Why did you leave?'

'The newspaper was losing money. I thought it was sensible to jump ship before it went under, or is that not a good enough reason? What now then, Rebecca? Do you want me to take one of those online tests to see if I'm a psychopath? Will that make you happy?'

'I just have a few questions, that's all.'

'Where was I on the night of your father's death being the first, I should imagine?' He seemed almost amused by this now. 'Unfortunately for me I was here, on my own, so I have no alibi, but I'm not a murderer, Rebecca, and I can't imagine why anyone would ever think I could be.'

'I never said you were.' She glanced over at the bookcase, as if noticing it for the first time. 'You do have a lot of books about the Nazis, though. I hope you don't admire them.'

He seemed taken aback. 'It's military history, an interest of mine.'

'All of it German?'

'I've always been fascinated by that period.'

'From the Nazis' point of view?'

'The books are written about them not by them.'

'So you don't think Hitler was misunderstood or that the Holocaust didn't happen?'

'Of course not.'

'I don't see any books on Stalin or anything about the Battle of Britain or Dunkirk. Just Germany.'

'A whole country lost its collective mind under Adolf Hitler. You might not find that fascinating but I do. What difference does it make whether I read German history or British?'

'It might say something about your world view.'

His eyes narrowed then. 'You've been talking to Graham, haven't you?' He shook his head as if in bafflement. 'He saw my books when I let him crash here and got freaked out by them. He is such a baby.'

'It wasn't just your reading material that bothered him.'

'He shouldn't be allowed out on his own. He's a fucking snowflake. You do realize that he's probably a virgin, don't you? Ask him. The whole time I've known him, he has never had a woman, let alone a girlfriend. You can't tell me that's natural.'

'What about you?'

He regarded her as if she had lost her mind. 'Are you serious?'

'Oh, I know you've had women, but have you had an actual girlfriend?' He didn't seem to understand the question. 'I'm asking if you have had a relationship?'

'That's none of your business actually, Rebecca. Why the hell are you asking me about my private life?'

'You brought it up.'

'No, I didn't.'

'You told me I should ask Graham about girlfriends. You said he has never had one and it's not normal, implying that *he* is not normal. So, have you ever had a relationship?'

'Look, just because I don't commit, that doesn't make me a killer.'

'I never said it did. But I should probably just file you and Graham together then.'

He gave her a look as if she was an unworldly fool and said, 'Think what you like. Not everyone fits into the same category.'

'What about your attitude to women? You don't seem to like them much.'

'Oh, I like women. You don't have to worry about that.'

'I don't mean sexually. You don't appear to like them as people.'

'Because I don't make them breakfast or hold their hands?'

'I meant the way you talk about them.'

'Here we go again. You're listening to Graham. That was just bants.'

'Bants?'

'Banter.'

'I know what it means. I'm just wondering if what you call banter really is just that. You joke about raping them.'

'Donald Trump jokes about grabbing women by the pussy. Lock him up.'

'Perhaps we should.'

'It's only words,' he said, folding his arms.

'Sometimes words don't matter and sometimes they do. You make jokes about rape.'

'And some women fantasize about being raped,' he said coldly. 'I read an article once that said between a third and a half of all women fantasize about being forced to have sex with a stranger and it was written by a female.'

'It doesn't mean they really want it.'

'Exactly,' he said, as if she had proved his point. 'If women are allowed to fantasize about being raped, why can't men fantasize about doing it? It doesn't mean a thing.'

'It's not common to say it out loud. Men don't normally talk about violent urges and women don't usually tell other people what they fantasize about.'

'I know the difference between fantasy and reality.'

'Do you?'

'Yes, I do. I knew a woman once who liked to be overpowered and tied up.' He looked Rebecca directly in the eye then, as if challenging her. 'She liked me to call her names while I was fucking her. Dirty bitch, cheap whore.' He smiled amiably at the memory. 'That kind of thing. It was the only way she could get off.' Then his tone became confiding. 'I reckon she had issues.'

'Thanks for sharing that.' She hoped her tone was contemptuous enough to make him stop.

'We had a safe word,' he continued unabated, 'because I didn't want things to get out of hand.'

'That was considerate.'

If he detected sarcasm, he didn't let on. 'I had to be careful. If I went too far without realizing it, she could have claimed I'd forced her to do things.'

'What a dilemma.'

'It was a legal minefield,' he said seriously. 'So I told her to use a safe word and I would stop instantly. Guess what she came up with.'

'I'd rather not.'

'Daddy.' And he smiled broadly then. 'Like I said, she had issues. A lot of women do.'

'Is that right?'

Then abruptly he said, 'What about you, Rebecca? Ever fantasize about being raped?' She deliberately ignored the question. 'Since we are *sharing*. You've asked me a lot of personal questions, so how about you? When you're alone at night and feeling . . . distracted. Do you ever lie there and wonder what it would be like if someone broke into your house and climbed into bed with you, held you down and –'

'I don't have a safe word, Jason. I am just going to tell you to stop right now.'

Even he could not ignore the hostility in her voice. He held up his hands to placate her. 'It seems you're comfortable talking about my sex life but not your own, which, if you don't mind me saying so, does make you seem a little uptight.'

Before he could say any more, she said, 'I'm going to

leave now.' She got out of the chair and saw that he was about to follow. 'I don't want you to get up.'

He laughed at the notion that he could not be trusted. 'See yourself out then, Rebecca. I've enjoyed our little chat. Do call again. Any time.'

She was already at his front door and relieved to pull it open. Rebecca had never left anyone's home so quickly.

28

The old newspaper office looked shabby from the out-side, as Rebecca would have expected from a building that had not had its windows washed or a lick of paint added to its exterior in more than two years. The TO LET sign had failed to attract anyone and it was easy to see why. The newspaper office was on the first floor above a large space that had once been a bustling arcade, filled with those coin-in-the-slot machines that devoured the money of parents desperate to amuse their kids on a rainy day in Eriston, and there were always plenty of those even in summertime. As a kid, she would walk past and experience a frisson of excite-ment. The flashing lights and whirring, bleeping, space-age noises coming from its games drew her to them but her dad would never take her there, declaring the place 'a waste of money'. She knew he was right but still, she would have liked to have experienced it at least once, though she never dared defy him by going in unaccompanied, certain he would choose that exact moment to leave the office and bump right into her.

The place was gone now and the newsroom was an empty floor above a large vacant lot. Soon it would be torn down and replaced with flats. It was only when she contacted the letting agent that she learned the site's new owner was none other than Connor bloody Owen. Was there a building in town that did not have his greedy fingerprints all over it? She would probably never know if her father had left the newsroom unlocked that night but if he hadn't, Connor would have been one of the people who had keys to the place.

Rebecca told the letting agent she wanted to finish the job of clearing the newsroom prior to its demolition. Sean Cole's untimely and suspicious death, in a building he was responsible for until it was finally levelled, made him particularly compliant and he granted her permission.

The letting agent turned up late to find her waiting on the doorstep for him. He mumbled an apology and some excuse about dealing with a difficult tenant, then gave her a key and left her to it. The front door opened on to a flight of stairs, which led Rebecca up to the first floor. She was revisiting the newsroom with mixed emotions: pride at her father's achievement in producing such a fine newspaper and sadness that it now seemed as if it was all for nothing. It would be if she did not at least salvage the newspaper archive her father had been trying to save the night he died.

Daylight was fading now, so she flicked the switch and light illuminated the stairs. At least there was still power in the building. As she reached the top, she remembered the first time she had come here, as a little girl, no older than five or six years old. It had seemed such an exciting grown-up place back then.

There was a woman on reception who made a fuss of Rebecca and told her how pretty she was before offering her a chocolate biscuit, which she politely declined because her father had told her to be on her 'absolute best behaviour' and she didn't want to smudge anything with chocolatey fingers.

There were four reporters then – unimaginable for a newspaper that was eventually whittled down to two, then one and finally just him. She couldn't imagine how much stress he must have been under, writing enough copy to fill that newspaper on his own every week, with no help from anyone apart from a centralized advertising department based in Newcastle, who were finding it harder and harder to sell space in any of the group's newspapers.

Now the newsroom was empty, apart from some office furniture stacked haphazardly against one wall. A single desk and chair had been set down to one side. Her father must have done that. As she drew nearer, Rebecca noticed a single leather folder open on the desk; an old article depicting Eriston Carnival and its numerous attractions stared up at her. There were photos of people dressed as clowns or TV characters from the eighties when these shots had been taken and pictures of smiling children eating ice creams. Was this the last photograph her father saw before he died?

She guessed he had picked this up to take a look inside and got distracted, like someone who starts to clean out an old room, then sits down with ancient family photos instead.

On the floor, piled beneath a row of large windows, were more of the big leather-bound binders, full of old editions of the *Eriston Gazette*. Their spines had dates embossed on them and each one contained two years' worth of the weekly paper's editions. The earliest ones went all the way back to the late sixties and each one was heavy and bulky. Where was he planning to store them all? Then Rebecca recalled the bare room that housed nothing more than a bed and a mattress. That's why he had cleared it out. He was going to put the whole bloody lot in his spare bedroom, the daft bugger.

As a journalist, as well as his daughter, Rebecca owed it to her father to finish the job. She had found the spare keys to his car in a drawer in the kitchen but the old Volvo was not by the house. She went to the far window and looked down. There it was, parked out back, where he had left it. Rebecca wasn't looking forward to making several journeys down to the car with the files before having to carry each one up to the top floor of the town house.

Maybe Alan would help her. It would be an innocent enough reason to get in touch with her old boyfriend and she guessed he probably wouldn't turn her down.

Rebecca started then at a sound that came from behind her. She whirled round, trying to work out if the noise had come from inside or outside the building. There it was again. Inside the building, definitely. It was the sound of a light tread on those creaky old stairs. Someone was coming up them to the newsroom, just like they had done on the night her father was killed and, like him, Rebecca realized too late that she was trapped, because the way up was also the only way down.

It was the letting agent, she told herself, but she knew that was unlikely. Was it Connor, the new owner, here to see what he was about to demolish, or a cleaner hired by them to . . . do what? Clean a place that would soon be reduced to rubble? No. She couldn't think of any good reason for someone to have followed her up here and she tensed, ready for whatever came next.

'Jesus Christ,' she blurted when she finally saw who it was. Dominic had reached the top of the stairs and stood there, looking at her questioningly. 'You scared the –'

There was no need to complete the sentence. He got the message but explained, 'You left the front door open.' So that's what he was investigating. A possible break-in at a murder scene?

Now it was her turn to apologize. 'Sorry. I was sure I closed it behind me.'

'It's an old door,' he said, meaning that it mustn't have shut properly because of its age. 'I was doing my rounds and I noticed it wasn't fully closed.'

'How come Eriston still has a beat officer?' she asked him. 'I thought there were, like, five PCs for the whole of Newcastle these days thanks to all the budget cuts, yet you walk around Eriston all day?'

He smiled. 'Sometimes I drive. Also, I cover a much wider area than that. There are a lot of villages and a couple of small towns on my patch but Eriston is the hub. I'm the only one around here in uniform and we still have twenty thousand people living here. I take their safety seriously but, to my own force, my presence here is little more than a PR exercise.'

'How do you mean?'

'Because of the murder rate,' he explained. 'Can you imagine the shit the politicians would get if they took away the town's only beat bobby and someone else was killed?'

'And you don't mind?'

'Doing the job? You have to play the hand you're dealt.' It struck Rebecca that this did not fully answer her question so she changed the subject.

'I wrote to Simon Kibbs in prison,' she said. 'I want to go and see him.' Just as her father had wanted to. *Ask him what he really saw.* 'I need to hear his version of what happened on the day Rose McIntyre was killed.' Then she added, 'My dad saw him.'

'I know,' he said, 'he told me.'

'He was planning on going to see Simon again.'

'How do you know that?'

'I found a note he wrote. It was like a reminder.'

'Interesting, and you have no idea why he wanted to do that?'

'No, but if I go I could ask Simon and maybe I could work it out.'

'It's worth a try,' he agreed.

'Only he hasn't replied yet.'

'Simon doesn't normally accept visitors. He's suspicious of them. I was surprised when your dad managed to get in to see him.' He considered this for a moment.

'I might be able to help you there. I know someone on his legal team. I'll give his solicitors a call and put a word in for you. It might help to get you through the door at least.'

'I'd really appreciate that.'

Then he glanced at the piles of leather-bound newspapers. 'What are you going to do with all this?'

'Save it,' she said.

Dominic didn't stay long. He was keen to get back to his beat and as soon as he left she called Alan.

'Hi,' she said when he answered, 'you know that thing we do where I ask you for help at really inconvenient times, then pay you in food?'

He laughed easily at that. 'What do you need, Shortbread?'

'You ever had a paper round?'

29

Alan helped uncomplainingly and never once questioned why she felt the need to save a load of old newspapers, even when it took them three trips in the ancient car and they had to carry each binder up the stairs to the empty spare room.

To thank him, Rebecca ordered Chinese food and opened wine. They talked until it got late and he admitted he would have to go, so she walked him to the door. He turned back then, just as she said, 'It's been lovely . . .' and he stopped any further words by slowly leaning in to kiss her, perhaps deliberately giving her enough time to pull away, but Rebecca let it happen.

It was a long kiss and almost a relief for it to finally happen but as soon as it was done, Rebecca started to overthink it. She broke free to tell him, 'I'm not sure if this is a good idea, Alan.' And he looked so disappointed she had to fight the urge to immediately kiss him again. Instead she said, 'I don't know if I'm going to be hanging around.'

'Do you have to sell the house?'

'I don't know how I could keep it. What is there for me here?'

He moved away from her and said, 'Nothing.'

'I meant work,' she said, and put a hand on his, then

squeezed it reassuringly. 'I'm just asking if we can take this slowly. It's a confusing time for me.'

'Of course,' he said. 'I'll message you.'

Rebecca was left to wonder if her lack of enthusiasm had ruined the moment. Did she just kill their relationship stone dead before it had a chance to begin again?

The following morning, to keep her mind from her complicated evening with Alan, Rebecca turned her attention to the next person she needed to see. Her father's last reporter at the *Gazette*, Leah Palmer, who had quit the newspaper in a hurry not long after joining it.

Leah wasn't that hard to find. She was the only person on site at the old lifeboat station, another empty building that had been the victim of the seemingly endless cuts in funding. The place had lain empty for years and the area was now covered by the lifeboat at Seahouses. Next door to this was the old cinema, which had closed long ago and hadn't shown a film in a long time.

She had been told where to find the former reporter by a council employee, who didn't seem unduly troubled by revealing her exact whereabouts to a stranger. Leah had a chair and a small desk with a PC on it in one corner of the room but she was standing over a much larger table right in the middle, which was covered with plans and architectural drawings. Her back was towards Rebecca at first and she was shocked to see that her father's former reporter seemed to have almost exactly the same hair style and colouring as

Katherine. Did she resemble Katherine Prentiss in every way? Was that the reason Dad had hired her? Was it also why he had to let her go? Could he not handle the reality of working with a permanent reminder of his murdered lover?

Then Leah turned to face her and the spell was instantly broken. Facially, she didn't look a bit like Katherine. The only resemblance was the hair and even that wasn't an exact match. Rebecca realized that her imagination had gone into overdrive, making her see the ghost of Katherine for no reason.

From the look on her face Rebecca wasn't sure if Leah was surprised to see her specifically or just a little shocked to see anyone at all. Rebecca introduced herself, then said, 'I understand you worked with my father, Sean Cole.'

'Oh, yes, I did –' she stared at Rebecca now, as if she was the ghost – 'and I am so sorry for your loss.'

'Thank you.' Rebecca knew it was a social nicety but wondered when it would end and she could finally stop fielding all these condolences. Rebecca decided against being quite as open to Leah as she had been with Graham and Jason and did not mention murder. Instead she told the young woman she was sorting out her father's estate and wanted to see everyone her dad knew before she left Eriston. She mumbled something about thanking everyone for being kind to him. To Rebecca's ears she sounded unconvincing but Leah seemed to accept this. 'You were his last reporter?'

'Yes,' she agreed. 'But not for very long.'

'What happened?' And when Leah looked blank she added, 'I heard you quit.'

'Only because your father asked me to.' She must have realized how bad that sounded. 'He heard there was a job with the grant team. Eriston was up for some EU money then and they needed someone to write the grant applications. It's more work than you would imagine. I've put together some massive tender documents.'

'But why would he want you to leave the *Gazette*?'

'He knew they were going to let me go. Not me, the job. I was doing fine and I enjoyed working with your dad, but I relocated here when I took over from the previous guy.'

'Jason.'

'That's him. I'd only been there three months when your dad realized they were making more cuts and he would basically be a one-man band. He felt bad because he was the one who had offered me the job and he thought I had a future in Eriston.'

And yet he told me no one has a future in Eriston.

'So he put a word in for me here,' she said.

That sounded like her dad. Always keen to help someone out, particularly another journalist and especially one left in the lurch because of him.

'You must have been annoyed when that happened.'

'It wasn't your dad's fault. Circulation was well down and there wasn't much advertising revenue from the website. It was a bit shit really and they wouldn't spend any money on it.'

'Did you get the grant money?'

'Yes.'

'But you're still here?'

'Applying for everything else I can get hold of,' she explained. 'There's funding available for the town, you just have to know where to look for it and more importantly how to apply for it.' She pointed at the plans. 'This is part of a submission to the Arts Council. I'm trying to get a hundred and fifty grand to do something with the place.'

'Do you think you'll get it?'

'I don't know. I hope so because it'll be my last grant application. There's nothing left to apply for so I'll be leaving afterwards. I'm not the one to oversee the building project.'

'What exactly is the project?'

'Redevelop this. Knock the two buildings into one.' She meant the derelict cinema and the lifeboat station. 'We're all ready to go, if we can get the cash.'

She showed Rebecca the plans. 'To get the grant it has to be arts-based, so a small single-screen cinema and theatre . . . here –' and she pointed to that area on the plan – 'you just raise the cinema screen when you want to put a live theatre performance on the stage.'

'Clever.'

'Here is the museum and art gallery, plus the café and the gift shop.' And she pointed to each section of the plan.

'What are you going to put in the museum?'

'All kinds of things. Maritime history, the fishing

industry . . . some other stuff to do with Eriston.' That sounded vague.

'The murders?'

Leah shifted uncomfortably. '*Some* of the murders. The very old ones, not the more recent ones.' Leah tried to show Rebecca another part of the plan, perhaps to deflect her from more talk of Eriston's grisly history, but this was her opportunity.

'You ever talk to my dad about them?'

'I did make that mistake once. I didn't realize he was the editor back then,' she explained sheepishly. 'He got quite angry with me and I apologized. When he calmed down, he explained that he knew Katherine Prentiss and that was why he didn't want to answer any of my questions. I was mortified and I kept apologizing. In the end he said, "Forget it," and we never talked about them again.'

'Did you see him around town after you left?'

'Once in the street a little while ago.'

'Did he seem OK?'

'He looked tired and stressed, but he had a lot on his plate by then. He said hello and I asked him how he was but he didn't really answer.'

There didn't seem to be any point in interrogating Leah further about her father, since it was clear she had only been part of his life for a short while and it appeared she knew nothing about the years following the closing of the newspaper.

'I hope you manage to get your grant,' Rebecca said.

'If we don't, this place will stay empty, but I'm not sure if we'll get the money.'

'Why not?'

'The museum is supposed to be interactive. I've never managed to think of a way to turn the exhibits from Eriston into a working museum. You can't replicate a deep-sea fishing experience or recreate a murder, thankfully. So if you have any bright ideas, I'd love to hear them.'

'I'll bear that in mind,' said Rebecca. 'And I really hope you get the funding.'

Eriston had already lost the *Gazette*. The museum might just be the town's last chance to preserve what remained of its heritage.

30

When she left the lifeboat station, Rebecca called Dominic on his personal mobile.

'Any news yet?' she asked. 'About the missing woman?'

'Not even a sighting and we usually get a number of those. Amanda Mayhew has vanished.'

'I've been thinking about the other cases,' she said. 'The ones that could be the work of a killer but were officially accidents or blamed on other people. Do you think you could get a look at the case files on those?'

'Maybe, but there are quite a few. Why?'

'I don't think we have all the information we need. I'm going to go through the newspaper archive and read up on them, and I'll see if I can find any court reports on the internet, but there is usually stuff that the public never hears. Perhaps some of it could lead us in the right direction?'

'Perhaps.' He didn't sound too convinced.

'It's just – I'll admit that I am struggling here. There's a lot of information in my dad's notes and the draft of his book, but sometimes it feels as if I can't see the wood for the trees. I'm sure there's something important that has been overlooked.'

'What makes you say that?'

'Instinct, I suppose. That and the fact that the guy hasn't been caught.'

'I'll try,' he promised. 'The files are at regional HQ. I should be able to get to them without anyone noticing.'

'I don't want you to get into any trouble.'

'Trouble is my middle name,' he said dryly. 'Actually, it's Paul. Paul is my middle name.' She laughed at that. 'Leave it with me. Should we meet tonight and compare notes?'

'Sounds good.'

Rebecca knew she would have a lot of reading to do before then.

Sunlight was streaming in from the top-floor window of the bare room while Rebecca leafed through old copies of the *Eriston Gazette*. The date at the top of this particular edition meant this one was special. It had gone to print days after Rebecca and her father found Katherine Prentiss's body in the woods and Sean Cole had struggled to keep his emotions in check. He had devoted pages of his newspaper to tributes to his fallen reporter and perhaps his lover too. Her fellow journalists weighed in as well, with pieces from both Graham and Jason. They must have been very hard to write with her murder still so fresh in their minds.

There was something about the tone of the pieces too. No one wants to speak ill of the dead but the articles written about Katherine by Graham, Jason and her father seemed to elevate her to a level above that of a mere human being. Rebecca did not doubt that Katherine was a bright, clever, ambitious young woman with personal magnetism and striking looks but was she really 'destined for greatness', as Graham had put it, and could she actually 'brighten anyone's day with a kind word, a small gesture, an offer of help with a story'? Was it true that she 'always lit up a room' simply by entering it, as her father had informed his readers? Did she have 'a one-hundred-watt smile and possess a heart that had room for everyone'? Did she never have an off day? Was she always so bloody perfect?

Rebecca stopped herself then. Why was she doing this? Was she looking for the flawed, imperfect person behind the tributes in order to better understand the murdered woman and make her more real, or was there more to this even than that? Rebecca had been doing quite a lot of soul-searching lately. She'd always had a tendency to judge herself harshly then find herself wanting. Was she examining these tributes so closely because she was jealous?

Her father's emotive words uncovered a truth Rebecca barely dared to acknowledge. The catalyst may have been tragedy but he had been able to express his feelings for this other young woman far more easily than he ever had for his own daughter. If, as Graham had assured her, he had been so proud of her abilities, why couldn't he just bloody tell her?

Where were his expressions of pride, affection and parental love when she had needed them most, as a girl then a young woman? When her self-confidence was low and he had dismissed her anxieties with a simple, 'You'll be fine', before returning to whatever he was doing that was more interesting to him? When she came to him for advice and help on how to become a journalist, why had he simply sighed and said, 'Are you sure that's what you want to do with your life?'

Feeling the need to torture herself further, she wondered why she felt so jealous of this tragic, long-dead woman. Was it because she felt as if she lost her father on the day that Katherine died and, if so, why didn't she blame the murderer instead of the victim? Maybe because Katherine was the ideal Rebecca could never quite live up to. Was this the reason she struggled to feel the right level of sympathy for a woman who had died brutally and far too young?

Rebecca abruptly closed the folder, dragged another one towards her and turned the pages of this older edition without really paying attention to them, so lost had she become in conflicting thoughts about her father. She had been through dozens of editions already, looking for information on the murder cases and mysterious disappearances in the area, while merely glancing at the headlines and accompanying photographs, without reading the mostly bland local news stories. Even Eriston didn't have a murder every week and much of the crime reporting was fairly trivial: fights outside pubs, burglaries and break-ins.

Rebecca turned another page and stopped. It wasn't the headline that drew her eye but the photograph accompanying a story about a talented young gymnast

MAKING THE GRADE. The girl was sixteen and had won a contest to represent the county. Rebecca didn't need to read her name. She knew it already from the picture, a younger version of someone she had seen in dozens of photographs over the years: Rose McIntyre, the Eriston Rose. She looked shorter, her body more compact and the hair was tied back to keep it out of the way but it was unmistakably a young Rose, dressed in a leotard that clung to her body without revealing too much for a family newspaper.

She glanced at the date of the article. It was written five years before Rose was murdered in the churchyard. Someone had interviewed her for the newspaper back then, but who? She scanned the article but there was no byline. Something else caught her eye, though. Rose was being presented with a winner's plaque by the event's sponsor, a local businessman who was in the photograph with her, and the company's logo was on a screen behind them both. OWEN LEASING it said. The young man presenting the prize was none other than Connor Owen.

They had agreed to meet up at the end of the day and share whatever they found. Dominic came to the house and seemed more upbeat than before. His perusal of the files had been fruitful.

'We are lucky,' he explained. 'A lot of this stuff is on the computer, so you'd leave a trail if you went looking for it but our chief constable is paranoid. A force down south got hacked and lost some crucial evidence, witness statements and the like, and they were slaughtered in the press for it, so he insists that everything has to be backed up with a hard copy filed away to duplicate the electronic version. You have to print everything but that's good for us. I found some interesting stuff. I think some of it backs up what I've been saying for years.'

'That the wrong men are sometimes convicted of the killings?'

'Yes. Take this one.' He leafed through his book of notes, then began to read. '*Seven years ago, Jane Anderson left her home for a night out and never returned, at least according to her husband. Friends confirmed that she went out for drinks with them. She left early and on her own. One of her mates said she was stumbling drunk. They would have made sure she got in a taxi but she ghosted from the room without them noticing. That was the last time anyone saw her alive.*' He looked up from his notes. 'This is where it gets interesting. No one ever traced a driver of a bus or taxi who saw her, so no one knows if she got home or not. She could have walked home. It was a bit of a trek but doable.'

'Even though she was "stumbling drunk"?'

'That was the theory detectives were working on. She got home; either with someone's help or on her own.'

'Why were they so convinced she made it back and wasn't just abducted along the way?'

'The husband,' he said. 'She was bad-mouthing him to her friends that night about his controlling behaviour and jealousy. That's a red flag. It's nearly always a woman's partner who hurts or kills her. Stranger killings are much rarer. This was enough for them to go to the house and look around. They found a small bloodstain on her pillow. That became the main piece of physical evidence against her husband.'

'How did he explain that?'

'He said she had a nosebleed. He claimed she got them occasionally but no one else could verify that. To the investigating officers it all added up. She went out and got drunk, he didn't like that, probably thought she had been with someone else and hit her, which caused the blood on the pillow. There were also tiny traces of it on some of his clothes. He said he must have got those when he tried to help her with her bleeding nose. Hall and his guys reckoned he got jealous, lost his temper then killed her. That's the theory.'

'So where did he hide the body?'

'Drove it out to a remote bit of coastland and dropped it in the sea below. It washed up days later.'

'Any forensic evidence?' she asked him.

'Nothing left by then. She'd been in the water for a good while. Also, crucially, there was nothing in the car.'

'So he was convicted on the basis of a tiny bloodstain and his wife complaining that he was jealous?'

'You have to understand it's not like it is on the TV. Most juries are fairly compliant and willing to be led towards a verdict. Hall's theory was reasonably convincing and the lawyers sold it well. The husband was jailed for life.'

'Did they never consider the possibility that she could have been abducted before she got home?'

'*I* thought she might have been and I told DI Hall that.'

'What did he say?'

'His exact words were "Why don't you just fuck off?"'

'Nice.'

'He is, isn't he?' he said dryly. 'And with such a limited vocabulary.'

'What was your theory?'

'We'd had some problems with unlicensed cabs, basically guys coming to the area and driving people home for a few quid, but it caused arguments with genuine cab drivers, who were being undercut. They have to pay taxes, prove their cars are roadworthy and have an actual licence. We had some public order issues around that.'

'Fighting?'

'Pushing and shoving mostly, but when word got round that there weren't enough cabs in the area to cope with weekend demand, we started getting other drivers who had no intention of getting you home safely. They would drive you out of town, take you somewhere isolated, rob you and leave you there. By the time you walked home they were long gone.'

'Anyone get hurt?'

'A couple of blokes didn't want to part with their money and took a beating. The guys doing this are bad people and won't take no for an answer. Then, a week before Jane Anderson disappeared, a woman came forward and said she was sexually assaulted by one of these bogus drivers. I don't think she was the first, just the first to report it.'

'You think one of these bogus cab drivers could have abducted Jane?'

'Or someone used them as a smokescreen so he could do whatever he wanted to do that night. Jane Anderson is just one woman from around here whose murder was never satisfactorily explained. There are others.'

'Tell me about them,' she urged.

31

By the time he was finished Rebecca was reeling. She'd had no idea of the scale of it all. Dominic was able to give her the names of half a dozen missing or murdered women with the background to each case. Some remained stubbornly unsolved, others had resulted in convictions that were, at best, unconvincing. The police were happy as long as someone went to jail for the crimes. It didn't seem to matter who.

Rebecca was impressed by not only Dominic's knowledge of these cases but the way in which he challenged the interpretation of the facts. 'Is that why DI Hall hates you?' she asked him. 'I would have thought he would welcome someone with such an analytical mind.'

'That's not the only reason,' he said slowly.

'Why don't the detectives like you, Dominic?' she asked, suddenly tired of his evasions.

'I told you,' he said, 'I messed up and I got the blame.'

'How do you mean, you messed up?' She spoke gently, trying to coax it from him. 'Everyone does from time to time. I know I have.' And when he didn't object or respond in any way, she asked, 'What did you do, Dominic?'

He wouldn't look directly at her at first and Rebecca wondered if he was annoyed that she had asked but then he must have reasoned he could trust her, because he began to speak, slowly at first.

'It was a crime scene,' he said flatly, 'but I didn't view it that way. I should have but I was young, inexperienced and what I saw –' he paused, as if remembering it anew – 'affected me.' He did look up at her then. 'Do you understand?'

She nodded but said nothing, not wanting to interrupt him now that he was finally explaining himself. 'I'd not been on the job long. The only dead body I'd ever seen was a fisherman, who fell overboard and drowned. Not nice,' he clarified, 'but not like *this*. This was . . .' He shook his head.

'What was it?'

'A young woman. I was called out to investigate a disturbance in her village and, as luck would have it, I was close by. I'm the local bobby so I'm never far away, which is a blessing and a curse. In this case definitely a curse. I was first on the scene and found the front door locked. I knocked and there were no signs of life, so I went round the back. I was half expecting the place to be empty but the back door was wide open, so I called out. No answer. I'd been told to go there for a reason, sounds of a struggle, some shouting, so I had to check it out, but at this point I'm half expecting to walk in on a couple having a row. There was no one in the kitchen, so I went into the living room and that's where she was, lying on the floor . . . and there was blood everywhere.' He stopped for a moment so he could compose himself. 'It was all over her. I could barely make out what she was wearing. There was arterial blood on the floor and even the walls. Anyway, I just froze. I don't know how I knew but I sensed there was no one else in the house by then. Call it instinct, but I knew that whoever had done this was gone. So I'm looking down at this woman, thinking there's nothing I can do to help her, but then a strange thing happened.' He looked at Rebecca in wonderment even after all those years. 'She made a sound. I heard it. She gasped or tried to say something to me and all these thoughts came rushing into my brain at once. I wanted to help her, to save her if I could. I wanted to comfort her too, because she looked like she was going to die right there in front of me but then my copper's instinct kicked in, and I'm thinking, "What is she trying to tell me? The name of the man who has more than likely killed her?" I needed to get in close to hear her, so I got down low. I had to kneel in the blood. I can remember how sticky it felt on the floor and the smell of it. I took her hand in mine and, like an idiot, I told her it was going to be all right. I'm about to get on the radio and get an ambulance out to her when I hear sirens outside. She gasps again but I can't hear her properly so I have to get really close to her mouth to listen. All I get from her is this kind of gurgle and then she's gone.'

He didn't say anything else for a while. Reliving the moment had taken a lot from him. She let him compose himself, then said, 'You didn't do anything wrong, Dominic. You couldn't have saved her. Why did you get the blame?'

'Because everyone arrived at once then. They were expecting a crime scene full of clues, forensic evidence that would lead them to the man who had done this terrible thing. Instead they got me, kneeling in the victim's blood, holding her hand, so close to her that she had bled out all over me and I'm covered in it.

'I tried to explain that she was still alive when I got there but she was in such a mess that no one believed it. I've just contaminated their crime scene.'

'But you thought she was alive.'

'I told them that and they said no one could have survived those injuries. They just thought I'd lost my head and fucked everything up and, do you know the worst of it, they're right. I did.'

'But you heard her?'

'Did I? I thought I did. I was convinced I had. Now, after all these years, I can't honestly say I know what I heard. They told me it was just air escaping from her body. I mean, that sounds like the most likely scenario, doesn't it?'

'I still don't see how it was your fault. You did what you did for the right reasons.'

'Well, it pretty near finished me. If I hadn't been in shock afterwards, I think they'd have just fired me. Even the guy at the Police Federation wondered if I might prefer to go and he was supposed to be looking out for me. I suppose he was in a way.'

'But you didn't. You stayed.'

'I felt responsible. This awful, truly terrible thing happened in my own town on my watch and everyone knew I'd messed up. The killer wasn't caught. He has never been caught. He is out there still and he keeps on doing it. I just wanted to get this man and I will, Rebecca, if it is the last thing I do.' He was quiet for a moment, then he said, 'I know what it's cost me, my obsession. At least one relationship. You know I go out at night after my shift sometimes and drive around the town?'

'You're hoping to catch him in the act?'

He nodded. 'It's stupid but I can't help myself. He watches these women. I know he does. He gets to know them first before he visits them. I am sure of it. If I can catch him doing that then this nightmare ends, for me and for all of us.'

She could tell that he meant it and even though she could see the toll it had taken on Dominic, it was good to know that he was even more determined to catch this killer than she was.

'How does he get in?' she asked him then. 'The cases my father was looking into, the ones he talked to you about, they are not break-ins. There are no signs of forced entry, which is one of the reasons the police don't look for strangers. Instead they hone in on the boyfriends, husbands, lovers. If these women were really not killed by the men closest to them, then how did the murderer get into their homes? Did he just knock on the door and march in or con his way in somehow? Some of these killings happened at night. What woman would open the door to a stranger and admit him like that? Why would they?'

'*Don't Let Him In,*' he said, as if that was supposed to mean something.

'What do you mean?'

'It was the name of a campaign we did years ago.' And he repeated it. '*Don't Let Him In.* There were posters and we did stuff with the TV and the radio stations, urging women not to open their doors to strangers, to always use the peephole on their front door and keep the chain on. We specifically told people not to answer their doors after dark, unless they knew the person standing there.'

'Was this because of the killings?'

'No one said that officially but the word came down from on high that we should focus on it. If people get knocked over by speeding cars or drunk drivers, we run campaigns to slow people down or get them to quit drinking and driving. If women are killed in their homes, then we get asked to do stuff like the *Don't Let Him In* campaign.'

'But why would your top brass want to do that if they were convinced the dead women were victims of domestic abuse or crimes of passion?'

'That's simple,' he said. 'They weren't. People were arrested, tried and convicted, but that didn't stop the other theories from doing the rounds. A lot of people had doubts about Simon Kibbs and whether he was capable of one brutal killing, let alone two.'

'Yet the police line from day one was that they had the right man?'

'Do you realize how much pressure they were under

to get that man? When he was arrested there was a collective sigh of relief at HQ.'

'I don't understand how detectives can act like that when they're not even sure. The whole police argument was full of holes from the beginning.'

'Yes, it was.'

'So why bring him in, why continue to argue it was him, why not just look for other, more credible suspects and some actual evidence, instead of scaring an innocent man into a confession?'

'You don't know how it works,' he said. 'It gets very political. No one actually says, "You must arrest someone and you have to make the charges stick." Your boss won't tell you that you can't let him go because it would be embarrassing and career-limiting for all of us, and do you know why they don't say that?'

She shook her head.

'Because they don't have to. Somehow everyone just knows. Then they figure it's all OK because it will go to trial and that's the safety net. If a jury thinks he's not guilty, he'll get off. If the jury says "guilty", then, well, he must have been all along.'

'But the jury is led to that conclusion by the prosecution.'

'Exactly, and sometimes by the man in the dock. If he seems evasive, can't account for his own movements or simply *looks* guilty, then the chances are they won't like him and he will go down.'

'And I used to have such faith in our judicial system.'

'Why?' And when she raised an eyebrow at that he

said, 'I'm serious. Juries are made up of normal people, so they are a cross-section of the general public. How many stupid, ignorant, easily led people have you encountered over the years? Now imagine some of them being on a jury that decides whether you go to prison for life or not. It's chilling.'

'You have a point,' she admitted. 'A scary one but a point.' Then she said, 'The detectives on the graveyard murder got a confession out of Simon. It was almost the basis of their case.'

'There were four detectives in that room with young Simon. Big scary guys who spent five hours taking it in turns to cross-examine him about every second of his day, deliberately trying to trip him up. As soon as one of them caught him in what they thought was a lie they went to town on him, threatening that he would be jailed for thirty years, that he'd get stabbed in the shower in prison, they told him he'd be raped there. They even roughed him up a bit, nothing that would leave bruises but, you know, twisting his ears, slapping him round the head, making him stand up then putting him in stress positions.'

'How do you know all this?'

'People talk and police officers are no different. Why wouldn't they boast about getting the graveyard killer to confess?'

'Does that kind of police brutality really still happen?'

'This was twenty years ago and two women had been slaughtered. Everyone was angry and out for blood. No one cared if Simon Kibbs got shoved around a bit.'

'I'm surprised he lasted so long.'

He smiled grimly. 'That wasn't what broke him. Towards the end of the interrogation he was still denying everything, then one of the detectives tried a different tactic. He asked everyone else to leave and he calmed things down. He gave Simon a chair to sit on and even brought him a cup of tea and a biscuit, then sat next to him while he drank it. He wrote out a short statement that was basically a confession to the murder in the graveyard, slid it under the lad's nose and told him a very simple lie.'

'What was that?'

'Sign this, son, and you can go home.'

'Oh, my God.'

'Simon signed,' he said, 'and he still isn't home.'

'I don't understand how that confession was allowed to stand and be presented in court. He was a young lad with learning difficulties and he had no legal representation; they kept him there for hours and lied to his face to make him sign.'

'And yet the judge did allow it. Still have faith in our legal system?'

'Not so much.'

'That kind of thing has happened more often than you would think over the years, but you haven't heard the best bit.'

'Seriously?' she asked in disbelief.

'The clever detective I told you about, the one who told Simon he could go home if he signed the confession – that was DI Hall.'

32

No good journalist believes anything unless it comes from at least two, preferably independent, sources. Rebecca trusted Dominic Green enough to work with him but he was hardly independent. It was time to confront DI Hall and challenge him on the seeming lack of progress in the investigation into her father's death. She called in advance, spoke to one of his detectives and he promised to pass on the message to Hall. He then phoned back a few hours later with an appointment for Rebecca to see Hall in his makeshift office at the major incident room.

'Some people you can reason with,' her father once told the teenage Rebecca, when she had unsuccessfully argued about politics with someone. 'Others, when confronted with facts that directly contradict their view, will simply double down on their beliefs despite all evidence to the contrary.' After little more than quarter of an hour in DI Hall's company, Rebecca began to understand what her father had meant by that.

CID was still looking into things; they were following . . . not leads exactly but 'lines of enquiry', none of which had led to anything concrete yet. These things take time, Rebecca was told, but she was assured they would leave 'no stone unturned'.

Exasperated with their lack of progress, Rebecca sought to put a little pressure on Hall by bringing Simon Kibbs into the discussion. If he wasn't the man behind the earlier killings, as her father believed, wasn't it reasonable to assume he may have inadvertently come too close to the real killer?

'Not this again,' was DI Hall's not very sympathetic response. 'No reasonable person could agree with the notion that an –' he seemed to be choosing his words carefully – 'amateur could have found something that an entire police force has been looking for, for years.'

'So I'm not a reasonable person?' she asked, and when he did not reply, she added, 'And it's not an entire police force; it's a small team from Northumbria CID, led by you and, on your own admission, you aren't even looking, because you refuse to entertain the notion that you might have put the wrong man behind bars.'

He folded his arms then. 'Show me some actual evidence to back up your theory that Kibbs didn't do it.'

Rebecca tried to stay calm, while she outlined the factors that had caused her father and now herself to doubt Simon's guilt. Hall was not really listening and was quick to dispute Simon's version of events.

'He's not right in the head.' And he tapped his own forehead to illustrate his point. 'The more we probed him, the more his story started to unravel. Simon said he didn't know Rose McIntyre but he had bought his sandwiches from her in the bakery almost every day for weeks. He claimed he just didn't recognize her. You want me to believe that?'

'That does sound far-fetched –' she began.

'You think?' he interrupted sarcastically.

'Until you consider that her carotid artery was completely severed during the attack so there would have been a lot of blood. When a major artery is cut like that, the blood doesn't just seep – it spurts out in an intermittent spray that's powered by the beat of the heart. A severed carotid will pump blood out from the neck for thirty seconds at sixty-five beats a minute. Her face could have easily been obscured, especially as she was lying on the ground when he found her. All Simon would have seen was a female figure covered in blood.'

'Well, aren't you the forensics expert?' he sneered.

'I googled that. It was very easy to find. Look it up, if you don't believe me. You probably should.'

'No, thanks. I've enough live cases to be working on without going over old ones that were solved years ago. Look, you've never met Simon. Everything he says is bollocks. When we first arrested him, he tried to pin the murder on someone else.'

'Who?'

He looked smug then as if he had been hoping she would ask. 'A detective.'

'Which one?'

He shrugged. 'He wasn't specific, anyone will do.'

'He actually said a detective killed Katherine Prentiss?'

'Yes, well, no. To be fair he didn't say that. What he actually said, in response to the question, "Did you see anyone else in the graveyard before, during or after the death of Rose McIntyre?" was "I saw a man leaving the graveyard." When we asked him who he saw, he said, "It was a detective." Now, even if we took that allegation even a tiny bit seriously, every detective in our region could account for their movements that day and none of them was in Eriston, not even me. Also, Simon had never met any detectives, so how could he recognize one?' When Rebecca was unable to answer him on that specific point he seemed to relax, as if he had won the entire argument.

'OK,' she conceded, 'so he's wrong about that, but Rose was meeting someone in that churchyard.'

'How do you know that?'

'Those graves were old and she had no family members buried there.'

'She could have just been walking through.'

'On her way to where?'

'I don't know. We'd have asked her but, unfortunately, she was dead.'

'You heard the rumours,' she challenged him. 'You must have.'

Rebecca didn't want to reveal what she knew or thought she knew; she merely wanted to see if Hall became evasive and he did.

'Which ones?'

'The ones about Rose having an affair, which might explain why she was standing in a secluded spot at the back of a churchyard. She was waiting for someone she shouldn't have been seeing. A married man possibly, with something to lose. Maybe she was going to tell his wife. Maybe –'

He held up a hand and said, 'Let me stop you there. We are not entirely stupid and we did hear rumours. We looked into them.'

'And?'

'I am not at liberty to inform you of the outcome of that part of our investigation.'

'Bullshit you're not! If you don't tell me, I have to conclude you didn't even follow it up.'

'We did follow it up and –' he was getting exasperated now – 'am I talking to you as a person or as a reporter now?'

'A person . . . either . . . I don't mind.'

'Well, off the record, and I do mean *off* the record, so you cannot use a word of this . . .'

'OK.'

'We found out who she was seeing and questioned him. The man was indeed married; he'd had a brief dalliance with Rose McIntyre, nothing too serious, and on the day she was murdered he had a cast-iron alibi.'

Rebecca processed this new information, then asked, 'So why was this never made public?'

'It had no material impact on the case, so it was decided to respect the privacy of the other party.'

'You should at least have revealed this information to the defence.'

'It wouldn't have made any difference.' But he looked flustered again.

'You don't know that! The existence of a third party, who was having a *dalliance*, as you put it, with Rose

McIntyre could have been enough to put reasonable doubt in the minds of the jury.'

'Yes, maybe,' he conceded. '*If* he hadn't had an alibi.'

'Who was it?' she demanded.

'I'm not going to tell you that.'

'Even off the record?'

'No.'

'Who are you protecting?'

'Let's just say it was a prominent member of the community.'

'Let's see then, who in Eriston is big enough for you to want to cover that up?'

There couldn't be many candidates in a town whose inhabitants tended to lack money or influence. It was then that she remembered the photograph of Rose McIntyre dressed in her leotard in the *Eriston Gazette*, getting that prize from the son of the wealthiest man in town. It seemed like too much of a coincidence. Rose was very young and it would be another five years before she was murdered, but Connor was young too back then, only a few years older than her.

'It was Connor Owen, wasn't it?'

'What? No!' But Hall was flustered and she could tell he was lying.

'Are you seriously going to deny this? What if I make it on the record?'

Hall looked as if he was about to say something, but must have realized that another denial might implicate him later. Hall's body seemed to sag then. 'Miss Cole,' he said, 'you are a right pain in the arse, do you know that?'

'Yes,' she said, 'yes, I do. So, Connor was seeing Rose on the sly because he was married and that had to make him a suspect but you reckon he had an alibi. So who gave him it?'

When he answered her, he spoke so softly she barely heard him at first. 'What did you say?'

'His father.'

Rebecca was incredulous. 'You took the word of his father? Are you serious? Wouldn't most fathers lie to the police to protect their sons from a murder charge?'

'Not just his father. They were in a meeting with some building contractors on one of their first big construction projects. They backed this up.'

'But if they were contractors, those people were reliant on the Owens for their money.'

'You think they'd give an alibi to a murderer to make sure they got paid? Come on!'

'Maybe not, but they did have a vested interest in keeping the Owens sweet so their alibi is hardly cast iron.'

He didn't seem to want to continue the argument, so instead he said, 'This is all coming from Dominic, isn't it? I told you not to listen to him.'

'I've barely seen him,' she said.

'Really? Because you have *been* seen with him. If it was down to me, I'd get rid of him, but he's unsackable. I'm not forced to listen to him, though, and nor are you.'

'Why won't you listen to him?'

'Because he has wasted everybody's time. You do know that, don't you?'

'I know he has theories and that you always ignore them.'

'The man ruined a crime scene,' said Hall, 'contaminated it till there was no evidence left.'

'He told me. He was trying to save her,' protested Rebecca.

'He was trying to save a woman who could not be saved. Lazarus was in better nick than she was by the time we found her, but it wasn't just that. Has he told you about the lighthouse?'

'What about it?'

'Strange goings-on.' He said it dryly, as if he was pretending to go along with this outlandish story. 'Spooky ceremonies, with chanting and singing, women held there against their will, and always just before we find one dead in the woods or washed up on the shore.'

'Well,' she said, trying to buy herself some time before she answered him because Dominic had never once mentioned this to her, 'why didn't you look into it?'

'Oh, we did,' he said. 'We spoke to people who live close by and they never heard a thing.'

She wasn't having that. 'The nearest house is more than a mile away from the lighthouse.'

'We sent a man up there to check it out too and you know what he found? Nothing. The place has been fenced off for years. Even teenagers don't go there any more.' He looked exasperated then. 'He wouldn't leave it at that, though. No. He said we'd gone up there at the wrong time. So he waited till the next full moon.' He shook his head in wonder. 'I can't believe I am even having to explain this. He went up there again and stood by the fence, reckoned he heard a woman's screams coming from the lighthouse. It was faint, mind you, but he was sure it was a woman and she was definitely screaming. He called it in, demanded back-up and told the desk sergeant a woman's life was in danger, then he cut the bloody fence.

'Do you know how many cars went up there? A lot. Nobody wanted to be the one who ignored that call. A lot of officers went to the lighthouse that night, lights flashing, sirens blaring and, when they got there, you know what they found? Him, standing there on his own, looking baffled, as usual. Half the lads who turned out for that call wanted to punch him and the other half wanted to call the men in white coats to lead him away. He is nuts.'

Rebecca didn't say anything. What could she say? That maybe he *had* heard screams and perhaps someone was there or, more likely, the strain Dominic had been under for years had caused him to hear something on the air, a gull's cry perhaps, something distorted on a coastal wind that convinced him he had heard a woman being tortured. The difference between Rebecca and DI Hall was that she did not feel anger or contempt towards Dominic, only sympathy or maybe pity. He had once been a bright, optimistic young man who had held the bloodied body of a savagely murdered woman in his arms and been derailed by the experience. His career had not so much stalled as become frozen in time at that point and now he spent his working hours and a good part of his free time patrolling the town, obsessively looking for the man who had done it. How could DI Hall not see this? Why didn't the force offer Dominic help instead of simply allowing him to stay in his job, while openly scorning all his ideas?

DI Hall seemed to know what she was thinking. 'I suppose I should feel sorry for him,' he said. 'But he keeps wasting my time. I'm telling you, young lady, stay away from him and don't listen to his outlandish ideas.'

Was it the condescending 'young lady' that irked her most or his lack of compassion for Dominic? Either way, she wasn't accepting that. 'We should just keep out of your way, is that it?'

'I am sorry for your loss. I understand your feelings of helplessness, but, yes, please leave it to the professionals.'

'Maybe I will,' she said, and his face immediately relaxed, 'then I can look forward to you pinning it on some teenager. That shouldn't be too hard. Just tell him he can go home as soon as he signs a confession.'

DI Hall's whole body tensed in anger. Rebecca had hit home with that, just as she had intended, but she had expected Hall to sneer or try to laugh it off. Instead his face turned quite red and his eyes reflected his anger. When he spoke it was a venomous hiss. 'What do you know about it? You weren't there.' He was so enraged she actually thought he might hit her. Then he seemed to force himself, through a considerable effort of will, to calm down. 'Reporters? You're all the fucking same. You hate the police until you need us to come and help you. Well, maybe when that day comes, we won't be there.'

'I think I should leave now,' she said.

'I think you should.'

'You've got a missing woman to find,' she reminded him, 'and I don't want to take up any more of your valuable time.'

She got up to go. There seemed nothing more to say. Both of them were angry and Rebecca was feeling the shock that comes with the realization that the worst thing she had heard about DI Hall was true. He really had tricked a confession out of a vulnerable young man and got him banged up for life.

Rebecca reached the door but forced herself to turn back to him with one final question. She wasn't even entirely sure why she was asking but she did it anyway. Perhaps she realized she would never get another chance.

'DI Hall?'

'What?' He looked up at her and spat the word.

'Why did you mention the wind chimes?' she asked. 'In your report?'

'What?' he repeated, sounding baffled. 'What report?'

'Amanda Mayhew has wind chimes at the back of her house?'

He looked at her as if she was quite mad. 'Does she?' Then he sounded impatient. 'What's that got to do with anything?'

'Never mind,' she said, and he frowned at her as she turned and walked from his office.

33

Dominic's revelations about DI Hall's role in the conviction of Simon Kibbs changed everything. Now Rebecca also had proof that Rose had been embroiled in an affair with Connor Owen, the man who wanted to buy her father's house from her. Worse, the details of that affair had been suppressed because the Owens were wealthy and prominent.

Rebecca realized DI Hall had a vested interest in keeping Simon Kibbs in prison. If he was ever pardoned or released, it would reflect badly on the men who had charged him with a murder he most likely did not commit. That would destroy Hall's career and he did not look like the kind of man who would allow that to happen.

It also meant he would never be able to keep an open mind whenever a link was made between the graveyard murder, the killing of Katherine Prentiss or any of the other suspicious slayings in the region, including her father's. He would always stick to the story that the murderer of those two women was already in jail. If Rebecca uncovered any evidence that might steer the authorities in another direction, there would be little point in passing it on to DI Hall. He'd ensure it was buried or ignored. Until she could find enough to conclusively prove the innocence of the wronged man and the guilt of another, Rebecca could not go public with it. When she did, she would have to go above Hall's head or leak it to the media, if that was what it would take to get justice for her father and the other victims. As far as Rebecca was concerned, she and Dominic were on their own and would have to watch their backs from now on.

Busy, busy, busy.

You're such a busy little bee, Rebecca.

Always running around, talking to people, asking questions: police and detectives, your father's friends and colleagues. Is there anyone you're not planning to speak to?

You stay up late every night too. I've noticed that you leave your lights on till the early hours. Spend all that time thinking, don't you?

What keeps you awake, Rebecca? Fear or guilt? Are you haunted by regrets and thoughts of what might have been or do you spend all your time searching for answers about Daddy? I think that's it. You're relentless, I can tell, and that makes you dangerous. I know your sort. One day you'll pop up on the local news being interviewed and asking more questions, appealing to everyone to help you find your father's killer.

People have a depressing tendency to listen to pretty girls, even when they don't have very much to say. You are different, though; you're more than capable of telling a story and a convincing one at that. If I let you do it, then who knows where it will lead?

There'll be more questions, awkward ones.

Frankly, Rebecca, I don't need the publicity, so I am not going to allow it.

You're done. You just don't know it yet.

Dominic had arranged to meet up once his shift was over. Defiantly she suggested the hotel bar. They had been seen together anyway so what difference would it make? She asked him if he had remembered to put a word in with Simon Kibbs's legal team and he assured her he had.

'What did they say?'

'Simon's solicitor was in court but I made sure his office will pass on the message that you can be trusted.'

Rebecca thanked him, then she told Dominic about her visit to DI Hall and his mood quickly darkened.

'What did he say to you?'

'Quite a lot actually.'

'Denied it, didn't he?' he said.

'His role in Simon Kibbs's confession? Surprisingly no. I reckon he thinks the ends justified the means.'

'Warned you off again too, I'll bet? What did he say about me? You can tell me. I'm used to it. Most of it will be lies anyway.'

Rebecca decided to be honest about DI Hall's views, namely that Dominic was stupid and believed outlandish theories. The police constable didn't like that but it didn't surprise him.

'We'll see who feels stupid when we catch the guy,' he said.

Rebecca wanted to gauge Dominic's reaction to Hall's taunts before she hit him with the most damning part of the DI's accusations. 'He told me about the lighthouse.'

Was that shame or embarrassment in Dominic's face? Whichever it was, he masked it well. He just said, 'The bastard,' as if that was sufficient explanation, but Rebecca needed to hear the full story.

'He said you called for a lot of back-up and when they arrived there was nothing there. He said you heard a woman scream –'

'I did.' He interrupted forcefully, then added with less certainty, 'I was *sure* that I had. I'd had my suspicions about the lighthouse for a long while. It wasn't a place kids and teenagers hung out in any more. They stopped going down there even before it was condemned. It was as if they knew, or sensed, that they shouldn't be there.'

'How could they sense that, Dominic?'

'You could just feel it was different. A couple of years later the whole place got fenced off by the council. Health and safety and all that.'

He said the last words scathingly and Rebecca interjected, 'Well, it was in a bit of a state and those stairs were crumbling away. They wouldn't want kids climbing up there.'

He ignored this. 'I used to drive to the lighthouse at night,' he told her.

'Why?'

'To get my head straight. I like it there. It was quiet

and I needed some peace after a long day. I'd do a day shift, then spend hours driving around the town.'

'Looking for the killer?' she asked.

'It wasn't just that. I'd try to get people to have more sense. If I saw an open window or an unlocked gate, I'd knock on their door and tell them to secure it.' He sighed. 'But they don't always listen. You can explain there are dangerous people out there but some of them just look right through you. I'd get tired but knew I wouldn't be able to sleep, because I never really sleep, so I'd drive up to the cliffs and just sit there in the car with the window open, letting some air in.'

'That must be cold at night.'

'I don't mind the cold and a sea breeze is refreshing. I was trying to make myself tired enough to go home and sleep,' he explained. 'Then one day I heard voices coming from the lighthouse. I was some distance from it, back behind the fence, but sometimes you pick up sounds carried on the wind.'

'What did you hear?'

'Voices, singing perhaps but more like chants. Someone was doing something up there at midnight and they thought no one could hear them.'

'Kids? Playing music or singing? Getting drunk?'

'No. It was all fenced off, remember?' He said that as if she had genuinely forgotten, but determined teenagers might still be able to get through or over a fence if they wanted to. 'And, I told you, teenagers don't hang out there any more.'

She wondered how he could be sure of that. 'Who then?'

'I went round the perimeter,' he explained. 'Couldn't see any sign of forced entry and the fence was intact but I knew someone was there. I didn't just imagine it.'

'So what did you do?'

'I stood as close to the lighthouse as I could and listened.'

'What did you hear?'

'Nothing. Whoever had been up there was gone.'

Rebecca wanted to ask *Are you sure it wasn't just the wind?* but knew Dominic wouldn't take kindly to someone else questioning his version of events.

'I tried to get CID to check it out and they did, reluctantly, in daylight.'

'And they found nothing?'

'Well, they wouldn't during the day.' She let him continue. 'I drove up there a few times. More than a few to be honest but I didn't hear anything else for weeks, until one night when there was a bright full moon above the lighthouse. I heard them then.'

'What did you hear?'

'It sounded like chanting and this time a woman screamed. I couldn't just go in there on my own and run the risk of whoever it was getting away but I had to move quickly because a woman was in immediate danger. So I radioed in, asked for back-up, then I cut through the fence.'

'And you went straight to the lighthouse?'

'Yeah. Trouble was I hadn't expected a bloody

cavalry charge,' he said in exasperation. 'By the time I'd got tools from the car to cut through the fence and was halfway down the old track to the lighthouse, I could hear them coming and so could *he*.' Rebecca assumed he meant the suspect he expected to find in the lighthouse. 'I should have told them not to go in with lights and sirens. I figured they would know not to do that. How else would we catch him?' He sighed. 'By the time I got to the lighthouse there was no sign of him. He had heard them coming and got away.'

'Would he have had the time?'

He picked up on her scepticism. 'You could hear them when they were leaving Eriston, Rebecca. Of course he had time.'

'But where would he go, with the sea down one side and the main road running from north to south on the other? If he had a vehicle on the perimeter you'd have seen it, so how did he get away?'

'Inland,' he said as if it was obvious. 'He'd head west.'

'In the dark?'

'Why not?'

'How would he get past you without being seen?'

'Like you said, it was dark. I couldn't see much. He could have slipped by me even if he was a few yards away.'

'What about the woman you heard?'

'He'd have carried her off or she could have described him.'

This didn't seem likely. 'That would slow him down, even if he knocked her out and threw her over his shoulder.'

Dominic didn't answer her for a while. 'You sound like all the others. You don't believe me either, do you?'

'It's not that I don't believe you.' And it was true that she didn't think he was lying or making up some exaggerated version of events. She did question whether what he genuinely thought had happened could have been possible, though.

'Oh, I don't blame you.' His tone suggested that might not be true. 'He got to you first. DI Hall told you I was a fantasist when all I really want to do is catch this man because *he* never will.' Then he said, 'But if you can't see it . . . '

'I can see it, but, like every credible reporter and any good police officer, I have learned to question things, so I can work out the sequence of events and determine what's plausible.'

'And you don't think my story is plausible?' He didn't sound angry, just sad. 'You weren't there, Rebecca.'

'If there was a man there, and I am not saying there wasn't, and if he had a woman with him, then why didn't you mention this to me before?'

'Because I knew you wouldn't believe it. No one does.'

'I want to believe it. I just need to work out how he could have escaped from the lighthouse, while dragging or carrying a woman against her will without anyone finding them afterwards.'

'They didn't even look for him,' he snapped. 'When they found me standing there and there was no sign of him, they gave up and started cross-examining me, just like you are.'

'Oh, come on, Dominic, I'm not cross-examining you. I'm just trying to get my head around it, that's all.' Then she asked him, 'Is there any word on that missing woman?'

He seemed happy to leave the topic of the lighthouse. 'Only that she's still missing.'

'Presumed dead or presumed alive?' she probed.

'You know DI Hall,' he said. 'Presumed alive.'

'But you don't think so?'

'You know I don't.'

She nodded in acknowledgement, then she asked, 'You ever go round to her house? Before we went there, I mean?'

'I told you I didn't. CID sent someone.'

'You did tell me that,' she conceded.

'What are you saying exactly?'

'I suppose I'm asking you if that was the truth?'

'You know it is.'

'I don't,' she said firmly. 'I don't actually know the truth of much that goes on in this town, including why my father was killed, which is why I will continue to ask everyone difficult questions, including DI Hall and you, Dominic.'

'It's not that difficult. I never went to her house until the day I took you there with me.'

'Then how did you know about the wind chimes?'

'I told you, they were in Hall's report.'

'No,' she told him firmly, 'they weren't.'

He looked taken aback by that. 'You've read it?' He sounded as if he seriously doubted that.

'I haven't but I know he didn't mention any wind chimes. Why would he?'

'I don't know. He goes into elaborate detail about lots of –'

'Dominic,' she interrupted him, 'I asked him about the wind chimes; he had no knowledge of the bloody wind chimes.' She took a deep breath in order to calm down. 'So how did you know they were there?'

'We heard them.'

'We heard the tiniest sound coming from somewhere to the rear of the house. You couldn't have known that's what it was.'

It was his turn to take a deep breath then and she knew she had caught him in a lie.

This'd better be good. This'd better be really good, Dominic.

'All right,' he said, holding up his hands, a gesture of surrender. 'I did go there.'

'When?' she demanded. 'And more importantly, why?' Then before he could answer: 'And why lie to me about it?'

'I wanted to see it for myself. I am convinced this woman didn't just fly away and I was looking for something that might back that up.'

'Then why not tell me?'

'Because no one in this town takes me bloody seriously, Rebecca! Because I walked into a crime scene once and fucked everything up. I have been hearing "every contact leaves a trace" for years now but I had to take a look inside that house. I just didn't want anyone to know about it, including you. I'm sorry but I thought

270

you would judge me.' He looked rueful then. 'And I was right, wasn't I? You are.'

'Only because you lied to me about it.'

'I'm sorry,' he said.

'You actually went inside?'

'Yes.' And when her face betrayed her feelings about that, he added, 'Well, the back door wasn't secured. I'm telling you, Rebecca, CID are fucking amateurs.'

'Did you find anything?'

It seemed to Rebecca that the last thing he wanted to do after admitting he had been there was to concede the truth. 'No,' he said quietly.

'I don't understand why you would risk so much – your job, everything – just to take a look around that woman's house. It doesn't make sense to me. I can't get my head around it.'

The shutters seemed to come down then. It was as if his mood suddenly changed and he had no intention of spending any more time explaining himself to her. 'You know what, Rebecca, I'm busy, and there are other things I could be doing right now.' He got to his feet.

'Dominic . . .'

'I'm going to leave you to it,' he said before she could protest. 'That way you'll have plenty of time to get your head around it.'

34

It had taken Rebecca a long time to get to sleep that night. As well as the usual sounds emanating from a house that seemed to groan under its own weight, she found herself thinking of Dominic's account of the unexplained presence at the lighthouse. She was conflicted. His story was hard to believe but she felt an innate sense of loyalty to the man and now he thought she was as dismissive of him as everyone else in Eriston.

When she woke, she was just as troubled, and was pleasantly surprised when Alan called her. She was relieved when he didn't mention their kiss or her reaction to it. He had just finished a number of jobs for Connor Owen and reckoned he had earned a day off. How did she fancy lunch?

They drove out of town to a quiet pub on a country road with only a farmhouse nearby. It was the kind of place that prided itself on the food, with local fish on the menu, as well as home-made steak and ale pies and sausages from regional farmers. The place was only a few miles from Eriston but it was so quiet out here that it felt a world away.

They talked easily over lunch and she decided to take the opportunity to ask Alan outright if he had been seeing anyone lately. 'Not recently, no,' he told her. But that didn't entirely satisfy her curiosity.

'Anyone special in your life before now?'

'There have been one or two, obviously, but I wouldn't say they were special.'

'No one you'd take home to meet the parents?'

'Not really, no.'

'*I* never met them,' she reminded him.

'I did not want you meeting my father,' he said firmly, and this came as a surprise to her.

'Why not?'

'I know you're not supposed to speak ill of the dead,' he admitted, 'but he was a miserable, hard-hearted old bastard with a violent temper, and to be quite honest I was ashamed of him.'

'Fair enough.' Then there was an awkward moment when she did not know what to add following his outburst so, instead, she changed the subject completely and said, 'Dominic told me he thought something was going on down at the lighthouse.'

'Talking of people with shitty fathers,' he said. 'What kind of something?'

'Something bad.' And she explained the policeman's suspicions. She finished the account at the point when he had called in back-up and been humiliated.

'I remember that,' said Alan. 'Police cars speeding up and down between the town and the lighthouse. We wondered what was going on. Some people thought they'd found a body but there were no reports of one.'

'And Dominic took the blame for wasting everyone's time,' she said.

Rebecca wondered if Alan might be dismissive of this or unsympathetic but instead he said, 'It did have a bit of a vibe about it.'

'What did?'

'The lighthouse,' he said. 'Not when we used to go there, but later.'

'How do you mean?'

'I remember we went to a party,' he said, 'this was years back. I must have been about nineteen or twenty, and a couple of my mates wanted to go there but it was boring, so we left. The town was dead too, so somebody suggested we get some cans and go down to the lighthouse one last time before they fenced off the Point for good. We walked all the way down there but . . .'

'What?'

He looked sheepish. 'This is going to sound strange.'

'Tell me.'

'The closer we got to the place, the more I started to feel bad about it.' He shook his head. 'I know it's daft but the atmosphere that night was very odd.'

'Are we talking ghosts or werewolves?'

'I told you it was stupid.'

'I'm sorry. You couldn't expect me not to take the piss but I am listening, really.'

'We got to the old drystone wall between the road and the Point and by then I was thinking, *I really don't want to go any further*. It was strange because we used to

274

hang out there all the time but, all of a sudden, I started to feel like wild horses couldn't drag me inside but I didn't want to bottle it in front of my mates.'

'What did you do?'

'I didn't say a word and we stopped there and looked at the lighthouse and no one moved, then one of my mates said something like, "I don't know. It doesn't look that great." And the other guy was like, "Yeah, this is a bit lame. Maybe we shouldn't." And I was bloody relieved. We turned and walked all the way back into town.'

'Do you think they felt the same way you did?'

'They definitely did. Everyone knew it and no one wanted to say anything but we didn't hang about.'

'What do you think it was?'

'I can't really explain it. There was just this atmosphere and we all felt it.'

'Do you think someone was there?'

He thought for a moment. 'I don't know, maybe, yes.'

They sat in silence for a while and Rebecca thought about this. 'Alan,' she said eventually, 'how would you feel about going down there now?'

She told him to say if he felt uneasy or didn't want to actually approach the lighthouse but he assured her it was OK because it looked different in the daylight and the place lacked the atmosphere he had felt as a teenager. They walked the perimeter, which was marked by a tall wire fence that cordoned off the whole area round the lighthouse, including a large clump of land that jutted out from the coastline, cutting it off from the mainland. The Point.

Alan nodded at a track that was on the other side of the fence and said, 'There's the old path.'

You could still just make out the dirt track generations of kids and teenagers had walked along to get to the lighthouse, though it was overgrown now. Rebecca followed the track with her eyes as it led all the way to the lighthouse, which stood on higher ground by the cliff edge.

'You can't get to it,' said Alan, but when he turned back to Rebecca she was already gone, making her way round the far side of the perimeter fence. 'What are you doing?'

'It's got to end somewhere.'

'I think the whole Point is cordoned off, so it ends at the cliff.' But she didn't stop walking, so he followed her.

Alan caught up with Rebecca and they carried on to the very end of the fence, until it finally halted right at the end of the Point, only ceasing when there was no more land to mark. If you tried to go beyond the fence, you would be stepping off the cliff, and there was a sizeable drop below to the rocks. To Alan's alarm Rebecca began to move along the fence right to its end until she was standing very close to the edge, while holding on to a thin concrete post that marked its finishing point. 'What are you doing?' he asked.

'There's a gap.' Rebecca had discovered that the

fence post was set back a few inches from the very end of the land, presumably to avoid it falling into the sea if the clifftop eroded. 'I can get round it.'

'Jesus, are you sure, Rebecca? That does not look safe to me.'

'It should be fine.'

'You know that part in the movie where the girl slips and the guy manages to grab her just in time before she falls?'

'Yes.'

'Let's not do that, eh?'

'I'll be careful,' she reassured him.

Rebecca took a firm grip on the post, then swung herself out and round the fence, until she could plant a foot firmly on the other side while trying not to think about the rocks below. She then lifted her other foot up and swung herself round. She was more relieved than she let on to find herself with two feet safely on the ground on the other side of the fence.

Rebecca looked back at him questioningly. 'OK,' he said doubtfully, then he gingerly followed her actions, and she stepped back to avoid getting in his way. 'Easy . . .' he said, when he was done, '. . . in theory, but actually quite terrifying.'

'Now let's check it out,' she said.

'What are we looking for?'

'I don't know.'

Maybe there would be nothing here at all but perhaps something would provide them with a clue to . . . what? The forbidding atmosphere of the lighthouse at night? The strange noises that could be heard from a distance, which might be a woman's screams but could just as easily be the sound of gulls squawking or strong winds whistling through the broken shutters on the lighthouse windows? It all seemed a bit ridiculous now in daylight, when logic was back in control, but something had bothered Alan that night years ago and Dominic Green had been so convinced by the sounds that he had called in carloads of back-up.

It had been a dozen years since Rebecca had been up here and Alan was with her that day too. Straight away she noticed something had changed.

'Where's the door?' she asked. 'There used to be a door.'

'I guess it rotted away or they took it.'

Rebecca remembered walking into the lighthouse and her friends closing the door, trapping her inside. It was a game. You put up with it for as long as you could bear until you banged on the door to be let out. Rebecca had coped with it for far longer than most, because she already lived in one of the creepiest houses in town.

As they grew older, the game evolved, and you went inside in couples for a few minutes of breathless snogging and anything else you had the nerve to do while knowing your friends could burst in on you at any moment. She wondered if Alan remembered that.

He had already stepped through the open doorway to check the place out. Rebecca followed. 'It hasn't changed,' he said.

Why would it? she thought. There'd be no point in

making the place look any better when it was officially designated as a hazard. They were standing just inside the gap where the door had been, looking down into a drop of several feet, where the floorboards used to be. There was nothing suspicious here, no evidence of anyone's presence since the place had been fenced off. There was no litter, no broken bottles or the remnants of a campfire. In short, it looked like a wasted trip.

Round the dip caused by the missing floorboards, there was a lip made of stone, which the boards must have rested on, so you could walk all the way round in a circle at floor level. When you looked down from there, there was a drop of about six feet to a stone floor that must have been part of the foundations. The flagstones were almost completely obscured by sand that had drifted in and settled there over the years. Large and ancient solid-metal rings were set into the walls but Rebecca could only guess at their original purpose because they were now as redundant as the rest of the lighthouse.

Rebecca remembered this dip as the place where teenagers used to climb down to 'cop off', because it afforded a little more privacy. Alan turned to her and smiled. It was an impish, mischievous smile and she knew why. He remembered too.

'Look at the stairs,' she said quickly, and pointed upwards. 'Even worse than before.'

'There's barely anything left.'

The stone steps still clung to the inner walls of the lighthouse, long after the floors they once supported had disappeared. Now they led to just one place, the very top of the lighthouse, where the floor was made entirely out of stone to support the additional weight of the huge light that was once housed there.

'Do you remember the dares?' he asked, as if that particular memory was unpleasant.

'I do.' She could still recall her terror when she had been the latest in a long line of kids challenged to climb as far as they dared up those partial steps. It was fine to begin with. The stone steps were wide enough to accommodate you but as you went higher they narrowed and had large pieces missing that had flaked away over time and fallen down into the sandy pit below. Once you reached a height where you could be injured if you fell, the whole exercise became way more frightening. Rebecca hadn't gone that high. Few did and none had ever reached the top, which was just as well, because a fall from that height would have been fatal, and the stairs were capable of giving way at any moment. It was a ninety-foot climb to the room that housed the light, only accessible through a rotted wooden hatch in the centre of the stone ceiling, more than half of which was missing. It was a tantalizing notion to climb up to that room to explore it, particularly as you would automatically achieve legendary status for the achievement, but Rebecca never came close to attempting it.

'I didn't even get halfway,' admitted Alan.

'I gave up after a few steps,' she said. 'I don't like heights.'

'I thought it might feel smaller, now we are older,' he said. 'But it's still a very long way.'

'It's scary.'

'We had some good times here, though.' He jumped down into the sandy pit below them, reached back and offered her his hand. She gave him a questioning look but decided to go with the moment for once. She slid down and joined him and, before she could say anything, he drew Rebecca to him and kissed her. This time she did not try to stop him.

35

So much for her intention to take things slowly with Alan. She realized how ridiculous that sounded now, as she adjusted her clothing.

Rebecca laughed. 'I can't believe we just did that. *You* are a very bad man.'

'You led me astray,' he replied.

'What?'

'I only pulled you down here for a snog and you completely took advantage of the situation.'

'Really?' She laughed. 'So now you're blaming me.'

He grinned then. 'I've missed you, Rebecca Cole.'

'I've missed you too, Alan Miller.'

Rebecca might have missed something else as they were leaving. She could have easily, in fact, now that she was feeling both light-headed and distracted by Alan's attentions, but on their way out she noticed a slight gap in the bushes behind the building, just wide enough for someone to pass through if they were not too broad and went sideways. 'I've never noticed that.'

'Neither have I,' he said. 'I don't think it was there before, only bushes. Maybe someone cut them back and went through it to put the fence up?' he offered.

Rebecca was already heading through the gap. Almost as soon as she emerged, she had to stop abruptly when she was confronted with a sheer drop from the cliff down to the rocks below and she almost lost her footing on the wet stone. Instinctively Rebecca took a step back from the edge. Alan joined her, placed a hand on her shoulder and said, 'Careful.' It was then that she noticed the path didn't actually end here but went off to the left and sharply downwards, into a series of weather-worn, stone steps. They glanced at one another and, wordlessly, decided to explore.

The stone steps were wet and slippery and had been eroded by centuries of biting winds and salt water but they were still just about manageable, if you trod carefully. It only took a few moments to reach the bottom where, disappointingly, they seemed to lead nowhere. They emerged at sea level on a platform of shingle-covered rock that must once have served as a jetty. It jutted out into the sea for a few yards before ending abruptly.

'The steps are only accessible by boat, and a small one at that,' Alan said. 'They might not have been used for years.'

'We just used them and it does prove one thing. The lighthouse isn't entirely fenced off at all.'

She left the rest of her thoughts unsaid because she didn't really want them to be true. Until now she couldn't imagine how anyone could have escaped from Dominic that night but here was a way out. What if someone had been bringing women here after it was fenced off and Dominic had been right all along? What if they were still doing it?

Rebecca had surprised herself. She looked back on those moments with Alan at the lighthouse and wondered at their daring. She might have described what they had done as teenage, if it wasn't for the fact that she would never have done anything like that when she was an actual teenager. They'd had sex in the same spot where they had once simply kissed and fooled around, their clothes in disarray and the cool air on her skin. Rebecca felt a strange combination of freedom, exhilaration and embarrassment as she recalled what they had done.

She was distracted for much of the following day. As she read the last of her father's notes on the Eriston Rose case, she kept having to stop and go back, because she found she hadn't taken a word in. Eventually she gave up on reading altogether and reached for her phone, then sent a hasty text to Alan.

Get here now. I'm waiting.

And she sat back to wait. Would he be turned on by that? Was he as excited by the memory of the previous day as she was?

When she didn't get an immediate response, Rebecca told herself he was busy and couldn't get to his phone. But after ten minutes she'd convinced herself he wasn't as into this as she was and cursed herself for sending such a blatantly unsubtle message.

After an hour she threw her phone into the corner of

the sofa in frustration and went for a run. Afterwards, she showered, then checked her phone again. Still nothing.

The letterbox rattled then and she retrieved a brown envelope sticking from it that was addressed to her. The letter looked quite formal and was on headed paper and she wondered if she had finally received a reply from Simon Kibbs. On opening it, she saw the letter was actually from Connor Owen and he was inviting her to come and see him to discuss the purchase of the house.

Great minds think alike, Connor.

At least this would save her the trouble of having to arrange an appointment to question him about Rose McIntyre. Connor Owen must have thought that bringing Rebecca to his office would be a more successful tactic than accosting her at her father's funeral or during a meal. Rebecca had taken an instant dislike to Connor and nothing she had seen or heard of the man since their first ignominious meeting had altered that view of him, especially now that she had confirmation of his affair with Rose McIntyre from DI Hall.

The dilemma for Rebecca was that Connor might possibly be the only one interested in purchasing her father's house, particularly when a private buyer might be scared away by his intentions for the neighbouring properties. Rebecca had no income and this house was the sole legacy from her father who, by the look of his bank account, was living a hand-to-mouth existence at the time of his death. *Like father, like daughter*, she thought ruefully.

Rebecca told herself there were good reasons to go ahead with the meeting even if she turned him down. Alan had predicted he would increase his offer, so at least she would have an idea of the property's worth. More importantly she had been wondering how to ask the property developer about his relationship with Rose McIntyre. She was highly sceptical of his alibi and doubted he would be keen to answer her questions but now she had an official invitation to come and see him.

Connor's office was opulent by the standards of the town he operated in, with large smoked-glass windows and modern office furniture. His PA was, of course, young, female and beautiful. She wore a short black dress and high heels and Rebecca wondered if that was her personal choice or at Connor's insistence. The PA brought in a tray with matching china cups filled with coffee and a plate of biscuits. She ignored Rebecca but set this down on Connor's desk then left.

Connor entered a moment later and went straight to Rebecca to greet her with a handshake. He gripped her right hand firmly with his, then tilted so that his hand was over hers, a dominance trick Rebecca recognized and was as unimpressed by as the strong whiff of after-shave that reached her at the same time. He was wearing another sharp suit and the signet ring was matched by a gold tiepin. He moved to the leather chair behind his desk and sat down. She noticed her seat was lower than his. Another device to make him appear more important than her.

Connor reached into his suit pocket then and, with some ceremony, withdrew a sealed envelope, white this time, which he handed to Rebecca. Her name was typed on the front. He said nothing, just waited for her to open and read it.

Inside was a formal offer to buy her father's house, with his company's name on the letterhead and the amount he was prepared to pay for it written in a larger font size and bold lettering to get her attention. The amount alone was enough to do that. As Alan would have put it, Connor had certainly sharpened his pencil.

Rebecca had done some research on asking prices for houses in the town and this offer was definitely on the generous side, reflecting Connor's urgent need to own all four houses so he could knock them down and build his apartments. He gave her a moment to take it in, then smiled indulgently. 'You drive a very hard bargain, Rebecca.' He stretched across the desk to offer his hand again. 'Now, do we have a deal?'

Instinctively she hesitated. This was a much better offer but she didn't appreciate being pressured like this. Even without her doubts about Connor, she would have liked some time to think about it. When Rebecca did not immediately clasp his hand again or betray any emotion at all, he said, 'You should know this is my absolute final offer.'

'But money isn't the only factor here.'

'What else is there?'

'You.'

'Me?' He turned his head to one side to show his bemusement. 'My credit's good. The cheque won't bounce, Rebecca.'

It was always money with Connor Owen. He couldn't see beyond it. 'I want to know I'm doing business with someone I can trust,' she told him.

He clearly didn't understand. 'There will be a contract. You can get a lawyer to look at it. It's no different from you selling your house to anyone else out there.'

'Except they most probably weren't a suspect in a murder case.'

She had wanted to drop this on Connor suddenly to see how he would react. Would he deny it or perhaps betray his feelings if the accusation was thrown at him unexpectedly? Connor looked shocked and immediately she could tell the cogs were whirring inside his head. She guessed he would be trying to work out what she had heard, what she knew and who had told her.

'What do you mean?'

'I know you were having an affair with Rose McIntyre.'

'Who told you that?'

'Let's just say I worked it out.'

'Gossip and lies,' he said, 'from my enemies.'

'You have enemies?' She would have rolled her eyes at that suggestion if he hadn't looked so serious.

'Jealous people,' he explained.

'I'm not jealous of you, but I'll only trust you if you tell me the truth.'

'Rose died a very long time ago. I don't understand what this has to do with you.'

'Firstly she didn't just die; she was brutally murdered, and it may have been a long while ago but my father was killed more recently.'

'Your father was killed?' Was he genuinely shocked to hear that or overacting? 'I hadn't heard that.'

'Under the circumstances you'll forgive me for not wanting to sell his house to someone implicated in a murder, however long ago.' She stopped short of making a direct link between the death of Rose and her father.

He held up his palms. 'All right, OK, I did have a bit of a fling with Rose, but it wasn't anything that intense. She was young and good-looking, so I messed around with her for a while, but it's not as if I was planning to, you know, leave my wife or anything.'

'Did your wife know about Rose?'

'God, no. Melissa is not the forgiving kind. She'd have taken me to the cleaners.' His face darkened. 'She did that anyway, about five years ago. Divorce cost me a bloody fortune.'

'You knew it would, even when you were seeing Rose.'

'Which proves I never would have run off with her.'

'And that gives you a motive.'

'What?' He seemed shocked.

'If she told your wife about the affair, it would have cost you a great deal of money. You just said as much.'

'Yeah, no, well, what I meant was . . . Look, it wasn't like that with Rose and me. She didn't want to be the next Mrs Owen.'

'Then why was she seeing you?'

'I was good in the sack.' Rebecca queried this with a look and he said, 'Her words not mine.'

'You must have been shocked when she was killed.'

'I was devastated.'

'But you kept your feelings to yourself. You and your father even persuaded the police to keep quiet about it.'

'I was married. What else could I have done?'

'You sorted out your alibi pretty quickly, though. I mean, you would have been a suspect without it.'

'I didn't sort out my alibi. I was in a meeting with my father at the time.'

'Your father was your alibi?'

'Not just him. There were others in the meeting too.'

'His contractors. Men who relied on him for their livelihoods.'

He didn't ask her how she knew that. 'You actually think they would lie about a murder for money?' He sounded very surprised, even though money appeared to be his prime motivating factor in life.

'Money can persuade people to do a lot of things.'

'You're very cynical for one so young, Rebecca. Look, there must have been a dozen men round that table. We were in Newcastle in a meeting room. The police didn't just accept my word for it. Everyone there had to vouch for me, including the deputy manager at the hotel. I can get you the details. They'll be filed away somewhere.' He looked around the room as if he might be able to actually see the documents from his desk.

Rebecca could see he was flustered but she was

tempted to believe him. A guilty man would have been calmer, less outraged by her suspicions, dismissive even. She could tell just by looking at Connor that his main worry was losing the deal on the table. This was currently in jeopardy because of her suspicions about him and he was desperate to allay them. It wasn't a good look but it was enough to calm her fears about him.

'Maybe you can find those documents for me then.'

He seemed to become suspicious. 'Is this about the bid? Are you looking for more? I won't be blackmailed, Rebecca.'

'No one is blackmailing you, Connor,' she said calmly.

Again, he took her lack of emotion as a sign she was holding out for more. 'This is Alan, isn't it? He thinks you hold all the cards because it's the last house on the block. Well, don't listen to him, darling. That property is only worth what I think it's worth and I could leave you stuck there high and dry.' He let out an exaggerated sigh, as if this was all so unreasonable of her. 'Don't you want to make a fresh start?'

Darling? It appeared the twenty-first century had not yet reached Connor Owen's office. He was still living in the last one.

'I'm not sure I do. I've been thinking I might stick around.'

'In Eriston?' His tone was disbelieving. 'To do what? There's nothing here.' Then he must have realized how that sounded. 'Not for a bright girl like you anyway.'

'Maybe I'll get a job in Newcastle,' she said.

'I *will* renovate those other houses,' he assured her, 'even if I can't pull them down. Do you really want to live next to all that crashing and banging for months with all the dust?'

'Maybe not,' she admitted.

'Well then.'

'But I have to live somewhere.'

He looked impatient now. 'What do you want *exactly*, Rebecca?'

'This is a good start,' she conceded as she held up the letter. 'Now, why don't we talk some more?'

36

When she left Connor's office almost an hour later, Rebecca immediately checked her phone. No text from Alan. What was he playing at? Had he still not seen it or was he playing games?

There was another possibility. He had wanted her but wasn't all that bothered about a repeat performance. He'd finally shagged his old girlfriend and now he was moving on. Maybe he had someone else. By the time she returned home Rebecca had convinced herself this was the most likely explanation and had begun to feel angry at being duped.

It was not until hours after her text that there was a knock on her door and she opened it to find Alan standing there on her doorstep looking apprehensive.

'What?' she asked him, her tone sharper than she had intended. So much for playing it cool.

'I'm sorry. I lost my phone. I thought I'd left it at home but I hadn't. I finally found it in the door panel of the truck. I didn't see your text, else I'd have been straight round.'

Rebecca's relief at discovering her old boyfriend was not really a twat who had instantly discarded her was replaced by a more urgent need. 'You're here now,' she told him, as she took him by the hand, brought him inside and closed the door. This time they made it as far as the living room.

Her doubts about Alan well and truly put aside, Rebecca agreed to meet him for a meal later. Now she could let her mind revert back to obsessing over the Eriston murders. Though she felt as if she and Dominic had made some progress, the truth still remained tantalizingly out of reach, just as it appeared to have done for her father. For days she had pored over every word he had written. He had investigated every suspicious death in the region in exhaustive detail and though he was often able to question the findings of the police he was not able to solve the cases for them. His book shed new light on old murders and had at least convinced her of Simon Kibbs's innocence but the jailed man had yet to even reply to her letter, so the prospect of speaking to him in prison was a distant one. What the book lacked was a conclusion that unmasked the real killer. If her father had been murdered because of something he had discovered, that revelation was not to be found within its pages.

If you added everything Sean Cole had written to the facts that she and Dominic Green had uncovered between them since his death, there was a hell of a lot of information to go on but still the truth evaded them. She had to find a way to cut through all this somehow.

Hours later, while she was waiting at the hotel bar for Alan, she resorted to a technique her father often favoured. 'If you can't understand it, write it down,' he used to urge her, 'then sometimes you start to see it for what it really is.' He always preferred the clarity of the written word.

Rebecca took out the Sheaffer Sagaris ballpoint, opened her notebook and started with a clean page. She began by listing all the factors that had to be present for someone to be the killer, assuming he was responsible for both murders twenty years ago and at least some of the others since then.

The first factor was age. The murderer had to be in his late thirties at least, to have killed the two women back then. If she assumed the killer had to be an adult, she could rule out anyone who was not at least thirty-eight years old now.

The second factor hit her quite suddenly. They had to have known Katherine Prentiss or at least known *of* her as a reporter. Otherwise how could she have posed any kind of threat to them? It didn't mean that whoever killed Katherine had to be a friend, colleague or lover, just someone who knew who she was and what she looked like. The newspaper had always put small photos of its reporters in the paper to accompany page-lead bylines, so that part was easy. They had to have worked out that Katherine was reporting on the graveyard murder and had somehow uncovered something significant, information that could destroy them, in fact. The list of people could then be narrowed down further, because it also had to be somebody who could set up a meeting with her in an isolated spot yet still leave her feeling safe. Katherine was no fool, yet she *was* fooled by someone.

Access. She wrote that word down too. They had to have had access to the other victims. Katherine and Rose were both killed outside in the open air and one of them in broad daylight but other victims were killed indoors, taken from their homes or picked up on their way back from a night out. Always when they felt least vulnerable, but who could have persuaded them to open their doors and admit a killer?

Journalists could.

She put Jason's name on the list. From the way he behaved when she met him it seemed obvious he had a problem with women. Graham had said Jason was upset when Katherine died, but he could have been faking that.

A moment later she added Graham's name. He claimed to love Katherine but she only had his word on that and love can sometimes turn to hate.

Both reporters could go to people's homes and they would be glad to see them because they wrote nice things about their achievements. They would knock on your door and you would let them in.

Don't Let Him In.

That was the name of the campaign the police had run, yet still the women let their killer in.

Who else would they trust apart from journalists?

The police.

On DI Hall's own admission Simon Kibbs had apparently claimed he had seen a detective walking away from the graveyard that day, just before he encountered the dying woman, but why would he say that? Hall claimed that Simon didn't know any detectives. Perhaps he did or at least knew what they looked like. If a detective knocked on your door, you would let him in. Rebecca had when DI Hall called. He or one of his detectives could visit a woman in her home on the pretext of asking a few routine questions, and Rebecca had never had a sufficient explanation for why these criminal investigations had been so poorly handled.

Rebecca wrote the names of Hall and his two detectives on her page and thought for a moment. In the interests of fairness she then added Dominic's name to the list. It went against her better nature but he was old enough, just, and had gained the trust of everyone in the town . . . but why, then, was he so tireless in trying to catch the killer? She put his name down anyway.

Dominic Green.

Who else could gain entry where others could not? There was an obvious candidate now she thought of it. Gregg Poole, the locksmith, could open any door in town. She should not rule him out simply because he had been so accommodating on her arrival. Didn't Dominic say he had been called out when Amanda Mayhew was burgled, months before she disappeared? He must have met her then and if he had fixed her lock, then surely he could open it again. He had made short work of the door barring Rebecca from her father's house. That was not a comforting thought now, knowing he could get in at any time he chose. Gregg had worked with the police so no one in authority was likely to suspect him of being a murderer. Would he have known Rose and Katherine, though? Possibly.

Gregg Poole.

Then there was Connor Owen, a predator, at least in the business sense. He took ownership of properties he could buy cheaply, then turned a quick sale into a profit. He'd had no scruples about accosting her at her father's funeral to try to buy the house. Clearly he didn't like to hear the word *no*. Maybe he thought rules were for other people. Could a man like that kill? Possibly. Would a woman let him in? If he was offering her a deal, perhaps. He had been having an extra-marital affair with Rose McIntyre that would have cost him an expensive divorce if she had revealed it. His only alibi was from his own father and their contractors. Connor had promised to prove he was in Newcastle on the day Rose was killed but she had yet to see evidence of this.

Connor Owen.

When Rebecca was done, she looked at the list of people who could possibly fit all her criteria, based on age, access, motive and the ability to set up a secluded meeting with Katherine Prentiss without alarming her.

Possibles

1. Jason Booth – reporter
2. Graham Walker – reporter
3. DI Hall – detective
4. DC Fox – detective
5. DC Carpenter – detective

6. Dominic Green – police constable
7. Gregg Poole – locksmith
8. Connor Owen – property developer

Eight names. That didn't narrow it down too much and it could still turn out to be a complete stranger. It was so frustrating. How the hell was she ever going to make a breakthrough?

Rebecca was so absorbed in her thoughts that she didn't even notice Alan enter the hotel bar, but she was happy to see him.

'That's old school,' he said. 'No one uses a pen and actual paper any more. They've all gone digital.'

'My dad drummed it into me. He used to say a reporter should never go anywhere without a pen, a pad to write on and a camera –' she tapped the screen of her phone – 'because you never know when you might need them.'

'Whatever you say, Grandma.'

'News has a habit of happening whether you are ready for it or not.' She was actually quoting her father now. *God, Rebecca, where did that come from? Now that he is gone, you're turning into him.*

'What are you writing?' he asked.

'Oh, nothing.' And when he gave her a questioning look, she deflected, 'You're late, Mr Miller.'

'I'm sorry,' he said. 'I left but I had to go back to the job.' Then he looked sheepish. 'Forgot my phone, again.'

'I'm going to buy you a special holster,' she told him, 'so you can clip it to your tool belt.'

Alan didn't sit down. Instead he said, 'I'll go and see if our table is ready.'

Before he could return, another familiar figure entered the room and walked up to Rebecca. Dominic seemed troubled. 'I've been looking for you,' he said. 'All over town.'

'Why? What's happened?'

'Nothing,' he said. 'I just wanted to say I'm sorry. I shouldn't have reacted like that.' And before she could reply he went on. 'It just brought back bad memories of never being believed but I shouldn't have walked out on you. The stupid anger-management course I went on taught me to walk away before an explosion and I wasn't about to explode. I was just . . .'

'Disappointed in me?' His affirming look told her she had read the situation correctly. 'I was about to apologize to you, Dominic, but you beat me to it. I wasn't doubting you, or at least not only you. I doubt pretty much everything these days and everyone, but that's because my father was killed and I have no explanation for it. When someone tells me a story like yours that's so –'

'Unbelievable?' he interrupted.

'I was about to say strange,' she assured him, 'but what *isn't* strange about this whole thing? I'm convinced my father was murdered but CID don't fully believe that, just as they don't believe you, so we have that in common at least. All I would say is that you have been a far bigger help to me since I came back to Eriston than any of the detectives.'

'Thank you,' he said. 'That means a lot.' There was an awkward moment then while each waited for the other to either say something else or end the conversation now they had a truce.

At that moment Alan came back into the room. Rebecca had been expecting him, of course, but Dominic had clearly assumed she was alone.

'He says our table is nearly ready.' Alan jerked his thumb back towards the restaurant, then he said, 'Hello, Dominic. What brings you here?'

The policeman's posture stiffened. 'Just a quick word with Rebecca,' he said. 'But I'll be off now. Enjoy your meal.'

37

It took a few days for the revised contract, containing the key changes Rebecca had demanded from Connor Owen, to come back to her. She then took it to a solicitor and he went through it line by line on her behalf before giving it the all-clear. As far as he could see, it was a bona fide agreement, with no tricks, catches or clauses she was likely to regret. In short, Connor Owen was not trying to con her. This was an above-board offer, and in one crucial way better than the last one.

Rebecca met Connor in a hotel the next morning for what he called a 'breakfast meeting'. There he gave her an envelope.

'What's this?' She opened it and withdrew some documentation.

'The hotel conference room booking form, signed by me,' he told her, 'and the receipt for the payment. Check the date,' he urged her and she did. 'The day that Rose was killed. I can't have been in two places at once.'

The document also showed that Connor had booked the conference room for the entire day and was there in person. Surely he could not have managed to slip out, travel back to Eriston, kill Rose then return before he was missed by those contractors who swore he had been with them all day.

'I'm surprised you were able to find it,' she said.

'It took a while but we keep everything. It was my alibi during a murder investigation, so I was hardly going to throw it away.'

Satisfied, she handed the contract over to him and said, 'My solicitor has been through every line.' He looked a little worried then and she couldn't resist pausing to take a sip of her coffee before concluding, 'He said it's fine.'

'Then we have a deal? You'll sign it?' he blurted.

'Yes, Connor. I'll sign.'

He looked as if he might collapse in relief, but instead he reached inside his suit and rummaged there, before using the other hand to reach into the opposite inside pocket and freezing.

'No pen?' she asked amiably.

He looked gutted. 'I left it in my other suit.'

'Oh dear.'

She could sense his alarm, as if the absence of his gold pen might actually put the deal in jeopardy. He tried to attract the attention of the waitress but she walked by without noticing him.

'Do *you* have a pen?' he asked Rebecca.

'Never go anywhere without one.'

She took out her Sheaffer ballpoint and signed the contract while he watched her intently. He then scooped it up and borrowed her pen so he could sign it too. She made sure he gave her a copy and then said, 'I'd better get going.'

'You're not having breakfast? At a breakfast meeting?'

'The quicker I get to the office, the quicker you'll get your money.'

'Fine.' It was not as if she actually wanted to have breakfast with him but at least she could now afford to pay for her own without worrying about it. 'It was a pleasure doing business with you.'

He frowned at that, obviously assuming she was taking the piss after driving such a long, protracted hard bargain from him. She watched as he got his things together and waited until he was just about to leave, then calmly said, 'Connor? Can I have my pen back, please?'

He fished inside his jacket pocket, retrieved her pen and said without a hint of an apology, 'Force of habit,' before handing it back to her.

Rebecca felt like celebrating but had to wait until that evening when she could meet Alan for a drink and surprise him with her news. There was a new place in town called the Rusty Dolphin. As well as a meaningless name, it had a first-floor bar with a large balcony that faced out to sea. It was the first time Rebecca had been here and she was surprised by how smart and modern it looked inside. Someone had spent some money doing this place up, so maybe there was a little more confidence in the town's future than she had realized. It was a cheering thought. Rebecca could easily imagine those commuters, who had turned their backs on Newcastle's nightlife, spending some time and money here.

Rebecca and Alan took their drinks on to the balcony and looked out to sea.

'I've been talking to Connor Owen about Dad's house,' she told him.

'He came back with a better offer? I knew he would.'

'He did,' she said, 'and I'm grateful to you for concentrating his mind.'

'How grateful?'

'You'll find out later.'

He looked anxious then, clearly assuming she was going to leave Eriston. 'So,' he asked, 'did you accept it?'

'No. I made him a new offer.'

Though most of the balcony faced the sea, it went round three sides of the building. She steered Alan to a corner, then pointed back to an apartment block no more than a hundred yards from the bar.

'That's one of Connor's buildings,' he said. 'I worked on it.'

'Then I'll know who to blame if the shower's not working,' she said.

'You're buying one of them?'

'It's part of the deal,' she explained. 'I get a lump sum plus one of his flats. I went to look at it a few days ago.'

'You mean you're staying?'

She nodded and he seemed very pleased. She was glad he didn't try to hide his enthusiasm. No games. It was one of the things she most liked about him – she always had.

'But what will you do? Was Connor's offer that good?'

'It was a good offer but I still need to work.' She laughed. 'I can't exactly retire.'

'What then?'

'I'm working on something but I don't want to tell you about it yet.'

'Why not?'

'Because it might not happen.'

'You and your secrets.'

'I told you about the flat.'

'Only after you bought it.' But he was still smiling.

'It's quite small but very nice and there's plenty of room for one.' Then she said, 'Or two, if I have visitors.'

'I like the sound of that.'

I see you, Rebecca.

Why are you so happy all of a sudden? Forgotten all about Daddy already, have you? Is that it? What a fickle little girl.

You're all the same when you have a boy on your mind.

I'm not sure if I can rely on you to be distracted for ever, though.

I'm trying to work out my next move. What to do for the best? It's a tricky one.

I'll visit you one day but I need to see how this plays out first. I reckon you'll give up, if you haven't already. You'll lose interest, say 'oh well' and leave here with the mystery unsolved. That's what I think you'll do, but is it just wishful thinking on my part? We'll have to wait and see, won't we?

Maybe I need to give you a scare to help you make up your mind.

Perhaps I should come to your house in the night and leave a dead rat by your doorstep for you to find in the morning. Not a very subtle message but an effective one, I think.

I don't know, though. There's a stubbornness in you, Rebecca, and it might have the opposite effect. Knowing the man you're looking for is watching may just encourage you, so I'll stay in the shadows for just a bit longer.

Rebecca stayed the night at Alan's house and it felt right. Any concerns she might have once had about moving quickly into this new relationship with her old boyfriend had largely dissipated. There was still a small logical inner voice that cautioned her against behaving so rashly. At the back of her mind she also wondered about the wisdom of a quick agreement for the sale of her father's house and whether she was doing the right thing on insisting on an apartment as part of the deal. She knew that if things didn't work out with Alan, their presence in the same small town might prove awkward, but somehow, in what she could only think of as a triumph of hope over reason, she didn't think things would end badly with him. Not this time.

She automatically chided herself. *No one ever does think that, Rebecca.*

Things were finally coming together, though. Rebecca felt hopefulness for the first time in a long while and it was a nice change. When Alan left for work, Rebecca returned home and made herself a late breakfast. She had just finished eating it when there was a faint knock at the door. At first she wondered if she had misheard and there was actually no one there but it came again, louder this time. She wasn't expecting Alan or Dominic. There was no peephole on the old front door, or even a chain, so Rebecca was forced to open it without knowing who was there.

A woman she had never seen before was standing on her doorstep, peering at Rebecca intently. She was a little older than her perhaps, possibly in her mid-thirties, but she looked tense, as if she had news of some urgency to impart.

'I'm Claire,' she said as if that would clarify everything.

Rebecca waited for her to explain her presence.

'Dominic's . . .' She shook her head as if whatever word she might choose would be inadequate. Rebecca wondered if she was going to say girlfriend or even wife. Dominic hadn't mentioned a partner. Was this woman here out of jealousy?

'I need to warn you. You should stay away from him.'

She must have seen Rebecca with Dominic and mis-understood the situation.

'You've got it wrong,' said Rebecca firmly. 'He's just helping me with something. I'm not seeing your boyfriend.'

'He's not . . .' She seemed frustrated that she hadn't explained herself clearly enough, then her tone soft-ened. 'He *was* my boyfriend, a long time ago –' she exhaled – 'then he ruined my life. And he *will* ruin yours.'

38

At first Rebecca felt a little uneasy, possibly even disloyal, inviting Claire in but she needed to hear what she had to say. Whatever it was, it had been important enough for her to track Rebecca down.

She explained that her full name was Claire Tilbury and she did not appear threatening, just nervous and a little intense.

'I used to live in the town,' she began. 'I don't any more, not since I broke up with Dominic. I had to get away from him.'

'It ended badly?' asked Rebecca, who had immediately lapsed back into the role of reporter, asking questions to get to the heart of the woman's story.

'It was almost all bad,' said Claire. 'Not just the end. I met Dominic six years ago, when I was teaching at the primary school. He came in to talk to the children about road safety. He was sweet and charming.' She said that bit as if she could barely believe it. 'I was new to the town and newly single. When he suggested coffee then a walk around Eriston, I accepted. My previous boyfriend had not been good to me. Having this big man, this policeman, by my side made me feel safe . . . though that sounds ridiculous now.'

Rebecca was listening to her intently, trying to work

the woman out. Had she and Dominic gone through a bitter split at the end of a bad relationship or was there more to it? He admitted attending anger-management classes and had been damaged by his experiences. Claire Tilbury certainly seemed authentic.

'We dated for months before he suggested we live together. He moved into my apartment, then everything changed.'

'In what way?' Rebecca probed.

'I couldn't do anything.'

'What exactly do you mean?'

'I mean, he wouldn't let me. At first it was fine but he slowly took control. It got to a point when he didn't trust me to go anywhere on my own. I couldn't meet friends or even family. He started telling me what to wear and what not to wear. He couldn't understand why I wanted to look nice when I already had a boyfriend. He always thought I was doing it for someone else, not just for me. It wasn't long before he accused me of having affairs with other teachers. He insisted on walking me to school in the mornings and tried to meet me there at the end of the day, even when he was on duty. We argued all the time and he would call me terrible names then threaten me.'

'He threatened to hit you?' Whenever Rebecca had seen cases like this in the news she had always believed the women involved, but she couldn't quite picture Dominic in the role of aggressor.

She shook her head. 'No. To destroy me. That's what he used to say. If Dominic thought I was seeing someone else, had any contact with my ex or any of the men I worked with at the school, that's what he would threaten to do. Destroy me.'

'What did he mean by that exactly?'

It took Claire Tilbury a while to continue and Rebecca could tell she was reluctant to go into detail. 'It was why I couldn't leave him. When we first got together, he said he wanted me to pose for him.' She seemed embarrassed. 'Pictures, you know.'

'Nudes?' asked Rebecca gently.

'More than just nudes.'

'Sexual things?'

The woman nodded. 'Some of them he took himself and others I sent to him.'

Rebecca's generation considered sexting quite normal but she had never done it herself, out of fear of what might happen to those images if a relationship ended badly. As a journalist, Rebecca knew how easily not just careers but lives could be destroyed if they were made public. Claire seemed to be living proof of the need for that caution.

'He said he would put them all over the internet if I left him and send them to everyone I knew.'

'Did you believe him?'

'He meant it,' confirmed Claire.

'So what happened when you broke up?'

'I put up with all of this for months because I thought I had no choice. I was terrified he would post explicit pictures of me and everyone would see them. It was awful.'

'But you did end the relationship. What changed?'

'The law,' said Claire.

Now Rebecca understood. She knew the legal system had finally caught up with the realities of that type of cybercrime. Distributing embarrassing images featuring nudity or sexual acts became a criminal offence more than five years ago and that had been Claire's chance.

'I didn't think he would dare do it,' said Claire. 'Especially with him being a police officer. He would end up in prison and his career would be over. That's when I asked him to leave.'

'And did he go?'

Claire shook her head. 'Not at first. He tried to bully me, then changed his tune and begged me to let him stay. He said he'd only been like that because he loved me and was jealous. We talked for hours and he kept on pleading for a second chance. He even deleted all the images he had taken and showed me they were gone but I knew if I backed down I would regret it. I never believed he could actually change and by then he had put me through too much. In the end he packed his bags and left, but it wasn't over.'

'What happened?'

'He phoned me all the time. I had to turn my mobile off, then change the number. I got the locks changed but he would turn up at the flat pleading to be let in. The neighbours would come out to see what was wrong but because he was a police officer they backed off. Sometimes I'd look out of my window and see his car parked across the road, with him just sitting in it. I didn't dare leave the building. Eventually I moved out of town but stayed at the school because I loved the job. It was all I had left.' She teared up. 'But then I had to leave because of him.'

'What did he do?'

'When he first asked me to send nudes, it was after we'd had a few drinks and I admitted I had done that before. I'd sent a couple of pictures to my ex. Dominic wanted to see them and they were still on my phone so I showed him. I think it turned him on but then later he got angry about it and asked why I had kept them if I didn't care about my ex. I had forgotten about them but I said I would delete them. He insisted on doing it so he knew they were gone and I let him because I could see he was so upset. I just put it down to stupid male jealousy. They were clearly old pictures. I was younger and my hair was a different style back then. They were obviously from a time before I came to Eriston.' She let out a sigh then that was almost a sob. 'Before he deleted them, he must have sent them to his phone.'

'Go on,' urged Rebecca when it seemed Claire was struggling to explain further.

'A few weeks after we broke up, I was called in to see the headmaster. He handed me an envelope that had been posted to him at the school. Inside were those old photographs that had been blown up, with messages scrawled on them, supposedly from me, telling the head that I wanted to fuck him.' Reliving the moment seemed to renew the whole ordeal for Claire. Her face was flushed. 'I was going to say that I don't know who was more embarrassed, the headmaster or me, but of course it was me.'

'Did he fire you?'

'He didn't have to. I told him I would leave that day and I never went back. How could I? It was awful. I don't know if he would have sacked me or not but he felt duty bound to tell me that someone had posted the photographs to him.'

'Did you go to the police?'

'Yes, but Dominic expected that. When they hauled him in, he said they were taken long before he met me, so my ex was in the frame for it instead. Dominic managed to convince everyone he was over me and wished me no ill. He said my previous partner was a bad and controlling man, which he was, but why would he wait all that time to get his revenge? No,' said Claire emphatically, 'it was Dominic.'

'And no action was taken against him?'

'None. I had no proof.'

Rebecca took a moment to process this. She could picture the polite, driven but considerate Dominic, a man prone to flashes of temper if he felt insulted or undermined but one who did not fully resemble the image Claire had painted of him, but why would she lie about any of this?

'You said you don't live here any more, Claire. Where are you now?'

'I moved down the coast to Craster.'

'You've not had any contact with Dominic since then?'

'Shortly after the incident with the pictures he came to see me. I was getting out of my car in town and he walked right up to me. He tried to apologize for everything he had done and swore he didn't send the photographs. I told him I didn't believe him and that was the last time I ever saw Dominic.'

'And you came back to Eriston specifically to warn me about him?'

'Yes,' she said, 'because he will do the same thing to you if you don't cut off all contact with him now, before it's too late.'

'But how did you know?' asked Rebecca.

'Know what?'

'That I had contact with him.'

Claire Tilbury looked confused at first, then she said, 'Oh, I see, because of my friend.'

'What friend?'

'I have a friend in Eriston that I keep in touch with. Linda Poole.'

'Poole? Is she related to Gregg, the locksmith?'

'His daughter,' Claire explained. 'She sees Dominic around town and the other day she saw him with you. Someone told her who you were.'

'And she told you?'

'Yes.'

'So you came up from Craster to warn me about him.'

Claire shook her head. 'I came to visit my friend. She

told me who you were and where you lived. I couldn't leave town without letting you know the truth about him. It took me a long time to get over our relationship . . .' She corrected herself then, 'Actually, I'll never be over it but I'm not afraid of Dominic any more. You should be, though.'

'I appreciate the warning but we've just been looking at old cases together. We're not in a relationship.'

'That doesn't matter,' said Claire.

'I think it does.'

'No.' The other woman shook her head. 'Not if he becomes obsessed with you.' She seemed to take a closer look at Rebecca then, as if examining her for certain qualities. 'And he will.'

39

Despite Claire Tilbury's warning, it was days before she heard from Dominic again. *Not exactly the behaviour of a man who is obsessed with me*, she thought, but Rebecca could not ignore his ex-girlfriend. Claire's words kept coming back to her whenever she considered her list of suspects and the possibility that Dominic might be chief among them.

Rebecca was sitting in the café when he spotted her. She had taken to eating out more often now, because staying in the house at night on her own was bad enough. During the day she needed to escape from it. The anxiety the place had caused her made her even more determined to go through with its sale.

Rebecca felt more comfortable seeing Dominic in a public setting. It was mid-afternoon and the place had thinned out considerably, so there was no danger of them being overheard. Dominic looked weary, as if he hadn't slept much lately. She knew how that felt. He bought a mug of tea and brought it to her table.

'I have some news for you,' he said. 'Ian Molloy.' The name meant nothing to her. 'That's the name of the man who broke into your father's house.'

'How do you know that?'

'Because he admitted it.'

'You got him?' She had given up hope of that ever happening but it seemed Dominic had been true to his word, at least over this.

'He tried to steal some food from a shop in the next town along but they caught him and we picked him up. He matched the description, so I spoke to him personally. He didn't even bother to lie. When I quizzed him on where he had been sleeping before, he told me that it was one of the Apostles.'

'You're sure it's him?'

Dominic showed her a photograph and it was definitely the man who had appeared in her bedroom doorway.

'Told you we'd get him.'

'What did he say? Did he tell you why he was living there?'

'Once he started talking, he wouldn't stop. I got chapter and verse. He used to have a job, a wife and a family, but ended up losing all three. That can happen these days. There's not much of a safety net for adult males because they are not classed as vulnerable. He had nowhere to go so he ended up homeless. One night, he broke into the empty house next to your father's, just looking for a place to doss. He knew someone lived next door and noticed the brickwork in the attic was loose. When his neighbour went out, he broke through and pinched some of your dad's groceries. He was at pains to tell me he only took what he needed to survive, if that's any consolation to you.'

'I am relieved to hear he isn't some kind of psycho.

You are *sure* that he isn't?' she asked, needing some reassurance. 'Did your missing woman turn up?'

'No, but there's nothing to link him to her and his story checks out. I spoke to his ex-wife this morning. She confirmed his version of events. It's quite a sad tale really.'

'I sympathize,' said Rebecca, 'but I was bloody petrified when I saw him standing there.'

'He sends his apologies for that too by the way. He was shocked to find you there.'

'Not as shocked as I was. What will happen to him now?'

'That's up to you,' said Dominic reasonably.

'How do you mean?'

'Do you want to press charges?'

Rebecca thought for a moment. 'What good would that do? Not if you genuinely believe he was only trying to survive.'

'I think that he was, yes. I can try to get him some help from social services, if you like?'

Rebecca assumed that a police officer would be more concerned with locking someone like Molloy up and was surprised Dominic took a more enlightened view. 'That would be good of you.'

Maybe that terrible moment, when Rebecca had woken to find an apparition in her room could finally be banished from her mind. The man Rebecca had confronted in her bedroom was no more than a scavenger down on his luck. Perhaps she could put this behind her. Maybe she would even sleep tonight.

'And I've been doing some digging in the files at police HQ,' Dominic told her. 'I found something very interesting. It had been buried there. I think, deliberately.'

'What?' Rebecca forced herself to listen to what he had to say, instead of focusing on the words of his former girlfriend. She wanted to challenge him about Claire Tilbury. At the very least she needed to hear Dominic's version of events, before deciding whether to cut off all contact with him. For now, though, she had to put that to one side in case he had made a breakthrough in her father's case.

'There has always been a lot of speculation about why Rose McIntyre was in the graveyard on the day she was killed. She had no relatives buried there. There was talk that she might have been meeting someone, gossip about a married man but no one knew who, and nobody ever came forward.' Rebecca opened her mouth to interrupt him but he carried on. 'Once Simon Kibbs became suspect number one, they never bothered to seriously search for this man or so everybody assumed.'

'But they did find him,' she said, and he mistook this for a question.

'According to a statement from one of the detectives investigating the Rose McIntyre murder, the married man she was seeing was swiftly identified. He was questioned in his own home and the alibi that he gave for that day was accepted, even though it came from a family member. It was also agreed that it would be in nobody's best interests to make the man's extra-marital affair public. It was covered up to spare him from the embarrassment. Now what kind of man gets to negotiate a deal like that with the police?'

'A powerful and wealthy one usually,' she said. 'Someone like Connor Owen.'

Dominic looked completely taken aback. 'You knew? Who told you?'

'I worked it out for myself. Guessed actually. Then I confirmed it with DI Hall.'

'You didn't think to tell me?'

'It didn't seem relevant and I've spoken to Connor, whose alibi checks out.'

'This changes everything,' he said.

'No, it doesn't.' Rebecca told him about the documentation she had seen from the hotel in Newcastle.

'Papers like that can be faked,' he said.

'They looked real.'

'Are you sure you're not just seeing what you want to see, Rebecca?'

'What do you mean by that?'

'You told me he's trying to buy your house. You have a vested interest in wanting him to be innocent.'

Rebecca stared back at him then and had to fight to keep control over her emotions. 'You're saying that I would knowingly sell my house to a man who might have killed my father?'

The ferocity of her glare must have registered with him then because he said, 'No, of course not!' He must have realized how damning his words had sounded. 'I'm sorry, Rebecca. I thought maybe we'd made a breakthrough, and I suppose I wanted it to be true. It wasn't just the alibi. It crossed my mind that Connor retains keys to the properties he rents or sells. It would explain how he could get in.'

'But not all the victims lived in Connor's homes.'

'No,' he conceded. 'They didn't. I did find out some other things, though, if you've got the time to hear me out?' When she didn't immediately answer him or express any enthusiasm, he asked, 'What's the matter?'

'There's something I need to ask you first, Dominic, and I need you to tell me the truth.'

He looked concerned. 'Of course.'

'What happened with Claire Tilbury?'

'Claire Tilbury?' For a moment she wondered if he was about to deny knowledge of her but then he said, 'My ex? What do you mean, what happened with her? How do you know about Claire?' He wasn't happy about this and it showed. 'Have you seen her?' Then he looked outraged. 'Did she come and see you?'

'Why did she break up with you?'

He went cold then and tried to shut the conversation down. 'I don't really want to talk about that, Rebecca. It's none of your business.'

'Ordinarily it wouldn't be, but you and I are working together on a case that involves violence against women.'

He straightened at that and waited for her to go on but she left it there. They stared at one another for a good half-minute and she wondered if he was judging her or was about to get up and leave. Instead he said, 'I don't want to talk about that –' he looked around at the near empty restaurant – 'especially in here.'

'Fine,' she said quietly, 'then I think we're through.'

Rebecca got up, but as she put her bag on her shoulder he ordered sharply, 'Sit down!'

40

An old man turned round to look at them then and the woman he was with frowned her disapproval at Dominic. When Rebecca shot him a look that told him his tone was too aggressive, he gently added the word *please*.

'I will if you have something to tell me.'

He nodded his assent and she retook her seat. It took him some time to decide where to start and Rebecca waited. Finally he began with: 'When I first met Claire, I'd had girlfriends but nothing like this. She was . . .'

'The one?'

'I thought so, yes, and at first I think she thought it too, but . . .'

'What happened?'

She was expecting excuses, some explanation that put the blame at least half on Claire's shoulders. Instead he said, 'I blew it. I totally did. I admit that.'

'How?'

'I was stupid.' He sighed. 'And jealous too, but it wasn't just that. There was insecurity on my part. I can see that now, with more years behind me.'

'What did you do?'

'It was more what I didn't do.' It was as if every word had to be painfully extracted from him. 'I didn't trust her. I didn't support her like a man should support his woman when she goes out to work or to see her friends. I questioned things.'

'Like what?'

'Where are you going? Who are you seeing? What time will you be back?' Rebecca was surprised he was admitting all this so freely. She couldn't make up her mind whether she was relieved by his honesty or alarmed that Claire Tilbury had been telling the truth. 'Honestly, Rebecca, I didn't realize what I was doing. I was so worried I would lose Claire I ended up driving her away and I cannot tell you how much I regret that. I tried to tell her how sorry I was when it ended between us. That didn't go too well.'

'Why not?'

He exhaled deeply then, because he must have known how this would make him sound. 'To tell you the truth I think she was scared of me. I should have called her first instead of just marching up to her like that. I was hoping she would hear me out then maybe we could draw a line under everything and move on and perhaps she could forgive me. I wanted to show her I could change.'

'But she didn't believe you?'

'I don't think she did.'

'I get that you were both young, Dominic, though not that young. You may very well have been jealous or stupid. What I don't understand is why she would be scared of you at all?'

'Do you really need to hear this?'

'Yes, I do.'

He looked embarrassed then. 'When she broke up with me, I lost my temper and I am ashamed to say that, in my frustration and because of my fear of losing Claire, I grabbed hold of her.'

'Grabbed her where?'

'Her neck,' he said weakly.

'You grabbed her round the throat?' She was appalled.

'And I am so ashamed of that. It's the worst thing I've ever done.'

'Was that all you did, Dominic?'

At first she thought he was going to say that was everything but then he continued. 'I threatened her, but I really didn't mean it.'

'What did you say?'

'I said if she left, I would destroy her.'

'Wow.'

'I honestly didn't mean it,' he protested, 'not then, not ever. I let her go and I did nothing about it. Nothing. Just ask her.'

I already did.

'You weren't just her boyfriend. You were a serving police officer. How could you not know that what you did was wrong?'

'I did know and it made me feel terrible afterwards. That's why I went to the anger-management classes. To try to sort myself out. Rebecca, I loved Claire so much that the thought of losing her made me completely lose control. The last thing I wanted to do was hurt her. Please believe me. It's not an excuse, but I think what happened to me, when I discovered that poor woman lying there dying, it . . . derailed me. I was told afterwards that I probably had undiagnosed PTSD. That can lead to irrational bursts of anger. I'm not justifying what I did, only explaining it.'

Dominic seemed sincere in his regret. He was older now and hopefully the intervening years had changed him. What he had done was bad on every level but perhaps he was telling the truth about it now. Maybe people could change, though at the back of her mind Rebecca knew they very rarely did.

'It wasn't just jealousy,' he said flatly.

'Then what was it?'

'Fear of losing her, I told you.'

'Isn't that the same thing?'

'I wasn't all that worried about losing her to another man, despite what she thinks.'

'I don't understand.'

'I thought if I took my eye off her for a moment, *he* would come and take her.'

Finally Rebecca understood. 'The Chameleon?'

'Whatever you want to call him. He's out there, Rebecca; he has been there our whole lives. You and I both know it. I realize I was too controlling but I couldn't help myself. I thought I was protecting her.'

Was that the cause of all this? People always talked about murder victims and their immediate families but rarely referred to the others who were damaged by their violence, including men like Dominic who had discovered what they had done. His explanation sounded heartfelt and plausible enough, if it were not for one thing.

'What about the photographs, Dominic?'

Rebecca wondered if Dominic would pretend that he didn't know about them. She swore that if he asked, 'What photographs?' that would be it. She would immediately end their association. Instead he said, 'That wasn't me. They were old pictures sent by her crazy ex-boyfriend. Because of the stupid things I said to her, she wrongly assumed I sent them to the school to hurt her but I didn't. Please believe that.'

'The timing, though,' she probed. 'Wouldn't the ex-boyfriend have sent them right after she broke up with him, not months later after she dumped you?'

He didn't react at first and she wondered if he was unable to wriggle out of that one until he said, 'She didn't tell you?'

'Tell me what?'

'He couldn't have sent them any earlier.' Then he added, 'He was in prison, Rebecca. Claire's former partner is a bad man. He is a crook and a fraudster who got two years. Those old photos landed on the headmaster's desk a couple of weeks after he got out.'

'Why didn't Claire think he sent them then? Why did she automatically assume it was you?'

'Because he's her weak spot,' he explained. 'Just like she was mine. I think she still loved him. It wouldn't surprise me if they were back together again now. When she talked about him, she would always make excuses for him, saying he hadn't done all the things people said he had. She can't allow herself to see the truth about him, let alone believe it, not ever. If she admits to herself that he sent those pictures, then her whole world comes crashing down.'

Rebecca greeted that statement with silence. Claire Tilbury seemed like a sympathetic and credible witness to the events of her former life, but now Dominic appeared contrite and genuinely ashamed. He had admitted a lot of what had been said about him was accurate, but was he telling the entire truth now and had he really changed? Had Claire been misled by a former boyfriend whose dishonesty was a proven fact?

'You know, Rebecca, it doesn't matter what Claire believes, only what you believe.'

He waited expectantly for an answer.

'I'll be honest with you, Dominic,' she told him, 'I don't know what to believe any more.'

41

Rebecca did not exactly end her working relationship with Dominic that day, nor did she leave him with the false hope that she could ever fully trust him again. Their eventual parting was an uneasy one, with him mumbling that he had to be going, while she said she had a lot to think about, and that was exactly what she did for the rest of the day. She hoped her guarded response to the allegations from his former girlfriend was enough of a hint for him to stay away from her, at least for a while.

As well as the trust issue, Rebecca reasoned it was possible she might not need any more contact with the policeman. Dominic had probably already told her everything he knew about Eriston's murders and missing persons cases. Perhaps she could simply continue on her own from now on.

Her mood was lightened when Alan paid her an unannounced visit that evening.

'Is this OK?' he asked. 'I'd have messaged you but I wanted to have a word.' His face told her it was bad news.

He's breaking it off. He's seeing someone else. He really is married with five kids.

But it was none of those.

'I've got to go away for a bit. I'm sorry.'

'Where are you going?' She didn't bother to disguise the disappointment in her voice. His timing was impeccable. She could have done with the one man she could rely on right now.

'Edinburgh. It's only for a few days. I do some work for a company that rents out student accommodation. I agreed to the job before you came back to Eriston. Will you be OK?'

She forced herself to sound brighter then. It wasn't his fault and he would only be away a few days. 'I'll be fine,' she assured him.

'I could leave you a key to my house. You could keep an eye on it for me.' They both knew what he really meant. If she felt edgy in the old house on her own, she could escape to his. She probably wouldn't actually take him up on this but it was nice to have the option and to know he was thinking of her.

For the next two days Rebecca was in limbo. With Alan gone and Dominic keeping his distance Rebecca had no one to talk to. She had spoken to everyone she needed to about her dad and felt as if she was no further forward. Even her negotiations with Connor were concluded. Now all she could do was wait for the sale of her house to go through, so she could move out and move on.

Rebecca had not heard the postman that morning but she found a letter lying on the mat by the front door. She picked it up and examined the envelope.

Rebecca's name and address were written on it in a childish scrawl. Her surname was misspelled as 'Coal'.

Intrigued, she opened the envelope and pulled out a single folded piece of thin cheap paper. The letter was from Simon Kibbs, a reply to hers just when she had started to give up hope of ever receiving one. The few words were in block capitals with no punctuation.

HMP FRANKLAND, BRASSIDE, DURHAM DHI 5YD

DEER MISS COAL

THANK U FOR YOUR LETTER AND FOR COMING TO
SEE ME SOON YOUR DAD WUZ KIND SO THAT IS OK
AND I HOPE U CAN HELP ME WITH MY PAYROLL
   I HAVE DONE THE FORM.
   YOU CAN COME AND SEE ME NOW
   SIMON KIBBS

Payroll? Then she realized he meant 'parole'. When they were out on the boat, Jack had said Simon sometimes got his words mixed up. Could she help him with his parole? Rebecca wasn't sure about that, but she hoped he could help her to piece together what had happened on the day Rose died, which might bring her one step closer to solving the mystery of her father's murder.

When Rebecca looked into the process of arranging a prison visit, she learned that Simon had to put her on his approved visitor list, by filling out a VO, visiting order, but then she remembered his letter. I HAVE DONE THE FORM. Sure enough, she discovered she was already on his list and able to book an appointment.

When she arrived at the prison, Rebecca waited almost an hour before they let her in. She expected to be shown into a busy room filled with prisoners and their families and wondered how she could speak to Simon openly in front of so many people without them being overheard. The prison officer assigned to escort Rebecca told her that this was not how things worked with Simon.

'He hardly gets any visitors and we make special arrangements when he does. You'll be seeing him privately but I will be in the room with you at all times. That's how the governor wants it.' His tone told her that if she was unhappy with that arrangement, they wouldn't be offering her an alternative.

'You don't think he is dangerous?'

'Well, he *is* a murderer,' he answered, as if she didn't know this. 'But that's not the reason. Simon is a VP.' When it was clear she did not understand what he meant, he added, 'A vulnerable prisoner. We have to keep him separate for his own safety. He's been attacked before. They all know about him in here and what he did to those women. He was front-page news. If we put him on a normal wing, he wouldn't last five minutes.'

With his explanation concluded they walked the corridors in silence until they eventually reached the interview room, which contained one of the prison's most notorious inmates. To the outside world Simon Kibbs was a beast, a modern-day Jack the Ripper who had gutted two women for little or no reason and would surely never be allowed to see the light of day again, but Rebecca saw a small cowed man who appeared deceptively harmless.

Even though Rebecca knew he would be older, she was still taken aback to see the almost middle-aged man the young boy had become. Simon was in his late thirties, his hair was receding, his glasses had thick lenses and his skin was as pale as you might expect from someone banged up on his own for most of the day. He didn't greet Rebecca, instead he just said, 'I thought I'd have to call it off. I couldn't find my glasses. They were under my bed. I'd lose my head, if it wasn't glued on.' And he laughed softly, as if he had just made that joke up.

She sat down opposite him, with only a table between her and the convicted killer. The prison guard stood off to one side, arms folded, watching them. 'Thank you for seeing me, Simon,' she said.

'I only did it because your dad was nice and now he is dead.' So he knew about that. 'I hope you are nice too.'

'I try to be.'

'You'd better not trap me,' he warned her. '*They* said you might.'

'Who did?' This seemed unlikely since he was not allowed to fraternize with other prisoners. Had the guards warned him about her?

'The solicitors. I have to tell them when someone comes in to see me. It's a rule. They're worried about you, though, because you're a reporter who works for one of them tobloids.'

'Tobloids?' She almost laughed at that but didn't think he would take kindly to it. 'You don't have to worry about that. I don't work for a tabloid. I don't actually work for anyone at the moment. I'm just trying to discover the truth.'

'Don't you? They said that you did.'

'Well, I don't and I don't know where they got that idea from, Simon. I am a journalist, like my father, but I'll be honest – I'm an unemployed one currently.'

'Your dad said that he had an open mind.' He leaned forward slightly and the prison guard unfolded his arms as if readying himself to intervene. Was Simon going to lurch at her? How long had it been since he had seen a woman close up like this? She hadn't thought about that until now. Would her presence be enough to make him dangerous again after all these years? Instead he asked her, 'Do you have an open mind?'

'I think so, yes.'

'And do you think I killed that lady?'

'Well, I don't know about that –' he sat straight then and it was his turn to fold his arms in a defensive gesture that indicated his displeasure – 'but my father thought you were innocent and that's a good start in my view.'

He uncrossed his arms and seemed to relax a little. 'He did and he is right. I did not kill that lady or the other one.'

'"That lady" meaning Rose,' she confirmed, 'and "the other one" meaning Katherine?'

'Yes. I never even met Katherine, so how could I have killed her?'

'That's a very good point, Simon. In fact, I was hoping you could help me to fill in a few gaps in the story today.'

'It's not a story,' he told her firmly. 'It's my life. It's why I am stuck in here for ever.'

'I'm sorry, Simon, I didn't mean anything by that. It's just a word journalists sometimes use.'

'You have to be careful with words,' he told her. 'Words are important.'

She could tell he firmly believed that. 'Are words the reason you're in here, Simon?'

He nodded at that. 'The police tricked me. They said I could go home if I signed under my words. Only they *weren't* my words. They were made-up words. It didn't matter, though.'

'You retracted your confession. You took it back.'

'Made no difference. The teacher still let the police tell the jury about it.' He was confused again and she realized he meant the judge. 'They didn't believe me. They believed the police. Everyone always believes the police.'

He started on a long explanation of being questioned by them and Rebecca was fascinated to learn of the many ways in which the police had exerted pressure on Simon to confess to a crime he most likely had not committed. He told her about being arrested shortly after Katherine's body was found and how he was accused of luring her to meet him somehow or following her into the woods, then brutally murdering her there, probably because she had worked out that he must be the killer. Then he said something very interesting indeed. 'I know she wanted to talk to me.'

'Katherine Prentiss wanted to talk to you?'

'Yes.'

'What about?'

'I don't know, but she phoned my mam, then put a note through the door of our house. My mam told me about it. I wasn't going to call her but then someone killed her and I was arrested. The police said the note was evidence but I don't see how when I never went to see her.'

It was evidence that Katherine had good cause to talk to you about something, thought Rebecca, *but what?* If the police thought she had evidence that Simon killed Rose, then that might give him a motive for also killing Katherine. That note must have been a pretty big piece of their case against him, yet Simon had not been charged with Katherine's murder, because it was too flimsy. He went to jail for one killing, not two.

They talked for almost an hour and during the visit Simon confirmed his account of the state of the woman he had found in the churchyard. 'There was blood all over her,' he said, 'that's why I didn't know who it was. I never realized it was the sandwich lady.'

It seemed Simon did not even know her name at the time; he just thought of her as the sandwich lady. Surely if he was as obsessed with her as the police had surmised, then he would at least know the name of the woman he was destined to kill?

'Wrap it up now, please,' said the prison officer as the hour mark approached, and Rebecca realized her time with Simon had flown by. It had been a useful exercise, but he had only confirmed much of what she already knew. It seemed he would not provide her with a significant breakthrough. Like her father before her, she had already concluded that Simon Kibbs most likely did not kill either Rose or Katherine, but she was no closer to identifying the real killer. Rebecca acknowledged the prison officer's warning and began to put her pen and pad into her bag when she remembered something. It was then that she belatedly recalled her father's note to himself. *Ask him what he really saw.*

'There was one last thing I wanted to ask you, Simon. I understand you saw a man in the churchyard that day around the time you discovered the body of Rose McIntyre?'

Simon looked down at the table then. 'I'm not supposed to talk about that ever,' he said. 'My solicitors don't like it.'

'Because they don't believe you?'

'Nobody believes me.'

'Come on, let's be having you.' The prison officer's tone was impatient and his voice louder.

'Just one more minute,' she urged him. 'Please.'

He didn't answer, just looked a little pained, but she took this as permission to finish her line of questioning

338

before Simon was spirited away, back to solitary confinement once more.

She turned back to Simon. 'Was it because you said you had seen a detective? Was that why nobody believed you?'

His voice was barely a whisper. 'Yes.'

'I see. Well, I believe you.'

His head came up and he looked her right in the eye then. 'You do?'

'Yes, I do. I don't think you would say something like that if it wasn't true.'

'I wouldn't,' he assured her.

She was trying to visualize the situation, to put herself in the shoes of this young man who had been little more than a boy really, a quiet, simple soul who sometimes got muddled and confused things, and yet seemed so sure about what he had seen that day in the churchyard.

'I just have one question for you, Simon. How did you know it was a detective?' He seemed torn, as if he couldn't make up his mind whether he should confide in her or not. She wanted to say *What harm can it do you, Simon? You're already stuck in here for life.* But instead she kept silent and hoped that would persuade him to say something before the prison officer lost his patience.

Rebecca wondered if Simon might claim that it was DI Hall or one of his colleagues, whose involvement in the case Hall had helped cover up by telling Simon not to mention it again. Had a detective been involved when Simon first got into trouble for touching that young girl? Was that how he knew the man? Maybe, instead, he somehow mistook Jason for a detective or even Graham. They both went around town asking questions. If he could confuse a judge with a teacher, then perhaps he didn't know the difference between a reporter and a detective.

'I could tell he was,' he said firmly.

'Yes, but *how* could you tell the man was a detective, Simon, if you didn't know him?'

'Seriously now, that is the end of the interview.' The intervention from the prison officer was not unexpected but the timing was awful.

Rebecca had to hear Simon out. 'Please,' she urged the man, 'just let him answer this last question.'

She was convinced he was about to say no but perhaps her imploring tone showed how important this was to her because instead he said, 'Hurry it up, Simon.'

Simon was accustomed to doing what prison officers told him to and he blurted out, 'Because of his uniform. He was walking away from me but I could see he wore a uniform.'

Rebecca blinked at Simon then and stared at him, as she tried to digest the significance of what he had just said. She felt a tingling sensation, a physical manifestation of something that was part shock and part excitement. When Rebecca spoke, she did so in a calm and measured manner that was directly at odds with her feelings. 'Simon, did you say that this detective was wearing a uniform? A police uniform?'

'Yes,' he said simply.

'But detectives don't wear uniforms,' she told him.

'This one did.'

Expecting to be cut off by the prison officer at any second, Rebecca quietly asked, 'Simon, what does a detective do?'

He looked at her as if this was a stupid question. 'Solves crimes, catches bad people.'

'That's right,' she said. 'They do.' Then she asked, 'Simon, what is the difference between a detective and a policeman?'

Again, he looked at her as if she was crazy. 'There is no difference.'

'So when you say you saw a detective that day, you mean you saw a policeman?'

'Yes,' he said. 'It's the same thing.'

42

Rebecca signed herself out of the prison, left in a hurry and swung her bag over her shoulder as she was striding out towards the car park. Her mobile phone was already in her hand and she turned it on as she walked.

Once she was back in her car, Rebecca reached for her keys so she could start the engine but her phone immediately rang with a message. She heard a familiar voice. 'Hi, Rebecca, it's Dominic. I just wondered how things went today.' He sounded like he was trying to be light and breezy. 'I heard you went in to see Simon Kibbs.'

How did he hear that? Those same contacts Dominic had in Simon's legal team? The ones she'd never met, who somehow seemed to think she was untrustworthy and worked for a tabloid. Where did they get that idea from?

'I was wondering if he said anything of note. Anyway, give me a call back when you can and let me know. Bye.'

Anything of note? Like the fact that he saw a uniformed police officer in the churchyard moments before he stumbled upon the body of Rose McIntyre. He had also told her that Katherine Prentiss had wanted to speak to him and had pushed a note through his door. This was significant but the police didn't understand why at the time. Rebecca thought she did now, though. Katherine wanted to talk to Simon because she had questions for him, including the one Rebecca had just asked Simon twenty years later. Who did you see walking away from the churchyard just before you discovered the body?

Like Rebecca's father, Katherine had contacts in the local CID. She might well have known Simon had claimed to have seen a detective walking away that day. Her contacts wouldn't have been shy in revealing that so they could rubbish his story, because there were no detectives in Eriston that day, according to DI Hall. Perhaps Katherine had decided not to accept that and wouldn't let it go. Rebecca hadn't after all. Maybe they were more alike than she would have admitted, at least as reporters.

If Simon had just used the word *policeman* instead of *detective*, then the investigation would have gone very differently from the beginning. Hall and the rest of the detectives on that case could all account for their movements, so they naturally assumed Simon was making it up to try to save his own skin. None of them realized the boy had actually seen a man in uniform but didn't know the difference between a policeman and a detective.

If someone knew Katherine was trying to speak to Simon, during the gap between his first questioning and eventual arrest, that might be sufficient reason to silence her. If she revealed what Simon had actually

343

seen, it would be a strong enough motive to kill her. Maybe it also explained why Rebecca's father had to die. He was the only person to visit the man in prison apart from the boy's mother, and he'd wanted to go and see Simon again. What if he had probed further into Simon Kibbs's story and found out what the boy had really witnessed that day? Her father had been silenced before that could happen.

If all this was true, then there was surely only one man who could have killed Rose, Katherine and Rebecca's father, and he had just left her a voicemail.

There was a bang on the side window then and Rebecca jumped. Her stomach lurched as she whirled round to see someone standing by the window. At first, in her shocked state, she thought it was Dominic. He had driven here to meet her, to find out what she had learned from Simon Kibbs. But, no, her eyes focused on the man who was staring at her now and it wasn't Dominic. He had a look of concern on his face. It was the prison officer who had watched her sign out. Tentatively she wound the window down, just enough to hear him speak.

'Miss, you dropped this.' And he held up his hand. It was her Sheaffer pen. Rebecca had left the prison quickly and gone to her car in such haste, she had forgotten to do up her bag properly and not heard the pen hit the ground.

'Thank you,' she said, as he handed it through the window to her. She took the pen and slipped it into her inside jacket pocket.

*

Rebecca drove straight home and moved swiftly from her parked car to the front door, unlocking it and getting inside as quickly as possible in case Dominic was nearby. She closed the door behind her, locked and bolted it and double-checked the back door was locked and bolted too, then went upstairs in case he showed up and tried to peer through her window to see if she was home.

Dominic phoned twice more that afternoon but Rebecca did not pick up. She couldn't face speaking to him. She desperately needed some time to think. She wished Alan was here with her and not miles away in Edinburgh, so she wouldn't be on her own tonight. She didn't have anyone to talk to about her new theory that Dominic Green might be the man responsible for the deaths of Rose, Katherine and her father. It still seemed incredible, impossible even, but what other reasonable explanation could there be for the presence of a uniformed policeman in the churchyard that day when Rose was killed and why would he walk away from the scene and not towards it? Why also would he not simply declare that he had been there just before the murder, unless he was leaving the scene of the crime?

Rebecca recalled Dominic's disgrace at that earlier crime scene when he was still a rookie police officer. The woman had bled all over him so that all the physical evidence there had been contaminated. He had sworn she was still alive and had hoped to save her. DI Hall, by contrast, had said, 'Lazarus was in better nick than her by the time we found her.'

Oh God, he killed her too, didn't he?

What about the latest woman to have gone missing? Was he responsible for Amanda Mayhew's disappearance too? Was that how he knew about the wind chimes?

How the hell was she going to convince anyone of this when she could barely convince herself? Who would believe that Dominic Green, the local police officer, known for his obsession with finding the killer of Rose and Katherine, was actually the man he was pretending to look for? If that was true, then it was genius.

No wonder women let him in.

But all Rebecca had was the word of a convicted murderer and even that was flimsy. He had seen a policeman walking away from the scene. Would that be sufficient to convince reluctant authorities to re-examine the case? She strongly doubted it. She could only imagine the scorn DI Hall would pour on her theory, if she was foolish enough to approach him with it. She had been defending Dominic all this time and now suspected him of murder. Hall would laugh in her face.

So why would Dominic be so obsessed with keeping that truth locked away? Was it because once people began to doubt him all his behaviour would then be challenged? Where was he on the day of the murder in the graveyard and did he have an alibi? Of course not. He was there. Who could have lured Katherine Prentiss to a meeting in the woods and why would she go? Did Dominic promise her information, then kill her before she could speak to Simon? Then there was his behaviour towards Claire Tilbury, his ex, who swore he had destroyed her life, just as he had threatened to do, and, of course, his contamination of a crime scene he himself had caused. When you added all this together, along with his ability to get close to her unsuspecting father, supposedly to help him with his own investigation into the murders, it began to add up.

Dominic had said he had links to Simon Kibbs's legal team and would put in a word on her behalf to secure her a visit. Instead that same team had tried to dissuade Simon from speaking to her, because they were convinced she was a tabloid hack who would trap their client. Only Dominic could have done that and now she knew why. She could probably get the solicitors to admit it too, if the policeman came under enough suspicion.

It wouldn't be enough, though, not to get the police to take it seriously.

So what could she do? *Think, Rebecca.*

No newspaper or mainstream news site would ever allow Rebecca to go public with her suspicions of Dominic Green. She could never name him. Even if they didn't think she was crazy, they would be too worried he would sue them for libel, but what if she could out him in a different way?

How could she get reputable, widely read news organizations to take her seriously? She knew how they worked and what to do to attract their attention. Give them a crumb, just enough to get them asking questions, so they would come to her and not the other way round. A blog page and maybe a podcast with a headline to entice even the most jaded editor. ERISTON ROSE KILLER IDENTIFIES MAN LEAVING MURDER SCENE.

That ought to do it. Even if they thought it was click-bait, they would be sure to read it, just in case. No one wants to be the one to miss an exclusive.

Rebecca wouldn't name Dominic but she could describe her visit to see Simon Kibbs in prison. This was almost news in itself, since he'd permitted himself only one other visitor, apart from his own mother, in twenty years and her father had not publicized the fact. She could describe how he saw a detective leaving the graveyard and was ignored by the police, then silenced by his own defence team because no one believed him. Her explanation that he really meant a police officer would lead her to ask an open question to Northumbria Police. Did they know where all their officers were that day and could they account for the movements of all their men at crucial times when other women had disappeared?

Rebecca knew her lone voice would not be enough. She would have to use all her skill to write a piece convincing enough to entice newspapers to start asking awkward questions of the police. Only then would they bow to pressure and investigate their own officers. The accumulation of circumstantial evidence against Dominic would be damning and if they delved more deeply into his life, they might even find the proof they needed.

She could write the piece, set up the web page, post the blog and send the links to every news organization she could think of. Then she would get out of town for a few days until it had been seen by enough people. A raised profile would be a form of protection against Dominic and he wouldn't dare come after her.

It was a plan. It might even work.

Her phone rang again then. It was Dominic, calling for a fourth time since he had left that voicemail. He was clearly rattled but what should she do? Rebecca didn't want to speak to him but if she failed to answer, he would become even more suspicious of her. He might realize she had extracted the truth from Simon and that would put her in immediate danger. Perhaps he would come straight round. Rebecca needed to stall him.

She tried to put his almost certain guilt out of her mind and told herself this was all about self-preservation. She picked up the phone and spoke in as breezy a tone as she could manage. 'Hi, Dominic.' She could feel the tremble in her voice, the words seeming to catch in the back of her throat, and she wondered if he could hear it too.

'Hi, Rebecca,' he said. 'I've been trying to get hold of you.'

'Oh, I'm sorry. I forgot to charge my phone and it went flat while I was out but it's charged now obviously.'

He didn't respond for a moment and she wondered if he didn't believe her. 'That's not like you.'

'I'm having an off day.'

'Did you get my voicemail?'

349

'Yes, yes, I was just about to call you back. I did go and see Simon.'

'And?'

'It was a bit of a waste of time, if I'm honest.' She was trying to sound embarrassed. 'I didn't get anything new from him.'

'Oh, really? I thought you might have.' Was he waiting for her to speak now? 'So he didn't tell you anything?'

'He talked about the murders, but nothing I didn't already know.'

'I see. That's a shame.'

Rebecca didn't answer. She realized she was actually holding her breath, hoping he would believe her, then hang up. Instead he said, 'I was going to pop round for a catch-up.'

Rebecca couldn't allow that, but how could she prevent it without him becoming suspicious?

'Are you at home now?' he asked her.

The very last thing she wanted was to be alone with him here.

'I am but I've got to nip out again now.' And she desperately tried to think of a reason before coming up with 'I've got to go to the doctors.'

'Really? Why?'

Shouldn't she just tell him to mind his own business? Wouldn't she normally do that if a man asked her such a personal question or should she invent something to embarrass him and put an end to his prying?

She settled on: 'I've not been feeling good for a while now and I need to get checked out.'

'I didn't realize you weren't well.'

'It's probably something I picked up on my travels.'

'Right.' His tone wasn't just unsympathetic; it was almost scornful. He didn't believe her, she could tell. Maybe he even wanted her to know he didn't believe her. There was a long pause on the line then and she wondered if he had gone until he finally said, 'All right then, Rebecca. Maybe we'll catch up tomorrow instead.'

'Yes,' she said, 'let's.'

She said goodbye and finished the call.

'Jesus Christ,' she said aloud, because now Rebecca was more convinced than ever that she had just had a conversation with the man who had murdered her father.

43

That evening Rebecca made sure her front and back doors were both locked and she drew the downstairs curtains but did not put the lights on. Instead she used the light from one small lamp in the living room to see by. She hoped that if Dominic drove up to the house, he would imagine she was out somewhere. She resolved not to answer the door to him or anyone else. She needed time to think about her next steps and how to go about them.

Her phone beeped then and she felt a sense of rising panic in case it was Dominic. She was hugely relieved to see that the message was instead from Alan. Rebecca was even happier when she read it.

Back early. Can you meet me?

When? she messaged back.

Now, of course, Shortbread.

She smiled at that. *Where?*

My house. Just come over. Please. I want to see you.

Alan was exactly what she needed right now to take her mind from all the fear and the worry, at least until morning when she could start work on her blog post. She would feel so much safer at his house too and could stay the night there. All she had to do was get out of here and into her father's car without being surprised by Dominic and she would be safe.

Rebecca peered out through a small gap to one side of the drawn curtains. There was nobody in the road outside, which was only half lit by that one flickering street lamp. A sea mist had descended but she could still make out her father's car, which was parked nearby. She could see the top of the road and the outlines of the trees and bushes opposite but little else.

Someone could wait right outside her door, of course, standing off to one side of it, but Rebecca banished that thought from her mind in case she lost the nerve to leave the house. Why hadn't she asked Alan to come and get her? She could ring him back now but this was stupid. The car was just yards from the front door and no one but Alan knew she was about to leave the house.

She grabbed her bag, phone and keys, positioning them so the sharp pointed end of her door key protruded through her fingers in case she was attacked, then she opened the door, stepped outside, closed it behind her and immediately went straight to the car at a brisk pace.

The car was nearby but not close enough and she heard something flutter in the bushes. Was he coming for her? Rebecca told herself it was a bird but broke into a run anyway. She pressed the key on the fob and the car's lights blinked at her, then she pulled open the door and was about to get straight in when she stopped and checked the back seat. That was how they always got you in movies. You sat down in the driver's seat, thought you were safe and they grabbed you from behind.

No one there. She did not hang about then. Rebecca climbed into the car, closed the door and immediately locked it in case that sound had not been a startled bird, then she started the engine and drove quickly away and down the hill. She had never felt more relieved to put her home behind her.

Rebecca rang the bell at Alan's house and waited but there was no answer. She knocked but still he did not come to the door. Perhaps he was upstairs or out the back and couldn't hear her but he had to be there because he had messaged Rebecca to come round and there were lights on inside. She still had Alan's spare key so she opened the front door and went inside. She turned on the hall light and called, 'Alan?'

No reply.

Was this a stupid joke? Was Alan mucking about and would suddenly leap out on her? Surely he wouldn't be that idiotic? Rebecca would be seriously pissed off with him if he was.

She opened the door to the lounge and reached for the light but when she flicked the switch it didn't come on. The bulb must have gone but she noticed movement in the far corner of the lounge and she stepped inside. The light from the hallway was no longer being blocked by her body and she could see more clearly. The sight that greeted Rebecca made her freeze in shock.

Claire Tilbury was sitting on the floor. She was tied up and gagged but conscious and staring right back at Rebecca, wide-eyed. Claire was distressed and more than likely in pain but the most immediate signal she was giving with her eyes was one of alarm.

Rebecca only had a second to work out what was going on. There was no sign of Alan or anyone else but someone had tied the woman up and, even in her fearful, shocked state, Rebecca could see they knew what they were doing. The gag was so tight round Claire's mouth that when she attempted to speak, whatever she was trying to say was horribly distorted and Rebecca could not make out a word of it.

Claire's face contorted then and Rebecca realized the other woman was trying to communicate with her eyes, which were wild and had an urgent look in them. Rebecca suddenly understood what Claire was trying to tell her but by then it was too late.

There's someone behind you.

Before she could turn to see who it was, Rebecca felt a sharp, searing pain in the side of her head. She toppled forward and fell to her knees, shocked and in pain. Her attacker was on Rebecca before she could move, pinning her head down with his hand, then letting his body weight force her towards the floor. Was he trying to kill or rape her? She felt a sharp pain in her arm then, which must have been the point of a needle. In a desperate panic to free herself Rebecca struggled harder, then suddenly found she had no strength left in her at all.

*

Got you.

I told you that you were done.

I admit you had me worried there for a while, Rebecca.

I was beginning to think you were the one who would work it all out. I could picture everything unravelling for me, but it looks like I overestimated you.

Now you are trapped and helpless.

It seems you're nothing special after all. No better than the rest.

All you've really succeeded in doing is taking up a lot of my time.

You'll pay for that now.

I've been looking forward to this.

She could not recall leaving the house. Rebecca must have been carried out because she was aware that she was outside now and it was very cold. Freezing water splashed her and this must have been what brought her round. She was vaguely aware of a rolling movement, a feeling like she was being pushed up then down and her clothes were wet in places. Rebecca tried to open her eyes but they were too heavy and she couldn't be sure whether what she was experiencing was real. More water splashed on to her face then and it felt like rain, but some of it touched her lips and she tasted salt. It was seawater and she realized she was lying in a rowing boat and it was moving. That was causing the up and down movement. She managed to open her eyes but was unable to sit up.

Someone was lying motionless next to her. A

woman. Claire Tilbury? She thought so. They were squashed together in the boat. A dark shape with his back to them was moving. Dressed in a black coat and cap, he was powering the oars, propelling the boat along. Rebecca tried again to sit up but she could not move. Whatever she had been given, it was strong and she didn't have the strength to fight it. She had no power over her limbs and her eyes felt incredibly heavy. She passed out again.

Rebecca couldn't tell how long she had been unconscious but she woke to find she was alone in the boat. The man was gone and so was Claire Tilbury. She could still hear the sea but the rowing boat was no longer moving. He had dragged it out of the water and on to the beach somewhere. He must have carried the unconscious Claire from the boat.

Close to her, looming above Rebecca, was a sheer cliff. She couldn't be sure but this looked like the very edge of the Point and she was directly below the lighthouse, which meant the boat was now on the exact spot she had surveyed with Alan when they had walked down the steps to the jetty.

Alan?

She remembered now. His text message to her, being in his house, Claire Tilbury tied up there and Rebecca attacked from behind, before she could help her. What the hell had happened?

It would have been the best time to at least try to get away but, when she tried to move, Rebecca found she was unable to get up. She concentrated hard and managed to move her leg. It twitched almost involuntarily. She focused on the other leg, managed to move it slightly, then flexed the fingers of both hands. They felt so numb it was as if they belonged to someone else. Next, she tried to sit up. If she could do that, perhaps she could get out of the boat and away, but she wasn't yet strong enough to manage it.

Then Rebecca heard a new sound. Urgent footsteps drawing nearer. Someone was walking along the jetty towards the boat. He was coming back. Her first thought was to try to call out for help but at this hour the only man within a mile of the place would be her attacker.

Rebecca closed her eyes and faked unconsciousness. She didn't dare open them in case he attacked her, injected her again or tied her up and then she would be done for, just like every other victim of the Chameleon. Rebecca would be killed, her body thrown into the sea or dumped in a shallow grave in the woods and no one would ever find her, unless she managed to stifle the panic rising in her now.

Think, Rebecca, think.

Strong hands seized her then, pulling her up by the lapels of her coat and hauling her into a seated position. Then the man stooped lower and levered her over his shoulder so he could pick her up and carry her.

He was off and moving with her now and she was rocked by the movement. She opened her eyes and found she could see nothing but the jetty below as she hung upside down from his back.

He reached the stone steps that went up to the lighthouse. She knew they were worn and would be wet and slippy, but he did not hesitate and was clearly used to walking here. She wondered how she might strike out at him, when and with what? She had no weapon and her limbs still felt like jelly from whatever drug he'd injected into her.

He carried her up the steps like a mannequin, then through the bushes and on into the lighthouse, which was illuminated by a large LED camping lamp he had already placed there. He stood on the stone lip that went round the edge, his back towards the lowered, inner section where she had been with Alan. Now she realized her life would probably end here.

He let go of her then and Rebecca slipped from his back as he dropped her and she landed hard on the sandy floor, which knocked the wind from her, the pain shocking her body back into life. Somehow Rebecca managed to stifle a cry, because she knew everything depended on her staying silent. She had to make him think she was unconscious until she got some strength back.

'Stupid, interfering bitch,' he said to what he must have believed was her still unconscious form. 'Taking me for an idiot.' And the voice was chillingly familiar.

There was a clattering sound then and he cursed. He had dropped something and it landed in the pit near to her, so he jumped down to retrieve it and she risked opening her eyes as he picked it up. The object was her phone, which he must have taken from her while she was unconscious. He bent low and she saw the side of his face and Rebecca's world seem to stop then.

It was Dominic.

44

Who else could it have been? But somehow it was still a shock. The Eriston police officer, Dominic Green, was standing there, pocketing her phone and regarding the now conscious, bound and clearly terrified figure of Claire Tilbury with a look of pure hatred.

'Should have stayed away, Claire,' he told the woman who was chained to one of the old metal rings. 'I'd have come for you eventually but it's going to be a hell of a lot sooner now, and when I'm done I'll go looking for your ex. When you both disappear, he'll get the blame. I wanted you to know that's how it's going to be.'

He turned towards Rebecca then and she closed her eyes, but did she do it in time to fool him? She didn't have a plan. If he came for her and she had some strength left, she could hit, scratch or kick him. It was a long shot but it was her only hope of getting out of there alive.

Rebecca could feel something sticky on the side of her head and she realized it had to be blood. What had he hit her with? The pain was agonizing but perversely that was a good thing. She was getting the feeling back in her body now, but what good would it do if he came for her, then chained her up too? Once that happened, it would be over for her and Claire. Maybe death would not be the worst of it. Nobody came up here any more and even if they did, they wouldn't be able to get in, so he would be in no hurry. Dominic would take his time.

She had to move now or it would be too late but did she even have the strength to do that? The decision was made easier by the incessant, despairing tone of Claire Tilbury's moans from behind her gag. She was urging Rebecca to wake up and do something. Rebecca risked opening her eyes again and fully expected her assailant to be standing over her but he was gone. She rolled over on to her back and realized Dominic had left the pit. That was why Claire was making those sounds. She was trying to wake Rebecca up. He had to have assumed she was still unconscious and probably would be for some time, so he had gone to fetch something from the boat. It meant she had a few precious minutes but what to do with them? He surely wouldn't be long.

Rebecca tried and failed to get to her feet and a sharp stabbing pain went through her head, and she immediately collapsed back down again. She knew she had to try once more. Rebecca rolled over on to an elbow and dug it into the floor. Ignoring the pain in her head, she pushed against it till she managed to get unsteadily to her feet, then promptly fell over again.

Rebecca went through the process of rolling on to her side then forcing herself up once more and this time she managed to stay on her feet. She staggered sideways, dizzy and disoriented and was greeted by the other woman's muffled pleas for help.

The harsh truth hit Rebecca then. She knew she

couldn't help Claire. Not now. There was no time. She had to save herself first if she was going to have any chance of escaping from Dominic, then return with others to rescue Claire.

Rebecca turned away and faced the door. She was about to attempt to run through it when she heard the sound of feet crunching the hard ground outside. It was Dominic and he would be back in seconds. She couldn't go out that way and there was no other exit from the lighthouse. With no weapon and only half her strength at best, she knew she had no chance of over-powering him.

There was only one course of action left and it was the very last thing Rebecca wanted to do. Her arms felt like jelly but she managed to haul herself up and out of the far side of the pit and on to the lip round it. Rebecca moved unsteadily towards what remained of the stairs, the stone steps she had been so terrified of as a teen-ager, and she began to climb them unsteadily. The difference now was that she was even more frightened of the man behind her than of the crumbling stone.

As feeling came back to her body, her thoughts also began to fall into some sort of order. Rebecca under-stood what had happened to her or at least thought she did. Dominic had stolen Alan's phone, which wouldn't have been that hard, as he was always losing it or leav-ing it in his truck. He had read their private messages, then sent Rebecca a text to summon her that looked as if it could only have come from Alan. Somehow he had managed to get into Alan's home while he was away, then waited for her to come over. She had no more time to consider this. Rebecca had to keep on climbing, putting her trembling hands out in front of her to feel her way up the broken steps and move higher.

Dominic burst back into the lighthouse. He was carrying a metal box and when he saw Rebecca climbing the old stairs, he let go and it crashed to the floor. 'Bitch!' he shouted. Whatever hard metal items were in that box there was a good chance he was about to use them to torture both women. He'd done this before, she knew it. He had even summoned a fleet of police cars down here on a fool's errand, to make them think nothing was going on at the lighthouse and dissuade them from ever looking here again.

The frustration Dominic experienced, as he watched her climb away from him, must have been short-lived because his tone abruptly changed and he became calm again. 'You're made of strong stuff, Rebecca. I'd have tied you up too, but you should have been out for another twenty minutes at least. Have you got ice in your veins where the blood should be? It wouldn't surprise me.'

Dominic didn't even try to chase after her. Instead he stood and watched as she reached a point where the stairs were so worn down they became little more than tiny ledges.

'You can climb, Rebecca,' he taunted her, 'but there is nowhere to go. You've no way to call anyone and nobody can hear you from here, even if you scream. No one comes here any more.' And he laughed. 'I'm the boy who cried wolf.'

Every time Rebecca placed a foot on a step, she expected it to give way and she would fall. Miraculously, one after the other, the partial steps stayed firm enough for Rebecca to lever herself slowly upwards and on to the next one. She was going round the inner walls of the building in a spiral, not daring to look down but occasionally catching a glimpse of the hard floor below where Dominic stood, taunting her.

'Careful, Rebecca. You've had a big dose of Midazolam mixed with Fentanyl. That's a powerful anaesthetic and I seriously doubt that it's fully worn off. You must be feeling very woozy. I'd hate to see you fall.'

She was already far higher than she had ever gone during those teenage dares. The only thing that frightened her more than falling was the prospect of being at the mercy of Dominic if she did. And so she climbed.

To take her mind from the drop below, she called out to him, trying hard to sound much calmer than she was. She didn't want him to know she was terrified, though it must have been obvious. 'You don't want to hurt Claire. If you did, you would have done it years ago. Let her go, Dominic. You loved her.'

He actually laughed at that. 'Loved this bitch? You're joking. I would have done this after we broke up but I couldn't draw attention to myself. When she came to see you, she forced me to act. I've waited a long time for this.' His tone became mocking then. 'Now come down, Rebecca, please, so we can get started.'

'If I disappear, you'll be the prime suspect.'

'Not when I tell them about that jealous, controlling

boyfriend of yours. The one with the violent father who scarred his childhood. It was Alan that messaged you to come over and you were never seen again. Don't worry, I didn't hurt him, just got into his house and took his phone. I need him alive and healthy to take the blame.'

'Because you usually only hurt women, don't you? You didn't contaminate that crime scene, did you, Dominic? You killed that woman!' She was moving more slowly now as she went higher and used untried steps. How easily they could give way.

'She deserved it!' he snapped back.

'Why? Because she turned you down?'

That seemed to anger him. 'Not just that.' And she knew she'd hit home. Rebecca realized that at least some of his anger at women was caused by their almost complete rejection of him. The one woman who had permitted him to get close to her was now chained at his feet. 'If you do it properly, all it takes is a slash at the carotid artery, then you can step back and see the look on their face as they die, but someone heard something and suddenly there were sirens.' He said that as if it had been most inconvenient. 'So I grabbed her while she bled out and it worked. After that they left me alone to do my thing.'

'Being a psychopath?'

'You should watch that mouth of yours, Rebecca. I can make this quick or I can make it very slow. It's up to you.'

The weight of her next step made a shard of stone

come free and it slid away from her. For a second she fully expected the rest of the step to crumble beneath her but somehow it held. 'Seriously, I want to know,' she asked. 'Why do you kill and why only women?'

That shut him up for a second. Was he actually lost for an explanation?

Then he said, 'The only way to avoid the pain of losing something is to destroy it yourself.' He seemed to warm to his subject. 'You don't know what it is like to stare into the eyes of another person while you take their life.' There was wonder in his voice. 'There can be no greater intimacy than that.'

'It wasn't enough, though, was it? You don't just kill any more. It's too quick.'

'You'd be surprised how quickly the novelty wears off,' he told her. 'And, just in time, they fenced off this place.' He said that like it had been done entirely for him.

'Mad people don't realize they're mad, Dominic.'

'I'm not mad. There is a limit to what I am prepared to take, that's all. I don't know how other men walk away from their humiliations but I won't.'

'It's not just that, though, is it?' She took another step and it held. 'You didn't know all those women.' And then another.

'You're all the same.'

'That sounds like an excuse to me. Why not admit you just enjoy what you do?' She was focusing entirely on the next step, taking one at a time and concentrating hard to keep her mind focused.

'You're going to find out just how much!' he shouted.

Dominic watched in impotent fury as Rebecca continued to rise and was soon far above his head. He yelled abuse at her then; it was the same shaming tirade of every man who thinks that women are all the same. She was a bitch and a slut and a lot of other foul things Rebecca barely registered, as she focused entirely on her next step. He told her exactly what he would do to her then, when he finally came up there and caught her. She tried to blot out his violent, vile words and kept on climbing. Periodically she would feel dizzy and like someone who had drunk far too much and could no longer fully control her senses or coordinate her movements. Rebecca forced herself to concentrate even harder and, by doing so, she managed to take another step then another.

'I've had enough of this, Rebecca,' he called. 'I'm coming up.' He had given up waiting for her to slip and fall and was following her, which increased her sense of panic.

Rebecca had almost made it to the top and in her haste to get away from him she neglected to test one of the final steps. Instead she put her faith in it and her weight upon it. It gave way immediately. Rebecca screamed in alarm and started to fall. Her hand flailed but could not grasp anything by her side. Somehow, as she fell, it went over her head, reached the roof directly above her and she wedged it there, which stopped her from tipping right off the ruined step. Her other foot stayed on the step below and, as her head dipped, she watched the broken remnants of rotten stone fall away below her. Dominic had to step aside to avoid them landing on his head as he climbed the lower steps.

'Ooops,' he said cheerfully, 'nearly,' and he laughed.

Astonished that she was still alive, Rebecca managed to reach high above her with her other hand. She pushed against what remained of the rotten hatch that opened into the room at the very top of the lighthouse. Most of it had rotted away and what remained was soaking wet, making it easier to push upwards. With the hatch open, she was able to grab the edge of the concrete floor and pull herself up. The worst part was having to let her feet leave the broken last step so she could haul herself upwards when she felt so weak. She was convinced she would fall.

Rebecca's head, then her shoulders went through the gap and she managed to pull herself up until both her elbows were on the edge of the stone floor, then she hauled herself in, expecting at any moment to either fall or have her ankles grabbed by Dominic who was coming up fast behind her. If that happened, she would be thrown all the way down.

'Do you think I haven't got the nerve to follow you up there? I'm coming, Rebecca,' he assured her.

Rebecca pulled the rest of her body through the hatch and crawled forward until she was fully in the room. Much of the roof here was missing, so there was some light from the moon outside. Rebecca pushed the hatch back in place and scrambled away from it, pressing herself back against the wall of the lighthouse. All she could do now was wait for Dominic to appear, and though she prayed he might slip, she doubted it. If she could make it up here in her weakened state, then surely he would manage it without falling.

'For what it's worth I always liked your dad,' he called. 'I felt bad about killing him.' He said it as if he was apologizing for some minor injustice. 'But I couldn't let him go and see Simon again. He was obsessed.' Then he asked, 'Why did your father have to be the one to find Katherine and why were you with him? I sometimes wondered if that was fate fucking with me, but there's no such thing. We make our own luck and yours just ran out.'

The mention of her father brought out a frustrated, impotent rage. She wanted to kill Dominic but had no means to do it. She wanted to delay or distract him, anything to keep him from reaching her, so she could think of a way to make him pay for what he had done.

'Why'd you kill her? Did she turn you down too?' She hoped her taunts might enrage him and make him careless, but he just laughed at the notion. She couldn't see him now, only hear his voice.

'Simon said he saw a detective leave the churchyard. Katherine heard that and wouldn't let it go. I was her secret contact in the force, as long as she promised never to reveal my identity. I told her Rose was having an affair and let Katherine assume she was screwing a detective. Maybe he killed Rose in a jealous rage? Slutty Katherine probably assumed everyone was as loose as she was. She *was* fucking your father, after all.' He said this with such certainty. Had he seen them together? Was this supposed to upset her? It didn't even matter any more compared to everything else that had happened. 'I told her I could prove there was a cover-up but was in fear of my life. I offered to bring proof after dark, somewhere neither of us would be seen and she couldn't tell anyone, not even her editor. I made her swear it. She knew the story would make her. I wasn't a detective, so she wasn't worried. If Katherine spoke to Simon and he told her what he had really seen, I had no alibi. I couldn't allow that so she had to go. Bye, bye, Katherine.'

Was he enjoying telling her the story? Had he paused in his climb to brag or was he slowly edging his way upwards while he distracted her? She listened intently and heard a grunt of exertion as he climbed over a precarious step. He was getting nearer.

Soon Dominic would be at the hatch and all he would have to do was push up against it. He would be in here with her and there would be nowhere left to hide. Rebecca's mind raced. What could she do?

She could pull open the hatch and try to prevent him from reaching her, but how? She couldn't reach down to push him. He would just grab her arms and pull her out, then down to her death. She could throw something at him, but what? Rebecca looked desperately around her, hoping to find loose bricks or stones but there was nothing there that would make a missile. The exterior walls were too sturdy to rip anything from them with her bare hands.

Stopping him before he reached the hatch was impossible. If it had been made of one solid piece of wood, then perhaps she could have stood on it, using her body weight to prevent him from coming through but so much of it had rotted away that she couldn't even trust it to bear her weight. He would be able to put an arm through and grab her, even stab her if he had a knife or swipe at her with a hammer.

There was no way to leave here and no prospect of fighting back. She was trapped and running out of time.

His insults grew louder. He was getting close to her now. If only she had a weapon.

Dominic's taunts had chilled Rebecca but at least they signalled his progress, as he carefully climbed the broken steps. As his voice grew louder, she realized he was almost at the top and yet she still could not think of anything to do, except sit there, frozen in fear, her back pressed against the wall. Rebecca would try to fend him off with her fists and feet when he reached her. She was determined to make it difficult for him, but knew his size and superior strength would be impossible to overcome. Rebecca had never been more terrified but there was frustration and anger welling up inside her too. This was the man who had killed her father and he was going to murder her too.

Think, Rebecca!

Seconds later, Dominic reached the top of the staircase, stretched upwards and easily pushed open the flimsy hatch.

'Now, you little bitch,' he said, 'let's get started!'

As he pushed his head up through the open hatch, he seemed surprised to find Rebecca kneeling right by it.

The last thing Dominic Green saw was Rebecca's hand moving in a blur, up then swiftly down in a hard, stabbing motion. Before he could move his hands away from the ledge to defend himself, she found what she was aiming for, the soft tissue of his eyeball. The chrome Sheaffer ballpoint pen went deep into Dominic's eye. He managed a scream before he let go of the ledge and slipped away from the hatch. The sound he made as he fell all the way down was inhuman. A howl of agony, anguish and fear that was only completely silenced when his body hit the floor far below.

The calm that followed was only broken when Claire Tilbury realized what had just happened. Dominic's body had missed the other woman by inches. Now he was dead at her feet and she was finally safe. Claire's muffled cry of alarm soon turned into loud sobs of relief. Rebecca slumped down, exhausted. Lying on her back, she tried to process what she had done. Rebecca had just killed a man and knew she should be experiencing guilt, shock or regret but, right now, like Claire, all she could actually feel was relief.

45

Getting down from the highest point of the lighthouse was almost the scariest part. With Dominic dead the fear that had motivated her to climb so far up the crumbling steps had disappeared. Now she was terrified in case she slipped or if everything gave way beneath her feet. If Rebecca fell, no one would ever know the truth about Dominic, and she would never get justice for her father and Simon Kibbs or any of Dominic's other victims. No one else knew that Claire was chained up in the lighthouse. She would probably die here too if Rebecca couldn't make it to the ground safely.

It was a long, slow journey down and every step was an ordeal she had to force herself to complete. More than once, fragments of stone became dislodged under her weight and she was convinced one of them would give way entirely. Somehow she managed to continue, until the drop slowly became less terrifying and she started to believe she might actually make it.

When she finally reached the floor, she felt an overwhelming sense of relief. Rebecca removed the gag from Claire's mouth and checked she was OK, even though they both felt far from it. Rebecca had to root inside Dominic's pockets, ignoring the mess she had made of him. She didn't have a choice if they wanted to get out of there. Rebecca retrieved her mobile phone and dialled.

It helped that there were two of them to tell the story and that one of them was still chained up when the police arrived. They had to use bolt cutters to release Claire.

DI Hall looked almost as shocked as they were. The killer he had been hunting, the mythical Chameleon, the murderer in their midst, was a police officer. Worse, he knew the man personally and had never taken him seriously, not once, even for a moment. More than that, every clue, every hint, every lead the man had given him, he had treated with prejudice and disregarded as the ramblings of an incompetent. Now he realized with a sudden clarity that he had been completely played.

'You're not the only one he fooled,' Rebecca told the detective, as they were taken from the scene to be checked over by a doctor.

'Do you think that will make any difference?' he asked her but he knew the answer already. The press would destroy him and the force would likely throw him to the wolves. 'It's over,' he said quietly, and he was not talking about the case.

Between them, they were able to piece a lot of it together but there were still some gaps and unanswered questions. Rebecca realized she might never know the full truth and had started to accept that until days later when the letter arrived.

She read it, then called DI Hall. He came round to her house with Fox and Carpenter. She showed him the letter and said, 'Are you going to bag it up and take it away or do you want to read it first?'

Hall looked older since the last time she had seen him. He seemed tired and worn. 'Why don't you just go ahead and read it?' he said, sounding like a condemned man waiting to hear his death sentence. They all sat and listened to Rebecca as she read the letter.

Dear Miss Cole,

As per our client Dominic Green's wishes, we were instructed to forward this letter to you in the event of his death.

> *Yours sincerely,*
> *Alexander Burton*
Ainshaw, Burton & Riley Solicitors

She then read from the previously sealed letter they had sent her:

Dear Rebecca,

Well, if you are reading this, you've won.
> *Or perhaps no one is reading this and I won.*
> *For argument's sake we'll assume you went one better than your father and worked it out. But life is for the living and I don't want to live a long and pointless one in prison, so we are going to end this soon, one way or the other. Everyone born dies eventually and nothing much matters in between.*

I do want you to know it all, though, Rebecca, the how and the why, because the truth matters to you, as much as it does to me, and I don't want the tabloids making up some Chameleon bullshit.

I expect you are wondering how it began.

My father used to make me walk our dog in all weathers and I'd take my time because I never wanted to go home to his quick temper. One night in the playing fields, I looked up at a window and saw her changing. Bill Mason's lovely new wife, Anna. That was the first time but I went back again and again to watch and she never realized.

It was years before I finally visited her.

That didn't go so well.

She was the first.

Bill did fifteen years for that one. Jealous hubby, prime suspect. Poor old Bill. Never mind.

I kept a record of the others. I knew I'd have to account for them one day. Some say the Chameleon has killed five. My own count is eleven. More than Brady, less than Shipman.

Ha, ha.

Some have never been found; others classed as unsolved; innocent men got the blame for the rest, thanks to DI Hall and his team. Please give him my regards by the way and thank him for everything. I quite literally couldn't have done it without him. There are four innocent men still serving life sentences because of DI Hall. I'll give you the details and, if it bothers you, you can sort it all out. I don't really care.

He thanked Gregg Poole next for being an unknowing accomplice. The police always used the local locksmith to secure houses after break-ins. Gregg was happy to show his local bobby how to get through any door so Dominic could understand the skills of burglars, and it was surprisingly easy to buy all the tools online.

It's a trust thing. No one expects a policeman to become a killer and they don't usually. With me it was the other way round. I knew I was a killer, so I became a policeman. Talk about hiding in plain sight. Do you know how easy it is to gain access to a woman's home or persuade her to climb into your car when you wear a uniform? There's no sport in it any more, so now I prefer visiting them in the night.

Dominic explained how he used a cocktail of his own invention to sedate women long enough to get them into the boot of the car, then out to the woods or the lighthouse, where he could 'work' uninterrupted. His knowledge of prescription drugs was the one thing he thanked his miserable old man for.

There were pages more. He talked about a woman who had been the easiest because she had left her downstairs sash window open. He confirmed he was the man who had offered a drunken Jane Anderson a lift home, then told how he had walked into the house of Amanda Mayhew, the victim with the wind chimes, a woman he had stalked for a long time.

Rose McIntyre had rejected him more than once. When they were at school together and years later, very publicly, in the pub on a Saturday night when she had told him, 'You can't afford me, love.' Everyone had laughed at Dominic and he had hated her for it. But then he found out she was having an affair with Connor Owen of all people, and he decided she didn't deserve anyone's love. Dominic had watched her meet Connor in the graveyard, because the path behind it led to one of his empty rental properties.

I pushed a note through the door. MEET ME AT THE USUAL PLACE, it said, with a time scrawled below it. I knew there would be no one else there, because all the graves are so old. I figured Connor Owen would get the blame. I wasn't expecting Simon Kibbs to see me but at least he took the fall.

It took Rebecca a while to read it all and, when she was done, she turned her attention to the list of the names at the back. Eleven of them. Eleven murdered women. Rebecca knew how close she had come to being the next one.

Each name came with a paragraph or two of explanation.

Just when she though it was over, she found another page.

Your dad had been haunted by Katherine's death for twenty years but it was only when he finally lost his job that he had the time to go over it all again in such obsessive detail. He came to talk to me about it and we were seen in the café together. I knew you would find out about it, so I told you first. I assumed he had written everything down but I couldn't find his laptop.

He did tell me he was going to visit Simon again. I could delay that but I knew Sean. He would get there in the end and I couldn't allow it.

You've seen Simon too and Claire. I reckon you've started to work it all out. You're a persuasive woman and I think it's only a matter of time before you start to convince other people that it was me. I can't let that happen.

Clever Rebecca.

Clever Katherine.

Too clever for your own good. Both of you.

Oh, how I despise clever little girls.

Rebecca stopped reading then. 'That's it,' she said.

Fox swore and Carpenter said, 'Jesus Christ.' They all looked deeply shaken but Hall said nothing.

'What happens now?' she asked him.

'Oh, I've got a pretty good idea what happens now,' he said. 'Let's just say you wouldn't want to be us.'

'I meant with Simon Kibbs.'

'Oh, him.' Hall shrugged. 'I suppose they'll let him out. He'll probably get a million quid in compensation.' He snorted at that, as if it wouldn't be richly deserved.

'And the other men?'

Hall shrugged again, as if he really didn't care all that much. 'We'll hand the letter in and leave it to the grownups, but all the cases will be reviewed in light of this . . . evidence. They'll most likely be released.' He didn't seem to be too bothered either way and she realized his overriding emotion was one of self-pity, as if he was the one who was really the victim of a miscarriage of justice.

'Can I have that?' he indicated the letter.

Rebecca gave it to him. 'I made a copy,' she said. It was a warning in case he failed to hand over the damning words.

'Of course you did.' He looked defeated then. 'You're going to write about this, aren't you, and you'll hang me out to dry.'

'Dominic fooled us both. I'll make sure that what I write reflects that.'

'Yeah, right.'

Rebecca hardened her tone. 'Do you really think anything I write about you will make any difference now, detective inspector?'

'No,' he admitted, 'it won't.' He turned to the others. 'Come on, you two.' And he made to leave.

'Things could be worse, DI Hall,' she reminded him.

He rounded on her then. 'Worse? How could they be any bloody worse?'

'You could be serving life for a murder you didn't commit.'

46

A year later

He was sleeping soundlessly next to her when she woke with a slight wine-induced hangover. It was Alan's day off so she crept quietly away without disturbing him.

Some people had expected Rebecca to leave the area for ever, like Claire Tilbury had, as if the shops and houses here were to blame for what she had been through, a permanent reminder of the night she was forced to kill Dominic Green to save her own life, but Rebecca wasn't superstitious. She didn't see his face reflected in every shop window or expect to see him standing outside her home. There were no ghosts in Eriston any more. Dominic was dead and that was that.

The new flat helped. Even before her father's death and her unwelcome intruder, Rebecca had never loved the family home. Nearly all her memories there were bad ones. When she was a child, the house frightened her and as a teenager she had watched her family slowly disintegrate there.

The amount she managed to prise from Connor Owen's greedy hands was enough to keep her going for a long while, particularly here, even allowing for the trade-in on the apartment. Rebecca finally had a base. On warmer mornings she could drink coffee on the tiny balcony, finally understanding why everyone wanted a sea view.

She didn't go and watch when they tore the Apostles down. Places changed every day and there was no point being sentimental about it. The new flats sprang up at a startling speed and soon you could have almost forgotten the Victorian houses had ever been there at all.

Things had finally calmed down now. Killing Dominic, and the fact that he was a policeman as well as a murderer, made Rebecca almost famous for a while. News organizations from all around the world contacted her and, for a few days at least, she was the story. Some of them said she was a hero for saving Claire and freeing the town of its predator but she dismissed this. Rebecca thought of her own actions as selfish. They were all about survival. Her desire to live was only matched by the rage she felt towards the man who had killed her father, then conned his way so ruthlessly into her life, before trying to take it from her. When she had looked down on his broken body, she felt no sorrow for him at all.

In the end Rebecca sold her story to one of the newspapers who had been hounding her, because it was the only way to make them stop, but she insisted on writing the piece herself. That way she could control the content. They weren't happy and paid a little less but, as she pointed out to the editor, 'This story does not need to be sensationalized.' And he had to admit she had a point.

She wrote the account of her experiences honestly until forced to describe what happened at the lighthouse. It took several attempts before she finally settled on an appropriate way to describe an act of such violence. In the end she wrote *I did what I had to do.*

Her father's prospective publisher got in touch then. Would she perhaps like to complete the book he had started now that it had an ending? Telling the story of the killer who had terrorized the people of her home town for two decades proved strangely cathartic, but she wondered how they would feel about it.

'It's your story, Rebecca,' Alan had said. 'You should write it.'

Others, like Jack, said it would be better for her to tell it before 'some other bugger makes it up'. She didn't ask DI Hall what he thought. He had taken early retirement within weeks of their final meeting and she very much doubted he would ever set foot in Eriston again.

It was strange to see the finished book in the shop window, bearing both Rebecca's and her father's name on the jacket. She had insisted on that. The process of writing it made Rebecca feel closer to her father than she had been for a long time and she found that she was able to forgive his affair with Katherine Prentiss. It had been a moment a long time ago and now they were both gone. Her mother had moved on, now so would she.

There was a black-and-white photo on the cover, of Rebecca standing on the dock in Eriston, gazing moodily out to sea. The publisher's title was still *The Chameleon*, followed by a short blurb on the cover, promising the book would tell *the true story of the infamous serial killer, by the woman who ended his reign of terror*. Those were not the words she would have chosen but it was, at least, a factually correct description of the book's contents. The modest advance was welcome too, and by the time it was published Rebecca had a job as well, just a short walk from her apartment.

Thanks to Rebecca, Leah got her grant. The old cinema and lifeboat buildings were renovated and the bound copies of the *Eriston Gazette* found a permanent home in the new museum. The town still needed a source of local news and Rebecca had offered to provide it. A new, leaner online-only version of the newspaper was launched, with Rebecca as its founding editor and sole journalist. The beauty of her idea was basing the newspaper here, so the building could achieve its status as a 'working museum', which finally secured its funding.

Rebecca grabbed a pastry from the bakers and ate it at her desk with a cup of coffee. She was halfway through editing a story when her mobile phone rang.

'It's your top stringer here,' Jack informed her.

She laughed. 'You're my only stringer, Jack.'

'I bet you say that to all the boys.'

'What can I do for you?'

'It's what I can do for you,' he said. 'I found something this morning.'

'What did you find?'

'A body,' he told her.

'In the sea?'

'Well, it wasn't in my back garden.'

She ignored that. 'Young or old?'

'Middle-aged.'

'Male or female?'

'Male.'

'Out at sea or washed up on the beach?'

'Out at sea,' he said. 'I saw him bobbing along, so I took a closer look.'

'That's the first one in a while. What do you think?'

'Well, he could have fallen in or jumped . . . but I'm guessing not.'

'Why?'

'A bloody big bruise on the side of his neck. I'm no detective but it looked like a blunt instrument to me.'

'Thanks, Jack, I owe you a pint.'

'You do,' he confirmed. 'Several, in fact.'

'Where's the body now?'

'I radioed and the police met me when I docked. You'll be wanting to speak to that new DI . . . Murrigan?'

'Mulligan,' she corrected him. 'Sarah Mulligan.'

'Aye, she's the one in charge.'

'Thanks, Jack, I will.'

'Do you think it might be a story?' he asked.

'It's always a story,' she told him. 'We just don't know

386

what kind yet.' Still on the phone, she stood up and grabbed her bag, then glanced at the half-eaten pastry and picked it up too so she could eat on the move.

'Knowing this town,' he said, 'it'll be the worst kind.'

'Leave it with me, Jack,' she told him. 'I'm on it.'

Acknowledgements

Huge thanks to my editor at Penguin, Joel Richardson, for his excellent advice and all his help with this book, and to Grace Long for her insights and valuable contributions. My thanks go to the brilliant team at Michael Joseph, especially Maxine Hitchcock, Sriya Varadharajan, Fola Adebayo, Jennie Roman and Emma Henderson.

My literary agent, Phil Patterson, at Marjacq is a constant source of support and encouragement and has been a great help to me for years now. I'd also like to thank Sandra Sawicka at Marjacq for ably handling my foreign rights.

I owe a debt of gratitude to the following people who have all helped and supported me during my writing career. Thank you, Adam Pope, Andy Davis, Nikki Selden, Gareth Chennells, Andrew Local, Stuart Britton, David Shapiro, Peter Day, Tony Frobisher, Eva Dolan, Katie Charlton, Gemma Sealey, Susan Jackson, Ion Mills, Peter Hammans, Emad Akhtar and Keshini Naidoo.

A huge thank-you to my wife, Alison, for all her faith and belief in me, especially during the early years. I hope you know I could not have done any of this without you.

Finally, a special thank-you to my wonderful daughter, Erin, who keeps me going and never fails to brighten my days.

He just wanted a decent book to read ...

Not too much to ask, is it? It was in 1935 when Allen Lane, Managing Director of Bodley Head Publishers, stood on a platform at Exeter railway station looking for something good to read on his journey back to London. His choice was limited to popular magazines and poor-quality paperbacks – the same choice faced every day by the vast majority of readers, few of whom could afford hardbacks. Lane's disappointment and subsequent anger at the range of books generally available led him to found a company – and change the world.

'We believed in the existence in this country of a vast reading public for intelligent books at a low price, and staked everything on it'
Sir Allen Lane, 1902–1970, founder of Penguin Books

The quality paperback had arrived – and not just in bookshops. Lane was adamant that his Penguins should appear in chain stores and tobacconists, and should cost no more than a packet of cigarettes.

Reading habits (and cigarette prices) have changed since 1935, but Penguin still believes in publishing the best books for everybody to enjoy. We still believe that good design costs no more than bad design, and we still believe that quality books published passionately and responsibly make the world a better place.

So wherever you see the little bird – whether it's on a piece of prize-winning literary fiction or a celebrity autobiography, political tour de force or historical masterpiece, a serial-killer thriller, reference book, world classic or a piece of pure escapism – you can bet that it represents the very best that the genre has to offer.

Whatever you like to read – trust Penguin.